A Cursed Heart Copyright © 2025 by Jana.C.Cser

This is a work of fiction. Names, characters, places, and incidents either are the product of the author's imagination or are used fictitiously. Any resemblance to actual events or locales or persons, living or dead, is entirely coincidental.

ISBN: 979-8-218-75791-5
First edition: August 2025

Warning

This book contains trigger situations such as gore, violence, arousal by murder and graphic sexual situations. This is suited for 18 above.

For everyone who believes they're without magic:
look deeper. It lies patiently beneath, waiting for you to awaken it.

Chapter One

Maeva Sinclair

My heart hammered against my ribs the moment I stepped inside. My once-fair skin had turned ashen with anxiety, the color drained from my face. Loose brown curls framed my shoulders like a tattered curtain. My jacket and trousers felt impossibly heavy, their fabric rubbing against my skin with the scratchy irritation of coarse sandpaper.

The walls seemed to inch closer with every session, their polished wood shelves sagging under the weight of countless volumes and framed accolades. Behind the cluttered desk, diplomas and commendations glinted under muted light—reminders of years I felt I had no part in. To my right, the couch beckoned—its plush cushions worn into inviting hollows—yet the muted emerald fabric felt as intimidating as a stage under too-bright lights.

I hesitated, tracing the coffee table's grain with my eyes before looking up at him. My fingers curled into the cushion as I tried to steady my breath.

"I—I think so," I managed, my voice softer than I intended. The vanilla candle flickered on the table, casting quivering light across the room. It smelled like safety, like forgiveness. "Thank you for asking."

He offered a small, understanding nod and settled into the armchair opposite me. His posture was open, inviting. The lamp beside him spilled just enough light onto his face for me to study his expression— concern tugging at his brow, patience in the tilt of his head.

I pulled in a shaky breath. Every muscle in my body wanted to bolt for the door, to escape the closeness of another person. But something in the way he'd carried me earlier—equal parts strength and gentleness—kept me rooted to the spot.

"Let me get you some tea," he said, rising. His hand hovered in mid-air, a silent question before he left the room.

I forced a nod. "Please."

As he crossed to the small side table, I sank deeper into the couch, watching his shadow pass over the wall. The candle's flame danced, and for the first time since I'd sat down, the room felt large enough to hold me. Maybe, I thought, it was enough to begin letting someone in.

He lowered his glasses just enough to peer over the rims—green velvet with gold stitching soft against his temples—as he settled into the old Victorian chair. A leather-bound notepad lay open on his crossed legs, every blank page a silent invitation.

Mr. Makenzie had been my Friday afternoon therapist for eight weeks. My previous counselor—Jerry—had decamped on a sudden midlife-crisis world tour, and I'd been shuffled into this office without a second thought. I needed help, after all. Insomnia was only the start of my problems. I'd assumed a sleeping pill would quiet my nights, but it wasn't sleep itself that betrayed me—it was what I saw when I closed my eyes.

My thumbs rubbed the worn rim of the China teacup resting in my lap. The warmth seeped into my palms like morning sunlight. I stared at the pale liquid and the tea bag bobbing at the surface, my breath shaking as I tried to gather my thoughts.

"We don't have much time today, Maeva. Would you like to begin?" he asked gently.

"I know, I know," I whispered under my breath.

My body sank into the couch as though into quicksand, each cushion pulling me lower. I willed my muscles to relax while my mind braced against the wall it had built in self-defense. Time stretched out, suspended until I found the words to resume.

"Please tell me what you saw this time," he coaxed, softer still.

I drew in a lung-full of air—my ribs protesting the desperate inhale—and exhaled with a low rumble of relief that lasted only a heartbeat. My shoulders slumped under the weight of that breath as I melted back into the couch's embrace.

Squinting against the lamplight, I lifted the teacup to my lips. Its warmth was a small mercy—a fragile shield against the storm raging in my chest. I should have felt comforted, but instead I clung to the cup as if it might soothe the ache within me.

My fingers trembled as I dug into my bag to retrieve the white-capped pill. I stared at it—both villain and salvation—cursing myself for needing it. Shame coiled in my gut at the thought of depending on chemicals to still my mind. And yet the memory of that darkness beyond sleep tugged at me, demanding I swallow.

With a resigned sigh, I tipped the pill onto my tongue and let it dissolve—its bitter promise sliding down my throat. I closed my eyes, bracing for the familiar fog that followed—my mind's only refuge, though it came at the cost of feeling real at all.

"I stood in a room filled with seven or eight women, gathered in a centuries-old cottage deep in the woods. They formed a circle around the table—some wailing, others speaking in hushed tones—while a small fire burned at the head of the room, its heat fierce and unyielding," I began.

"What else did you see?" he asked.

"There was a young woman lying in the middle of the circle," I said nervously.

I lifted my chin and watched Mr. Makenzie's pen glide across the notepad, the ink flowing as if it were discovering the words for the very first time. He didn't seem to notice my gaze until our eyes met. With a subtle nod, he silently invited me to continue.

"I paced the room, each sob tearing at my ribs until I felt their grief in my own chest. The air thrummed with their anguish, a living thing pressing against my skin. Finally, at the edge of the circle, I saw her—lying still, death written across her body. Crimson soaked the hem of her skirt, and a thin rivulet dripped from her nose onto her blouse. Her face was a map of violence: bruises dark as bruised fruit, halos of yellow and green blossoming around her eyes. Blood streamed in rivulets from her ears, pooling at her neck like a warning I could not ignore."

My breath hitched, and I pressed a trembling hand to my chest as my pulse thundered like a war drum. Dizziness swirled at the edges of my vision, and I sank back into the couch cushions, the room tilting beneath me. It felt impossibly hard to breathe.

Then the medication claimed me—warm fog seeping into my limbs, dragging every ounce of strength from my body. Helplessness washed over me in suffocating waves. I closed my eyes, unable to fight, allowing the darkness to swallow me whole.

I've always been weak. Even as a child, I crumbled under the smallest burden, leaning on others because I couldn't bear my own weight. I've never had an ounce of resilience, just a string of people who held me up when I couldn't stand. Why should I expect more of myself now? In moments like this, I'm nothing but a fragile petal in a storm, destined to wilt. And even that feels generous.

They could help carry the burden with me. That's why I needed people more than they needed me. I had nothing significant to offer them, but they had given me everything I needed: support.

I laid my head back on the cushion of the couch. The cold leather was soothing against the back of my neck, offering relief from the redness of my skin I knew was illuminating in the dark room.

As I sat there quietly fighting back tears, I lifted my head to meet his gaze. We hadn't spoken for what felt like an eternity. The ticking clock on the wall was the only stable sound on which I could focus. Our eyes met, each of us trying to read the other's thoughts.

"Are there any more details you can recall?" he pressed.

"Anything at all?" His legs uncrossed and then re-crossed the opposite way, weight shifting from one armrest to the other. He leaned forward; the pen poised over the notepad like a sprinter at the starting line.

His focused intensity calmed me—I felt less like a patient and more like a collaborator. The soft lines of his face relaxed into encouragement as he met my eyes.

I lowered my gaze to the carpet, searching for stray fragments of the dream. "I can't think of anything," I admitted, voice barely above a whisper.

He let out a gentle, "Oh," then prompted, "There was a woman there who seemed extremely angry."

"Explain her to me," he said, curiosity sparking in his tone.

"She was older—her long hair-streaked gray with black, pulled back in a braid. She wore a brown dress cinched by a heavy metal belt buckle…"

"What was on the buckle?" he interrupted, firm but patient.

"I—think it was a bird?" I offered hesitantly. I hadn't focused on their clothing, but her rage had made her unforgettable.

"She kept whispering, 'Our poor Anna,' over and over." I shivered at the memory of her anguish—so fiercely it felt like it pierced my own soul.

"Was the bird a raven?" he asked, a hint of a smile playing on his lips.

My eyes flew open. "How did you know?" I breathed.

He tapped his pen against the pad, poised to write. Confusion crept over me. I hadn't told anyone a single detail—how could he know?

He sighed deeply, the kind of exhale you make when a weight finally lifts. He dropped his pen onto the notepad and snapped it shut. Uncrossing his legs, he stretched them out before the chair, then planted both feet firmly on the floor. One hand rested on the closed notepad, the other on the armrest. Lifting his glasses from his face, he set them atop his head and rubbed the bridge of his nose, eyes closing as his eyebrows arched in relief.

He let out a slight, hysterical giggle. With each breath, his chest rose and fell in time with his laughter, as though an electric thrill coursed through him.

I scanned the room awkwardly, searching for the joke I'd missed. I fidgeted on the couch, sipping my tea, a jittery smile curling my lips. How could my harrowing dream provoke this amusement in the middle of a therapy session?

I replayed every word I'd spoken, desperate to identify my misstep—and came up empty. Tension coiled in my shoulders, and irritation seeped into my posture. My face flushed, eyes narrowing in mounting anger. I sat up straight, uncrossed my legs so both feet were planted firmly on the floor, and leaned forward. With a sharp clink, I set my teacup on the coffee table, making sure he heard it. Then I raised my hands in a questioning gesture.

"What is so funny?" I snapped, my voice sharp enough to crack the silence. Without waiting for an answer, I swept my bag off the floor and pushed to my feet. I wouldn't tolerate disrespect in a paid appointment. My boots scraped angrily across the hardwood as I rounded the coffee table and strode toward the door.

Just as my hand touched the knob, a vice-tight grip closed around my elbow. I yelped and froze—the force so sudden I hadn't even noticed his reach until I slammed into his side. I looked down to find Mr. Makenzie unmoved in his chair, his eyes locking onto mine with unsettling intensity.

Shock and fury warred in my gaze; his was cold and unblinking. His grip bit into my arm, unyielding and surprisingly callous. I couldn't pull away. Panic shot through me as my heart pounded; I counted the few steps left to the door, each one feeling unbearably distant.

My heart sank into my stomach. Tears welled in my eyes as anxiety washed over me, and my lips began to quiver—terror was closing in. I needed to escape; I had to run as fast as I could to get away.

Frantically, I scanned the room for anything within arm's reach I could use to defend myself. I wasn't strong, but if I screamed maybe someone would hear.

I spun toward the coffee table, moving as swiftly as I could—and then he was upright too. Still holding my arm, he was suddenly right beside me.

He seemed to have grown overnight. Where I once barely met his gaze, now I had to tilt my chin skyward to look into deep, impossibly blue eyes. His height had surged—he towered over me in a single bound—when only weeks ago he'd stood no more than an inch taller than I. The man I'd trusted was gone.

The fine lines around his eyes and mouth—proof of midlife's wars—had vanished, leaving smooth, ageless skin that caught the lamp's glow like marble. His complexion was flawless, his jawline chiseled to perfection, and where his hair had once been streaked with silver, now it lay thick and midnight-black, each strand shimmering with youthful vigor.

Mr. Makenzie, the gentle, world-weary therapist who'd welcomed me to his Friday sessions, was replaced by someone half his age living sculpture in his mid-twenties. The difference was so stark that my chest tightened with a fresh wave of disbelief. This could not be the man I thought I knew.

My face registered a mixture of shock and awe at the sudden transformation. I couldn't tear my eyes away from him—his perfectly youthful features were magnetic. Forcing myself to look past his beauty, I searched his face for some clue.

"Who are you?" I whispered, panic rising in my throat.

Then, as the enormity of it struck me, I tried again, voice quavering, "No—what are you?"

A wicked smirk curled his lips as he herded me backward toward the couch, our eyes locked in a silent battle. His grip on my elbow was iron-clad as he pushed me down into the cushions. I braced myself, hands pressing into the leather, jolting at the force that plopped me back into my seat.

He loomed over me—his frame impossibly large—and I shrank against the pillows like prey before a predator. Tears pooled unbidden at the corners of my eyes. Even then, neither of us dared break the fierce intensity of our gaze.

He shifted slightly and settled onto the couch beside me; his long legs tucked almost to his chest as he folded into the too-small seat. Even sitting, his broad shoulders and towering frame seemed to swallow the furniture—my own form beside him felt small and swallowed up.

My breath hitched, growing shallow and quick as my heart pounded in my ears. I watched every deliberate movement as he got comfortable: one arm draped casually over his bent knee, the other resting against the back of the couch, reaching almost behind me. Despite his ease, I felt the tight coil of tension in my chest tighten further at his proximity.

I could feel his warm breath stirring the hairs at the nape of my neck, each exhale like a flicker of flame against my skin. My pulse thundered in my throat as the heat of his body pressed in around me, leaving me suffocating in its wake. I turned my face away, desperate to escape the intensity of his gaze, but he seemed to track every inch of me, his eyes gliding over my cheek, my collarbone, the curve of my shoulder.

Instinctively, I tried to shrink away tucking my chin to my chest, my shoulders creeping up toward my ears. My hands gripped the cushion's edge, knuckles whitening as I inched along the couch, searching for any sliver of space between us. With every millimeter of distance, I put behind me, he simply shifted—his arm sliding further along the backrest, his hand now inches from mine.

My heart pounded so loudly I thought he must hear it; my stomach fluttered with equal parts fear and something I couldn't name. Even as I leaned away, my body betrayed me—drawn as much to him as repelled—caught in the gravity of those cobalt-blue eyes refusing to break their hold.

He drew in a slow, deliberate breath—one that felt less like air and more like he was inhaling me. I caught my own breath, uncertain whether the sound came from me or from him leaning so close. His face hovered at mine, the space between our noses vanishing. Instinctively, I turned my head, angling my cheek toward the bookshelf; the familiar spines offered more comfort than the heat radiating from his body.

Still, I couldn't escape the whisper of his exhale against my neck, moist and warm as a summer storm. The soft, tremulous shudder of his breath sent a chill down my spine—though I couldn't tell if it was fear or something altogether more complicated. Every sense screamed alarm, yet a strange pull held me captive, caught between warning and wonder.

"Are you scared?" he whispered, his warm breath ghosting across my ear.

"Yes," I admitted, voice trembling in the sudden hush.

A predatory smile curved his lips. "I can smell it on you, Maeva."

I snapped my head toward him, heart pounding so fiercely I feared he could hear it. In that instant, he seized me by the throat, pushing me back onto the couch with brutal strength. My arms shot up reflexively, but before I could even brace for impact, I felt a sharp pinch—

He bit me.

A strangled gasp escaped my lips as he threw back his head in triumphant laughter. My fingers clutched at the fresh ache in my neck, but hot blood welled between them, dripping in a dark ribbon down my throat and staining his chin scarlet.

He leaned closer, eyes bright with triumph. "I guess you were telling the truth," he murmured, amusement dancing in his voice as my life slipped away with every terrified heartbeat.

I lurched to my feet and bolted for the door, lungs burning, vision narrowing at the edges. Panic propelled me across the room, but my momentum stalled against the heavy oak of the bookcase—its shelves rattling under the weight of my back. He laughed then, a low, delighted rumble that made my skin crawl.

My legs trembled as I pulled myself upright, hands pressed against the cool wood grain, while the world swayed around me. No words came; the only sound in my ears was the frantic pounding of my own heart. I willed my senses to steady, to clear the fog creeping in at the corners of my vision.

Staggering toward the door, I risked a glance over my shoulder. He was at the table now—calm, methodical. In one hand, he pinched a tissue and pressed it to his blood-smeared lips. He tilted his head back, and the light caught on with two impossibly long, glinting fangs.

Time snapped back into focus with a jolt of terror. I realized there would be no escape from what he truly was. Whatever lay beyond this door suddenly felt like a distant dream.

I couldn't fight it anymore; I felt completely defeated. I dropped to my knees and slowly fell forward. Exhaustion overtook my body. I must be losing a lot of blood, I thought, that I'm hallucinating.

Next, my eyelids fluttered shut against my will. With my remaining strength, I rolled onto my back. I looked up at the ceiling—crown molding etched across each wall. Dim light cast the lampshades' shadows into giant, unblinking eyes that stared down at me, watching me succumb to the horror of dying in a pool of my own blood.

Helpless, I felt my eyes close without consent. Then a breath ghosted against my ear, followed by a sultry voice that sent chills racing down my spine:

"Do you know how long it has been for us to find you?"

Chapter Two

Maeva Sinclair

My hands clutched the silky-smooth, warm fabric beneath me. My bare legs rested against something surprisingly soft. My pajama pants scrunched up to my thighs. Blinking against the morning sun, I tried to focus through the haze. The ornate golden light fixture on my ceiling snapped me fully awake, and I bolted upright in bed—dizzy from the sudden movement.

A flood of questions burst behind my eyes. How did I get here? What happened last night? Heart racing, I swung my legs over the side of the bed and stumbled toward the bathroom. The cold hardwood under my feet stung like ice; my blankets still clung warmly to the footboard. Arms outstretched, I ran my fingers along the furniture, searching for balance as I crossed the room.

I pressed both palms against the chipped paint of the doorframe before slipping into the washroom. My breaths came shallow and rapid, as though I might hyperventilate. Fragments of conversation, flashes of pain, and a fleeting, agonizing memory teased at the edges of my mind— but the full story eluded me. A sharp migraine throbbed at my temples as I willed those fragments into a coherent whole.

I found the bathroom mirror centered on the back wall. The gold-trimmed frame only heightened my anxiety as I stared at my reflection. I swept my hair to one side, searching my face for any clue—there was nothing there.

I slid my hands behind my neck and interlaced my fingers at its base. Leaning my chin toward my chest, I felt my neck muscles stretch before releasing in a relieving crack. I exhaled deeply, then raised my head and met my own gaze.

Maybe it was all a dream, I thought, rubbing the tense muscles on either side of my neck. When I felt the pressure ease, I let my arms drop. But then I noticed something odd. Brushing my hair aside once more, I angled my neck toward the light and peered closely at the skin just below my hairline.

I dragged my fingertips slowly down the side of my throat and felt them brush against two small, tender knots. I jerked back in shock, my hand dropping away from the mirror as my heart pounded. Staring at my reflection, I leaned forward again—nothing. Yet I knew they were there. Fingertip after fingertip, I shifted positions, pressing and prodding against the glass, desperate to see what I could so clearly feel.

Panic rose in my chest. My eyes and my touch contradicted each other, and I couldn't tell which to trust. "I'm not losing my mind," I whispered, scrubbing at my neck as if friction might reveal the truth. But the knots remained stubbornly hidden.

Defeated, I pulled away and sank onto the edge of the sink. My hands braced me as I dropped my head to my chest and let out a shaky sigh. I closed my eyes and forced my breathing deep and steadily, willing the dizziness and doubt to fade. My fingers clenched the porcelain rim until my knuckles went white grounding myself in the only solid thing left: the sink beneath me.

When I began therapy, I wasn't ready to start medication immediately. Mr. Makenzie had taught me simple breathing exercises to use whenever my anxiety spiked. He believed these techniques could change how I experienced life—and somehow, I came to believe it too. They'd worked well in the past: focusing on pressure points on my hands or wrists was enough to ground me and bring my attention back to the present.

Lately, however, my dreams had grown so vivid that I sometimes lost the sense they weren't real. I'd found myself second-guessing my decision to delay medication. Still, I kept reminding myself that if I ever needed it, there was no shame in taking medicine to help.

Once I'd calmed my mind and eased the tension in my chest, I returned to bed. The night air felt less hostile than before, and the sheets beckoned with their warmth. Despite the lingering undercurrent of anxiety, I let myself slip back under the covers—determined to rest, at least for a little while longer.

My queen-size bed sat against the far wall, its dark wooden platform frame topped by a headboard carved with a single blossoming flower. On either side, matching nightstands held oversize lamps whose soft pools of light stood ready to chase away the night. Each tabletop bore a small stack of books—some well-worn, others still waiting for me to delve into their pages.

To the left of the bed, two large windows framed the city skyline. Across the floor lay a plush velvet rug in vibrant blues, its softness echoing the cool wood of the bed frame.

Still shaken by my earlier terror, I drew the curtains closed against the brightness of the morning sun and eased myself back under the mountain of silk sheets and fluffy down comforter. As my tense muscles melted into the mattress, the blankets wrapped around me like a protective cocoon, trapping the warmth of my body in a comforting embrace.

I rested my head on soft pillows and closed my eyes, willing my flickering lids to still. My breath slowed, and I surrendered myself to the promise of sleep.

Constant thoughts jostled in my mind like frantic bidders at an auction. I tossed and turned, searching for a comfortable position. I counted deep inhales and long exhales, bringing my focus back to my racing heart. Gradually, the residual worries began to fade, and at last I surrendered to the soft embrace of sleep.

Then a sudden chill crept up my spine, sharp as ice. Tiny needles of cold pricked my fingertips until they burned red. My hair whipped across my face in an invisible wind, and a wave of frost crawled up my legs, chilling me through the fabric of my pajamas. My long sleeve thin shirt barely keeping any warmth, while my thin pants kept no heat from escaping my skin.

I looked down and realized I was standing in a field of freshly fallen snow. Each step sent powdery flakes crunching beneath me. It was only a dream, but the memory of my last nightmare—its grief and panic—surged back, knotting my chest with dread. I steeled myself against the rising fear.

I was deep in the woods. Towering trees loomed overhead, their outstretched branches weaving together like the walls of a living fortress. Gaps in the canopy framed shards of gray sky. Needles of pine and fir hung heavily on every limb, and moss draped the trunks as if donning armor against the relentless cold.

Winter's beauty toward the natural world was unwavering yet gentle—a quiet white blanket laid down when the sun's warm embrace retreated. The forest, locked in seasonal slumber to conserve life through its coldest hours, felt hushed and whole. I stood motionless, listening to snowflakes whisper against branches, each soft "pssh" the only sound in that frozen cathedral.

I squeezed my eyes shut against the stillness, bracing for what might come next. My mind raced: What if there are predators here—wolves or worse, humans bent on violence? I knew how badly I overanalyzed everything, how I habitually sabotaged my own peace with a thousand "what ifs."

But even as panic fluttered in my chest, I reminded myself—you will be okay. I will be okay. The mantra steadied my breath. Those haunting dreams had taught me a harsh lesson: I was alone in the dark. And yet, surrounded by winter's silent resilience, I realized that sometimes alone wasn't the same as helplessness and that, for now, had to be enough.

My anxiety coursed through my veins, tensing every muscle until I felt like a rigid statue. Each breath came shallow, puffing out in little clouds of white mist. But there was nothing here—no screams, no blood—just the cold air and the silent woods. Frustrated, I shouted, "What the hell am I doing here?" hoping for an echo, some clue carried back on the wind.

I stretched out my arms, as if embracing the forest might yield an answer. Stupid—I hate this quiet. My dreams were usually violent, full of chaos and pain. This silence felt like standing on the edge of a cliff, unable to leap forward. I slumped to my knees, resting my arms on my thighs. I'll have to wait for morning—or at least until I wake up. Better to freeze here than stay trapped in suspense.

As the sun sank below the horizon, the sky shifted from gold to deep indigo. The remaining light danced on snow-laden branches, each flake sparkling like a diamond. But the warmth was gone; I could feel the cold seeping in, my body shivering uncontrollably. Every mile of fabric between me and the snow felt too thin. My hope faded with the light— and with it, any notion I might survive this dream.

My breath caught in my throat as I heard it again—a wet, crunching shuffle through the snow. I snapped my gaze upward, spinning in place, scanning the tree line for movement. My pulse thundered: was it a monstrous animal, its heavy paws sloshing through drifts? Or something far more human—and far more dangerous?

My legs wobbled beneath me, my pajama pants cold as the night when I stooped to scoop up a fist-sized stone, its icy surface numbing my fingers even as it felt like my only hope. Cold sweat beaded on my brow; heat flooded my cheeks, the remnants of my body's last warmth fleeing into the winter air.

This is just a dream... this isn't real... I whispered, teeth chattering. My mind rattled against itself—until a shape emerged from the shadows.

A woman's silhouette, tall and still, stepped into the dappled moonlight. The trees parted silently for her, and for a heartbeat I felt her gaze lock onto mine, as if she could see every terrified thought racing through my mind.

I tightened my grip on the snow-slick rock, knuckles white, ready to throw—whatever she was, I knew I had to defend myself.

Her gaze flicked across the trees as if she were reading their hidden pathways; lips pressed into a thin line of steel resolve. Not a tremor shook her stance, yet every muscle in her body seemed coiled, ready to spring. At her hip, the ivory-hilted dagger caught the moonlight—its leather sheath worn smooth by countless journeys. She wasn't afraid; she was the storm.

Under the hood of her heavy woolen cloak, stray waves of strawberry-blonde hair escaped in tendrils, dusted white with fresh snow. High cheekbones and a slender nose cast sharp half-shadows, lending her face an almost carved, statuesque beauty. Freckles scattered across her cheeks like flecks of copper, and her long lashes framed eyes so pale they seemed to glow in the darkness. Each booted step left a half-melted imprint in the snow, as though the forest itself had yielded to her passage.

I pressed the rock tighter in my fist, heart pounding so fiercely I could barely hear the soft rustle of snowflakes. Here, in this frozen silence, she was both guardian and harbinger—an echo of something ancient and fierce. And as she met my unblinking gaze, I knew I was no longer alone in the woods.

The familiar, hefty buckle—its surface embossed with a raven in mid-croak—was cinched snugly at her waist by a wide band of weathered brown leather. My pulse thundered as I recognized it: the very same sigil I'd glimpsed on that furious woman in my dreams.

Standing so close I could see the frost in her lashes; I watched her reach behind the sack slung over her shoulders and draw it forward. From its depths she produced a long wooden staff, its tip wrapped in tightly bound cloth. With slow deliberation, she laid it on the snow-crusted ground at her feet.

I leaned in, each careful step a silent plea that she does not notice me. Her slender, gloved hands hovered above the stick, knuckles white against the biting cold. I braced for the warmth of her breath—only to see her whisper some word of power, then lift her palms. Between them, a tiny flame flickered to life, dancing like a living ember.

Startled, I lost my footing and splintered backward into the snow, a sharp pain shooting through my back as I landed hard. My mouth fell open. She had summoned fire with nothing but her whispered words and open hands.

My soaked pants and cold limbs vanished from my awareness; every shred of me was riveted to her. She knelt, lowering the flame until it kissed the cloth wrapping her staff, which ignited in a swathe of crimson light. Smoothly, she rose, cradling the torch before her like an offering.

As she stood, I finally noticed the rune etched on her middle finger: a vivid, azure sigil that pulsed with its own inner glow. The hood of her cloak fell back, letting her braided strawberry-blond hair spill free. With a slow, satisfied exhale, she shouldered the sack once more, the torchlight illuminating her face in warm contrast to the forest's chill.

For a moment, the woods held its breath—branches laden with snow, the hush of falling flakes—while she lifted her chin and surveyed her handiwork. The torch's flame, pure and defiant, carved a circle of comfort and power in the gathering dark. And there, in its golden glow, I understood I was no longer alone. Frozen in the snow, I could only watch as she beamed at her creation.

"A tiny flame can be just as deadly," she whispered to the dancing torchlight.

She kept her gaze fixed ahead and pressed on, walking straight toward me with unwavering purpose. Each stride was long and deliberate, as though she had a destination she could not afford to reach too late. I stepped aside to let her pass, watching the glow of her torch fade into the forest's depths, growing dimmer with every determined step.

The sky darkened until only night remained, and the rustle of nocturnal creatures echoed through the trees. Panic seized me—I was alone and defenseless. I couldn't stay; I needed to get home, back to my warm bed where I was safe. My voice caught in my throat as I screamed,

"Wake up, Maeva—wake up, dammit!"

Tears streamed down my cheeks in icy rivulets. My breath came in ragged, shallow gasps, each spasm more violent than the last.

I couldn't remain lost in these woods. If I wanted to survive this dream, I had to keep moving. I turned and followed the path she'd taken, but the glow of her torch had vanished. Now only the pale moonlight and distant stars illuminated the snow. It was faint—no match for her fire— but enough to guide me onward into the darkness.

I followed the faint footprints she'd left, straining to catch a glimpse of her torchlight. But the relentless snowfall erased her tracks almost as soon as they formed, so I broke into a run—

Through trees draped in ice I stumbled, boots slipping on hidden patches of black ice. Brambles and jagged rocks tore at my arms and legs as I scrambled over fallen logs. Slush and mud slicked the hillside, each slide leaving me soaked and chilled to the bone.

My clothes clung to me, heavy with forest debris; my feet numbed with cold, every toe threatening frostbite. Still, something in me—a deep, urgent pull—drove me onward. I couldn't face the darkness alone; I needed her light, however fleeting.

As my eyes adjusted to the moonlit gloom, my steps grew surer, my pace quickened. I tore ahead until I burst into a small clearing—and there, half-buried in snow, stood a massive boulder. Heart hammering, I scrambled up its side, hands scraping on frost-slick rock, until I perched atop it and surveyed the silent forest below, searching for the faintest flicker of flame.

Perched atop the boulder, I lay sprawled on my back, ice-cold wind whipping my tangled hair across my face. Below me, the moonlit valley stretched like a silver tapestry, trees swaying in the breeze, their black trunks etched sharply against the pale snow. My elbows throbbed where I'd scraped them raw—each pulse a reminder that I was alive, blood warm against the unforgiving stone.

I eased myself into a seated position, brushing crusted snow and rock dust from my torn sleeves. The lacerations burned, but I pressed my fingers into them, stanching the flow with damp mittens. My breath came in shallow gasps, steam curling into the night air. Through blurred vision, I scanned the distant tree line for any glimmer that betrayed her passage.

Below the cliff, the canyon yawned in darkness, broken only by the silvery gleam of a frozen creek winding through the valley floor. If I descended here, I might lose sight of her entirely, swallowed by shadows. But higher still, another ridge beckoned—just within reach if I dared another climb. I swallowed back a wave of dizziness, planted my booted feet on the granite's edge, and hauled myself upright.

Every tendon in my arms protested as I leaned forward, hands splayed against the cold surface, sliding only inches before catching in a shallow crevice. My legs trembled as I lifted one knee, then the other, finally pulling myself to my feet. The wind bit through my coat, every breath a razor's edge on my lungs.

Standing atop the rock, I felt both the triumph of survival and the weight of exhaustion. Knuckles white from gripping the stone, I swept my gaze across the horizon one last time. There—in the distance, where the trees grew thick and the night was absolute—I thought I saw her: a solitary figure, torch raised high, moving with purpose into the darkness.

Heart hammering, I set off down the boulder's steep flank, careful not to slip. Each footfall brought me closer to that distant point of light— and I prayed, closer to the fierce, mysterious woman who had lit this frozen forest with her single, deadly flame.

There was no time for doubts or lingering pain, I told myself, voice cracking like dry twigs. I forced my back upright, every muscle protesting, and swept my gaze across the dark stand of pines. Frost clung to low branches, glittering faintly in the moonlight, but I ignored the bite of cold in my lungs—my mission burned sharper than any winter chill.

Through the silent valley, I caught it: a pale ember hovering above snow-laden ground. It bobbed like a will-o'-the-wisp, drifting toward the distant copse. My heart thundered as relief blossomed in my chest. I found you.

Gingerly, I slid down the slick surface of the cursed boulder, its rough grain scraping my palms. Snow crunched underfoot as I plunged into the open, each step weaving between gnarled roots and broken limbs. The air smelled of pine resin and damp earth, but with every stride, the terror of solitude melted away.

The light grew stronger—a soft, iridescent glow swirling as if alive. Branches overhead arched in cathedral silence, framing the woman I recognized. Her profile was half-hidden beneath a hood, but when she lifted her head, the torch's flame danced across high cheekbones and steady eyes.

She stood motionless on a small rise, the snow at her feet undisturbed. The flame enveloped her like a halo, painting her hair in molten gold and casting long shadows behind her. My knees trembled, but I pressed forward, boots sinking into fresh powder. Each beat of my heart echoed in the hush; a drum summon to our reunion.

Finally, I reached the crest. As I stepped into the soft circle of light, the world beyond faded—only her calm smile and that living flame remained.

My heart lurched at the promise of company, and the fog of angst that had clouded my mind began to lift. I noticed her pace slowing, and through the trees I caught other sounds: the sharp crackle and distant snap of burning wood. I followed her lead as we wove between trunks into a small clearing.

At its center roared a great fire pit, flames hungrily devouring dry logs. A ring of women sat around it, their faces half-lit by the blaze, brows knit and eyes blazing with fierce intensity. I hesitated at the edge of their circle, the cold seeping into my bones, and inched closer to the heat, desperate to thaw my frozen limbs.

The woman I had trailed stepped forward without hesitation. All eyes snapped from the fire to her as she approached, snapping their trance of flickering embers. With deliberate grace, she pulled back her hood, letting moonlight gild the top of her hair, then dipped her head in quiet greeting. One by one, the women inclined their heads, granting her passage to the flames.

The inferno should have seared her flesh—its heat was a living thing—but she stood unmoved, as if the fire bowed to her will. I watched, breathlessly, as she lifted a torch to eye level. The dancing flame reflected in her steady gaze, and a slow smile unfurled across her taut features.

Then, in a gesture both swift and serene, she swept her hand through the torch's roaring blaze. The fire licked her skin, yet she neither winced nor faltered. When she withdrew her hand, a small, perfect flame hovered in her palm—an orb of molten light. The torch's shaft, once alive with fire, lay smoldering and spent at her feet.

A hushed awe rippled through the gathered women. In that suspended moment, the fire pit's roar dimmed, and every eye turned to the sigil on her finger, glowing in rhythm with the stolen flame.

Chapter Three

Maeva Sinclair

I watched as the women settled onto stones arranged in a perfect circle around the fire. One of them—taller and more imposing than the rest—strode forward and claimed the seat at its head.

Without warning, the flames leapt skyward as if someone had poured gasoline into the pit. One after another, the women took their places; the fire's crackle surged into a thunderous roar that echoed through the sleep-darkened trees.

I studied each face by firelight: a grandmother's weathered wrinkles, a mother's determined jaw, a girl's fierce wonder—each at a different stage of life yet united by the raven-shaped buckle glinting on their belts and sashes. The flames danced across their skin, igniting strength in their eyes.

Creeping along the tree line, I skirted the edge of their circle, awed by their silent power. Here was a sisterhood woven into the fire's very essence—a cult bound by raven's call and flame's embrace. I paused before the woman I had followed, her gaze unwavering as embers spat at her feet. In that moment I understood she did not command the fire. Together, they were the fire.

"Thank you all for traveling such great distances to meet," the elder's voice rang out—gentle yet unyielding. I whipped my head toward her, breaking my gaze from the flames. The oldest woman in the circle rose, hands folded before her, her carved seat still marking her place at the head.

Silence fell as every pair of eyes fixed on the elder. I felt a shiver—her face was the same woman from my dreams, only older now: once-sharp lines deepened into permanent furrows, and her hair lay pale and thin against her skull. A murmur rippled through the group, hushed and urgent.

"Tonight," she continued, voice cold as winter's edge, "we lay all fears to rest. There will be no secrets here." She paused, letting the weight of her words press into the circle. Then, with deliberate grace, she swept her gaze side to side, pinning each sister under her scrutiny—like a preacher calling out sin, leaving no one unchallenged.

Heads turned, shoulders stiffened, and eyes flashed—some in irritation, others in barely concealed dread. A few bristled into defiant postures; most sank back, mouths clamped shut. The tension coiled tighter than a serpent ready to strike.

I crossed my arms, every nerve alight with curiosity. The elder, unmoved by the silent currents swirling around her, let her gaze linger on each woman, naming their whispers without uttering a single name. I leaned forward, waiting for someone—anyone—to break the hush. But no one dared. Respect or fear, I could not tell; only the unrelenting silence remained, as heavy as the darkness pressing in from the trees.

"Meridith," the elder intoned, her voice echoing against the quiet woods, "voice your concerns for the Knight family and their business." She lifted a knotted hand—palm up, fingers curved like raven's talons—inviting Meridith's words into the circle.

Meridith's chest rose and fell in shallow breaths as she stood at the circle's mouth, the firelight painting her cheeks in flickering amber. Her midnight-feathered hood draped heavy across one shoulder, and she clasped her hands at her waist to steady them.

The elder slid back onto her frost-chilled stone, adjusting the hem of her moth-eaten skirt before folding her gnarled fingers into her lap.

Moonlight glinted off the raven-buckle at her hip, her rheumy eyes fixed on Meridith with unwavering patience.

I pressed against the trees' hem, snow crunching faintly beneath my boots, each step a reminder of my isolation. Knights? My heart pounded like a war drum. My breath formed clouds in the cold air as I strained to catch every nuance of Meridith's next words—yearning for a foothold in their ancient secrets.

Around us, the circle held its breath. Only the fire's roar broke the hush, sparks spiraling skyward as if eager for Meridith's answer.

Meridith rose at last, shoulders trembling under the weight of every gaze. My breath caught—this was the woman I had followed, her name finally falling into place.

She drew in a wavering breath, voice barely above a whisper. "I feel… I feel our coven is in danger."

A harsh voice cut through the silence. "Louder, Meridith!"

Her eyes dropped to the frozen ground, as if the earth itself bore their sorrow. She swallowed hard, hands twisting her gown's hem into tight knots. The raven-buckle at her waist glinted like a silent witness to her fear.

When she spoke again, her words tumbled out in a rush: "They want to use us for our power. They promise goodwill—help for our people—but their interest lies only in our magic, in what we can give them. Leaders who covet our gifts cannot be trusted."

Her posture straightened; vulnerability gave way to resolve. "We must protect our coven," she pleaded, eyes sweeping the circle. "If we do not, they will come and take it by force."

For a moment, the fire's roar muted in my ears as her gaze met each sister's. Sadness and fierce determination shone in her eyes— embers calling to the rest of the circle. I held my breath, waiting to see if her passion would ignite theirs.

I watched the firelight flare across Meridith's face, casting harsh orange shadows—yet still she found no affirmation. Her eyes darted to the elder, and when the woman at the head of the circle gave the slightest nod, Meridith exhaled and sank back onto her stone.

Before her cloak had even settled, a sharp clap of movement drew my eye: Rebecca sprang to her feet, finger jabbing through the glow as though Meridith was a recalcitrant pupil.

"You do nothing but spread fear," she hissed. "They have only helped us—remember Anna? They found her when we lost hope!"

"Rebecca," the elder snapped, voice cold as ice, "that is enough."

But Rebecca's anger only brightened, her words cutting through the crackle of the flames. "What good is a leader who won't lead?" she spat, chest heaving, eyes aflame.

A hush rippled through the seated women—shock and disbelief warring on their faces. The elder rose, cloak whispering across the stones, irritation flickering in her pale gaze. The fire seemed to roar in agreement, embers dancing like sparks of outrage.

"Every elder equals every member," the woman at the head declared, voice sharp as a blade. "We are the trunk of the tree—steady, rooted—and you are its branches. Each of us has our part to play."

Her words were a spark to tinder. Shouts and jeers erupted around the circle; insults hurled over the flames like burning missiles. The fire hissed, wind fanning its anger, until the clearing felt alive with fury.

I skirted closer, heart pounding, trying to thread through the cacophony. Voices overlapped so fiercely I could not discern a single argument. Determined to understand, I edged toward the center of the maelstrom, each step crunching in the snow, the heat of their conflict pushing me onward.

Pressing myself just behind Meridith's shoulder, I narrowed my focus on her and Rebecca as they hurled accusations. Around us, the circle of women flailed their arms, voices shrill with indignation, eyes alight with outrage. The fire roared between them, tongues of red and orange licking skyward as if stoking their fury.

Inch by inch, I moved forward, straining to isolate their words from the din. Suddenly the edges of my vision blurred. When I blinked, the flames—once crystalline in their heat—softened into hazy halos, and the women's faces fused into shifting silhouettes. The forest's dark greens bled into molten firelight; every shape and color melted together in a dreamlike haze.

My heart thundered as panic coiled in my chest. I fought to steady my gaze, but the world spun. Then, through the roar of voices, a faint jingle rang out—clear, metallic, insistent. I jerked my head toward the sound. Another jingle—so close it felt as if it rang inside my skull.

Reality snapped back. I found myself cocooned in blankets, fingertips brushing the familiar grain of my nightstand. My breathing came in ragged gasps. Groping along its edge, I wrapped my fingers around the cold metal of my phone.

The dream—its firelight, its sisterhood in turmoil—receded like smoke. As I silenced the soft jingle of notifications, my mind raced: What had I witnessed? And why did it feel so startlingly real?

I blinked the sleep from my eyes and swiped up without looking. "Yeah?" I croaked.

"Hey—I'm around the corner. Come meet me!" chirped a familiar, perky voice.

My best friend from third grade, Lori Whittens. We grew up together when her and her mother moved to my hometown. When I decided to move to France, she excitingly wanted to come with me. She was my foil—bold where I was shy, a social butterfly where I flitted at best—and yet we fit together perfectly. Lori had unraveled every secret I'd ever kept; there wasn't a corner of my life she hadn't explored.

Her world was electric—late-night bars, impromptu road trips, the kind of laughter that echoed down empty streets. Mine was safe: morning coffee, a stack of books, the same routine stretched endlessly ahead. I loved her stories, lived through them vicariously, even as my chest tightened at the thought of stepping outside my comfort zone.

But today felt different. My heart fluttered with anticipation, not dread. Throwing off my blankets, I dressed in all black—a long-sleeve tee, ripped skinny jeans, and scuffed leather boots—and paused before my favorite mirror. It stood nearly five feet tall, its bronze frame ornate with curling leaves; I'd rescued it from a dumpster months ago, hauling it home like a trophy.

I twisted my hair into a messy bun, loose tendrils escaping where my grip was too light. I skipped makeup—dark circles under my eyes felt like honest badges of fatigue. Grabbing my jacket and bag, I gave myself one last look: nervous, yes, but alive.

With a quick exhale, I rushed out the door.

Chapter Four

Maeva Sinclair

I stepped into the Pavilion Bistro and paused at the threshold, eyes sweeping over neatly draped tables and mismatched wooden chairs. Delicate vases held single blooms—pale peonies and sprigs of lavender—centered on crisp linen cloths. Floor-to-ceiling windows bathed the space in golden afternoon light; the city's bustle reduced to a gentle hum beyond the glass.

Then it hit me—a curling plume of burnt tobacco smoke that wrapped around me like a velvet cloak. My chest tightened and vision blurred as the scent washed over me, warm and intoxicating. A tremor ran along my spine with each breath, the air thick with a strange longing I'd never known.

I spun in place, heart hammering, scanning every patron and passing waiter. Each table became a blur of faces and shifting shadows. My feet felt rooted to the ground, as if the smoke itself had chained me to the threshold. Every instinct screamed to follow the scent deeper into the room—yet my body refused to budge.

This place felt familiar, but never like this. Desire coiled in my veins, pulling at me with magnetic force. I swallowed hard, determined to find its source … if only I could tear myself away from the smoke's thrall.

A sudden crash of plates and the clang of cutlery from the kitchen ripped through the haze, yanking me back to the present with a jolt. The lingering tobacco scent dissipated like morning mist, and my racing heart slowed as I refocused on the bistro's warm glow.

Lori sat in our usual nook beneath a wrought-iron chandelier, the petals of a half-wilted peony nodding in a slender glass vase beside her napkin. She glanced up from her phone, sunlight dancing in her blonde hair, and the crease in her brow spoke volumes—she recognized the tension tightening my shoulders. Wordlessly, she rose and tucked a strand behind her ear, then tilted her chin in a silent invitation. Concern softened her features, and I knew she'd guessed every thought before I had the chance to speak.

Relief bloomed in my chest. I managed a shaky smile and closed the distance between us. Lori enfolded me in a confident embrace, her coat brushing my arms, and I felt the last tremors of anxiety drain away. The gentle sway of her hug was steady and sure, like roots growing deeper into the earth.

Our waiter—a tall young man with a neat bow tie—appeared at the table's edge, offering a polite nod. "Can I start you off with something to drink?" he asked, voice low above the restaurant's murmur.

"I'll have a White Russian, please," I said, sliding onto the cushioned bench and smoothing the sleeve of my jacket. The cool leather under my fingertips grounded me further in reality.

He turned to Lori. She beamed, tipping her head toward the windows where traffic shimmered like distant stars. "A shaken margarita for me—and, um, keep 'em coming," she added with a playful lift of her brow.

Lori's wink was her way of saying we had a mountain of stories to unpack. We leaned back into the banquette, exhaling together as the tension eased from our shoulders and our minds unclenched. At last, the dam of unspoken thoughts broke, and we dove into a torrent of catch-up: her whirlwind escapades, my quiet anxieties.

I nudged my purse to the floor and settled deeper into the leather seat, drinking in Lori's energy like a spectator at a fireworks show. She lived a life I only dared read about—late-night bar crawls, impromptu road trips, dance floors under neon lights—adventures that would paralyze me with panic if I ever tried them myself.

That smoky lure lingered at the edge of my senses, curling through the air like a living thing. My breath hitched; warmth flooded my cheeks and spine. My thighs pinched together as hunger—not hunger for food, but for something wilder—crept up my back, tightening every muscle. A shimmer of sweat surfaced on my upper lip, and for a heartbeat, I felt utterly consumed.

Clawing my gaze back to the present, I caught sight of our waiter hovering at the edge of the table, leaning in as Lori laughed at something he'd said. He was a handsome young man with easy charm—his bow tie slightly skewed, eyes twinkling. Lori fluttered her eyelashes and tilted her head, her golden hair catching the overhead glow like spun sunshine. She was magnetic; I'd seen men orbit her table like moths to a flame.

I envied her light, even as I resented the unwanted attention it drew toward me when I ventured out. My own flirtations stumbled—half-smiles and thumb-twirls around a straw in my drink. I forced a laugh at Lori's teasing comment, pretending I belonged in their banter, while my heart still pounded from that smoky whisper in the air.

I felt my pulse spike as he swept into view—dark hair slicked back, hooded eyes smoky with intensity. He wore an all-black silk suit that clung to his broad shoulders, the fabric tracing the ridge of muscle beneath. His tan skin gleamed in the warm light, creating a perfect contrast against the midnight sheen of his jacket. My gaze drifted to the unbuttoned collar of his shirt; the subtle dip at his throat sent a jolt of electricity racing down my spine.

He produced a slim tablet and flipped it open with a practiced flick, setting it on the table. I couldn't tear my eyes away. Every line of his body—powerful quads outlined beneath his trousers, the elegant curve of his calf—pulled my attention like a magnet. I sipped my White Russian, pretending to study the swirling cream, but my eyes kept drifting back to him, captivated by the taut strength in his stance.

His shoes—sleek, sockless loafers—completed the dangerous elegant look. I tilted my head, tracing the clean line from his ankle up to the rippling fabric at his thighs, then let my gaze rise to rest on his face. I bit my lip, breath catching as I soaked in the subtle arch of his brow and the set of his jaw.

A tremor of heat pooled in my belly. I shifted in my seat, heart hammering, desperate to remain inconspicuous as desire coiled tight in my core. Just as I summoned the courage to look up again, our waiter glided between us, expertly blocking my view and shattering my private reverie.

"Everything okay?" Lori's teasing voice cut through my embarrassment. She was propped on her elbows, chin in hand, grin playing at her lips.

I blinked, forcing a casual smile. "Yeah, all good."

She launched into her drama-filled recount of office chaos, but my attention drifted—my senses still electrified by the stranger across the room. My ears heard Lori's words, but my eyes remained fixed on him in my periphery. In that moment, I realized I was utterly, hopelessly entranced.

I opened my mouth to reply, but the stranger at the next table had already begun gathering his things. My chest tightened as disappointment bloomed, he rose, his broad shoulders blocking the light, and stepped toward the main aisle. As he passed, his arm brushed mine—cool silk against warm skin.

"Excuse me," he murmured, voice low and velvety—a tremor of heat tracing up my spine. I lifted my eyes to meet his—deep pools of midnight that beckoned me to drown.

"It's okay," I managed, voice hushed.

A crooked smile curved his lips, bright teeth flashing against stubble-shadowed skin. He offered a silent nod to Lori, then vanished into the swirl of the bistro. Even after he was gone, the memory of his sculpted jaw and powerful frame lingered like an echo.

Then the scent returned—tobacco and something darker, richer— seeping into my lungs and stoking a wildfire of desire. My throat went dry, vision narrowing to that intoxicating fragrance.

"That was a little weird," Lori sighed, breaking through my daze.

I downed the last of my White Russian in one long swallow, then reached across and emptied hers too. For the next hour, we traded stories and laughter, unraveling all the missed moments of the past weeks. With Lori, words flowed easily—no need for daily check-ins when every fortnight felt like a homecoming.

When we finally stepped back into the afternoon sun, I hugged her tight. "Thanks for everything," I whispered.

She held me a heartbeat longer, then grinned and teased, "Maybe if you got laid, you'd loosen up."

I pulled back, my eyebrows arching. "Thanks for the tip."

Her eyes twinkled wickedly. "Just saying—your hair might even shine more."

"Yeah, yeah. Love you," I laughed, brushing off her tease.

"Love you too," she called as she hailed a cab.

I watched her disappear into the traffic, the tobacco-sweet memory of the stranger still lingering in my senses. With a final wave, I turned homeward, heart pounding with questions I didn't yet have the answers to.

Determined to reclaim the rest of my day, I headed for the little bookstore a few blocks away—the one wedged into a corner, its battered sign half-hidden by ivy. I hadn't slept well in days and figured a new story might lull me into dreamland.

The air turned sharp as I walked, a cold breeze slipping beneath my jacket and crawling up my spine. I stopped mid-sidewalk, half-expecting someone to be lurking behind me—only to find empty pavement and frowning strangers brushing past. Embarrassed, I forced myself onward, but then that scent returned: burnt tobacco, rich and smoky, twisting through the city air. My pulse quickened as I glanced over my shoulder, half-hoping—and half-dreading—to see him there.

Finally, the bookstore's weathered façade appeared: a tall, narrow door with an antique copper handle worn smooth by decades of readers. My fingers closed around its chill weight, and for a moment I savored the promise of quiet aisles lined with paper and ink.

Then another hand settled over mine—warm, large, veined, the skin etched with intricate tattoos. I looked up, frozen, as the mystery man from the bistro stared down at me. His dark pupils were endless, drawing me into a silent command.

My heart hammered so hard I thought I might scream. The world tilted: my face drained of blood, then flared crimson. I yanked my hand back, every instinct screaming to flee—but my feet felt rooted to the spot as his presence swallowed me whole.

In that breath, the cobblestones, the copper handle, the scent of tobacco—all of it became a single, trembling question: why was he here?

I felt his shadow engulf me as he closed the gap—an imposing silhouette that made my heart pound against my ribs. My fingertips pricked with anxious energy, hovering too close to his side, and I struggled to keep from flinching.

He studied me with an intense curiosity, the sun illuminating his flawless skin and making every feature seem impossibly perfect. When his gaze drifted back to my face, he spoke, low and intimate.

"You are very beautiful," he murmured.

My cheeks flamed—I'd never been called beautiful, and the compliment sent a jolt through me. My gaze shot to the ground, my mind scrambling for something—anything—to say. Instead, I managed a strangled, "Th-thank you," my voice cracking in my own ears.

He took another step forward, and I felt the heat of his body so close that I could count the breaths rising and falling on his chest. My legs threatened to give out; I shifted from foot to foot like an awkward schoolgirl with a crush. The air between us pulsed with something electric, and I could feel every drop of blood rushing to my face.

When I dared to glance up again, his dark eyes held me captive, and a fresh wave of mortification washed over me. My heart raced as he reached out, his hand brushing the small of my back—an intentional touch that sent a shiver of embarrassment through my spine.

His breath brushed my ear as he whispered, "Are you going to walk through?"

My head spun. "W-walk where?" I stammered, my cheeks blazing so hot I could feel the heat in my scalp. My words tumbled out, nearly tripping over one another.

He arched a brow and gestured behind him. "Through the door," he said gently, still holding it open.

Mortified, I realized I'd been standing frozen in the threshold, mouth parted in silent awe, as he waited for me. I cleared my throat— loud in the hush—then sucked in a shaky breath. With one hesitant step, I brushed past him so close our elbows knocked together. My heart thundered, palms slick against my thighs, as I forced myself inside, determined not to collapse in a heap of red-faced embarrassment.

I bolted down the nearest aisle, spine tingling as if every book around me were watching. My cheeks burned; I prayed no one had seen me stumble. Pressing my back against a shelf, I inhaled slow, steady breaths and reminded myself why I loved these quiet treasures.

The shop was chaos incarnate—stacks bleeding into aisles, no neat labels to guide me. Finding a hidden gem demanded patience (and a strong back), but the reward always outweighed the hassle. I ran my fingers over crinkled dust jackets and cracked leather spines, savoring each title as if it held a secret.

Then I spotted it: an unassuming volume bound in deep chestnut hide, its surface mottled and cool under my fingertips. A thin leather strap looped around its middle, as if keeping something precious—or dangerous—locked inside. My pulse quickened. Why was this blank book here with no title, no author, no hint of what lay within?

Despite my better judgment, my hand drifted back to it. The moment I touched the cover, a jolt of adrenaline shot up my arm, and I reeled backward—almost colliding with a teetering pile of books. My heart thundered so loudly I was sure the whole store had heard. With my fingers shaking, I righted the stack and ducked behind it, cheeks still scorching.

Peeking around the corner, I checked that no one had witnessed my retreat. When I dared look again, the cover remained blank. Curious dread prickled at my skin, but I set my purse beside me and eased it open. Inside, the pages were pristine—aged parchment, dust-flecked but utterly empty. No preface, no handwritten scrawl—just endless white space.

I swallowed hard. A journal, perhaps? Or something far more cryptic? My fingers hovered over the first page, and for a heartbeat I hesitated—then, steeling myself, I leaned in to inspect it…

"Can I help you?"

A soft voice drifted from the aisle's end—one of the clerks making her rounds—and jolted me upright. My pulse lurched in my throat as I stammered, "I-I'm fine, thank you." I snapped the book shut, hiding its mystery from view.

"I see you've discovered one of the rarest volumes," the low voice murmured, and I jumped, nearly dropping the book.

"It's not rare," I blurted, cheeks flaming. "There's nothing inside—just blank pages. Maybe it's a journal?"

My pulse thundered as he stepped into view: tall, dark-haired, every bit as unnerving as the last time I'd seen him. Sweat prickled at my temples, and the scent of tobacco curled around us again, tugging at something deeper. He reached out and plucked the book from my grip. My breath caught as I watched his long fingers splay across the leather cover, then fan opened the volume. The pages remained as empty as mine—dust-dimmed parchment without a smudge.

"Only because you can't see the words written there," he teased, handing it back with a half-smile that didn't touch his eyes.

"Invisible ink?" I shot back, forcing a laugh that caught in my throat.

His expression sobered, jaw tightening. "Perhaps not the ink you know. But the words are there." He leaned closer, voice dropping to a whisper that vibrated against my skin. My heart thudded so loud I could feel it in my throat. I dared a glance up—his dark eyes unreadable—and my breath hitched. Was he flirting or warning me?

Embarrassment and curiosity warred inside me as I returned the book to its shelf, determined to escape. I pivoted toward the door.

He extended a hand—long, veined, the skin etched with intricate tattoos. I froze, then lowered my hand into his. His grip was firm, warm—almost electrifying.

"Elias Knight," he said.

My stomach fluttered. "Maeva," I replied in a flat tone, though my pulse betrayed me.

He cocked an impressed brow. "Does Maeva have a last name?" His lips curved into that same enigmatic smile.

I swallowed, voice barely above a whisper: "Sinclair."

Elias Knight's eyes flickered with something of—approval or amusement, I couldn't tell—but the air between us crackled with unspoken promise as he released my hand and stepped back into the shifting light.

I felt his gaze burn into me as he tilted his chin down, lifted my hand, and pressed a soft kiss to its back. "It's very nice to meet you, Maeva Sinclair," he murmured.

My hand dropped to my waist; heat pooled in my palms. He smiled, dark eyes never leaving mine. "That's a beautiful name—it suits you perfectly."

"Th-thank you," I managed, voice catching.

He straightened and circled behind me, the whisper of his movement stirring the leather-bound volume in my arms. His scent— tobacco and something warmer—washed over me again, and my legs went weak. From behind, he reached out and reclaimed the book, his fingers brushing mine as he handed it back. Our eyes locked in the soft light of the aisle.

"Do you know a Sinclair named Meridith?" he asked, voice low. "She's been a dear friend of my family for generations."

I shook my head, brows knitting. "I don't believe so."

He let out a slow, rueful smile. "I thought as much—Sinclair's are a rare breed these days."

He stepped forward again, closing the gap until I could feel the warmth of his breath. "Would you care to join me for dinner?" His tone was gentle, earnest—an invitation that echoed in my chest.

My throat tightened, alarms ringing in my mind, but something in his deep gaze calmed me. Lori's teasing echo— "Maybe if you got laid…"—flitted through my thoughts. I drew in a shaky breath.

"Sure," I whispered, surprise lacing my words.

"Excellent," he said, relief lighting his features. "Meet me at The Fork House at eight on Saturday."

"I'll be there." I tucked a strand of hair behind my ear, trying to steady the flutter in my stomach.

Stepping toward the door, I dared a last glance back—only to find the aisle empty. My heart lurched. He'd vanished as mysteriously as he appeared.

Clutching the leather volume to my chest, I paused. Though its pages were blank, something deep inside urged me to keep it, to protect it. With a steadying breath, I carried it to the counter and purchased the strange journal—eager, anxious, and inexplicably hopeful for what Saturday night might bring.

Chapter Five

Elias Knight

I paused over the scattered photographs on my desk, each one an imperfect echo of her presence. No camera could capture the full gravity of her beauty—the way her dark chocolate curls framed a face both youthful and knowing, or how those penetrating brown eyes could unnerve the most steadfast soul. Petite and lithe, she moved with a quiet confidence, her soft voice a disarming counterpoint to her fierce gaze.

Daniel Black returned from one of her routine therapy sessions, offering only a curt nod. His silence spoke volumes—appearance was secondary to the truths hidden in her dreams, which formed the cornerstone of our investigation. From the instant he confirmed her identity, I knew I had to see her for myself.

Daniel is my right hand in the field—an ageless ally bound to me by the centuries. He commands a covert cadre, each recruit tasked with unearthing descendants of Meridith Sinclair and extracting the faintest clues from their bloodlines. When a lead runs dry, Daniel severs that lineage without mercy. Over time, our family retreated from the hunt, outsourcing our task in exchange for promises of immortality that we could never fulfill—our curse alone condemned us to eternity, and Meridith's covenant ensures we endure.

Though Daniel is not of my blood, he has stood by me since our fathers forged alliances between distant villages. We are brothers in every sense that matters, united by a purpose older than memory. For us, centuries collapse into moments—each day another turn in a cycle that only ends when Meridith does.

It is said that "A curse set takes blood and love—a curse broken takes heart and peace." For centuries I hunted Meridith's descendants, each lead a fleeting whisper in an endless night. Time stretches forever, yet sifting through generations of Sinclair blood felt like an eternal slog.

Over the years, the curse transformed my family. Humanity slipped through our fingers as we became something else—monsters dwelling in the same frozen moment for centuries. But now, at last, we had a chance at salvation. I'd met many Sinclair's, yet none bore the key memories hidden in Maeva's veins—clues as vital as the grimoire we'd reclaimed long ago.

Memories woven into blood are both curse and gift. Once we began feeding on their lifeblood, shards of ancestral recollection flooded our minds—visions Meridith hid behind generations of secrecy. We chased her trail from one distant kin to the next: the grimoire rescued from a dusty crypt, the bloodstained blade used in our father's assassination, its magic branded by her ancient spell work.

But when Maeva Sinclair stepped into that dusty bookstore, the grimoire's leather bindings gleamed with purpose, and the air itself thrummed with power. No other Sinclair had awakened its magic so fully. Daniel's scheme—guiding her to the volume's hidden perch—had worked perfectly.

As the book pulsed like a living heartbeat in her hands, I knew she was the one. Maeva carried the final piece of Meridith's puzzle, and with her, our family's centuries-long nightmare could at last come to an end.

For centuries, my family scourged the world for Meridith's bloodline—tasting flesh and blood from every Sinclair descendant—yet none awakened the ancient memories, none felt the grimoire's call. Fate can be cruel, but sometimes she chooses favorites.

Maeva Sinclair intrigued me: delicate of frame, blissfully ignorant of her heritage. Meridith was the most formidable woman I'd ever known—

untamed, effortlessly powerful, her presence commanding every council from distant villages to grand courts. How would Maeva react when she learned her ancestors had fallen short of that legend? I suspected Maeva carried Meridith's blood still smoldering in her veins—and if she ever discovered that spark, she might unleash a power our curse could not contain.

I could not coerce her outright; risking her wrath would be folly. No—this required subtler feints. Women, I'd learned, are labyrinths of heart and emotion, yet drawn by the faintest ember of desire. I needed to seize Maeva's heart first—bind her willingly—before commanding her true power. She was already ensnared by the strange magic I'd guided her toward; it was only a matter of time before her loyalty—and more— became mine.

A firm knock on the petrified oak door shattered my reverie. I set aside the small cup of dark, metallic brew that had become my morning ritual.

"Shall we bring the… witch here?" Daniel's voice rumbled from the threshold. His hulking form leaned against the frame, arms folded, his patience practiced over centuries. I met his gaze only briefly before turning back to the window.

Outside, dawn's pale light touched the still lake, its surface a mirror to the evergreen pines. I once greeted mornings with hope; now I watched each sunrise through the same centuries-old dread, never daring to exhale. Below the water's glassy calm lay the shadows of what had been—and what was yet to come.

Even amid the fondest recollections, it was the bodies beneath the water that haunted me most. In my dreams, I wakened to their desperate thrashing—pale limbs clawing at the surface, mouths open in silent screams that never reached the air. Villagers and wandering travelers alike had once flocked to our doorstep for healing, unaware that the very hands they thanked were the ones that drew their blood.

Night after night, when our hunger was sated, we bound stones to our victims' ankles and cast them into the lake's inky depths—alive or not, it made no difference. Their weight dragged them down into eternal silence, hidden beneath a placid surface that bore no trace of our atrocities. And through it all, Meridith's visage remained unruffled, her expression as still and dark as the water itself.

Daniel's amused smirk flickered into something more calculating as he stepped away from the doorframe.

"Consider it done," he said, voice low. With a final nod, he turned and vanished down the stone corridor, boots echoing against ancient tiles.

I drained the last of the copper-tinged spirit, the burn trailing its warmth through my chest. Pushing the empty glass aside, I rose from the oaken table and crossed the chamber in long, measured strides. The dawn light danced on the walls, but I no longer sought its comfort.

Instead, I peered out once more at the placid lake, recalling those thrashing forms beneath the surface—reminders of our hunger, of the secret atrocity that built this fortress.

A slow smile curved my lips as I let my plans take shape. Maeva Sinclair—so delicate, so ignorant of her own power—would learn quickly enough that some gifts come with a price. She thought I invited her to dinner; soon, she would discover the true banquet I had in store.

Chapter Six

Elias Knight

Soft clicks echoed on the flagstones as Abigail's heels advanced—precise, measured, each tap an unspoken command. Daniel's easy confidence wavered; his shoulders stiffened, and he rose to full height before swiveling to face her.

"Mistress," he intoned, voice steady despite the tension coiling in his stance.

She stepped into the doorway, pale light glinting off her perfectly coiffed waves of golden-blonde hair. Her gaze bored into Daniel's, untouched by surprise or warmth.

"Daniel," she drawled, voice silk laced with steel, "I never expected you here. I assumed you'd be out draining some poor girl's life for your amusement."

Daniel's jaw clenched, but he held his ground as she closed the distance, her skirts whispering over the stone. He tilted his head just enough to study her—petite, impossibly poised, every line of her tailored gown flawless, from the delicate embroidery at her cuffs to the way her lipstick matched the rosy arch of her cheekbones.

"Not today, Mistress," he replied, each word clipped. His deep blue eyes flickered with unease, betraying the respect—and fear—he carried for her.

Abigail's lips curved into a thin, knowing smile. Even here, in the shadowed halls of our ancestral fortress, she radiated authority: sun-kissed strands framing a face that never tolerated imperfection, and makeup applied with the precision of ritual.

Daniel's posture straightened still further, as if she alone could tame the centuries-old beasts that raged within him.

Between them hung a fragile silence—charged, ancestral, and inevitable—before Abigail inclined her head, as if granting permission for what was to come next.

Beneath Mother's flawless façade lay the same hunger that cursed our bloodline. She bore the gift of eternal youth—skin like ivory, hair glinting with sunlight—but her beauty concealed a predator.

Long ago, she walked the village at night, coaxing unsuspecting souls into shadowed alleys, then sinking her fangs into their throats. By lantern's glow, she left dismembered bodies scattered like grotesque offerings; panic rippled through the streets until Father intervened.

Daniel moved with preternatural silence, each footfall muffled by fallen leaves as he stalked his prey. He selected those who stood out— scarlet-haired waifs, gaunt peddlers whose hollow cheeks whispered of hardship, even small children clutching tattered dolls—anything that would send their hearts hammering. Under a pale moon, he trailed them through skeletal birches and tangled underbrush, the forest closing in like a cage.

When he struck, it was with ruthless precision: first a silencing hand over their lips, then a sudden, brutal tearing at muscle and sinew. The air filled with the sickly-sweet tang of spilled blood as he sank his teeth into warm flesh, crimson rivulets coursing over his skin. A final, rasping gasp died on their throat, and Daniel stood amid the ruin, his breath slow and steady as he watched the life fade from their eyes. Then, without a shudder of remorse, he dragged the body deep into the woods—no footprints, no witness—leaving only the quiet hush of the night to swallow the horror.

His animalistic fury eclipsed even his darkest seductions. Status, family name, or social standing meant nothing—if Daniel set his sights on you, you were marked. When he delivered prey to our stronghold, torture followed that no beast would dare enact. I sometimes feared he reveled in our curse, his eyes alight with savage delight.

All that changed the night he brought Sarah into our midst. She arrived under the guise of a simple village girl—soft-spoken, demure, skirts dusted with road dirt. Yet beneath that innocent facade lay the hands of a master bladesmith.

As she stepped across our threshold, her fingers toyed with a slender knife concealed at her thigh, its polished steel catching the torchlight.

We welcomed her as we did any newcomer—offering warmth by the hearth, the comfort of food and drink. But Sarah's gaze never wavered from my father; she moved with studied grace, as though gauging each man's strength, mapping our vulnerabilities. Then, in a blur of motion, she struck.

Before anyone could shout alarm, her blade flashed—a silent arc of light slicing through the hush. It plunged into my father's heart; the steel snapping ribs with a sickening crack. He gasped, eyes widening in shock, and sagged into her arms as her hand twisted the knife deeper. His warm blood spattered across her sleeves, vivid against the pale linen.

He collapsed onto the stone floor, the impact rousing a swirl of ash that drifted upward—his final curse upon this place. My mother's scream ripped through the corridors, raw anguish echoing off the cold walls, a sound that will forever haunt these halls.

Sarah stood over him, chest heaving, eyes glinting with righteous fury rather than fear. Her blade, slick with life's essence, trembled only slightly in her grasp. She had come for vengeance—her target stained with our atrocities—and in that single, brutal moment, she revealed that we had more enemies than we ever imagined.

The line between hunter and hunted blurred that night: her justice as sharp and uncompromising as our own bloodlust, her purpose clear, while ours was reckless survival. In Sarah's cold triumph, I glimpsed the full cost of our centuries-old curse—and the reckoning that now loomed for us all.

Years later, we discovered the truth: Sarah had been sent by the Raven Coven itself, armed with a cursed blade forged to pierce our immortal hearts. In all our years of bloodletting, we never suspected that our own arrogance would become the instrument of our undoing.

My family once feasted indiscriminately—travelers, merchants, nobility alike—never troubling ourselves with the grudges we amassed. Yet that fateful night revealed our fatal flaw: only Meridith's enchanted weapon could end us. A single devastating wound, and years of unchallenged power crumbled in an instant.

In the wake of Father's death, we vowed to be more cunning. Survival demanded selectivity: prey hidden behind false identities, villages circled like chess pieces, alliances forged in shadow. But grief is a poison that is more potent than any blade.

Mother, consumed by fury and despair, welcomed death's embrace. She prowled the countryside like a vengeful storm—enticing warlords to challenge her, razing entire hamlets in her path. Daniel and I scrambled to bury the evidence, binding bodies for the lake and burning our tracks, but her wrath was unstoppable.

Her single mistake—slaying the wrong target in her grief—ignited a rebellion. Villagers rose with torches and pitchforks, storming our ancestral fortress, dragging our banners into the dirt. They torched our halls, looted our treasures, and left our legacy in smoldering ruin. Heads impaled on pikes marked the final insult.

Forced into exile, we scattered to the far corners of the earth. For a century, we watched as generations passed into myth, our name fading into folklore. Then, when the embers of our lineage cooled, we returned— ever more refined, more insidious.

We adapted. We traded wanton slaughter for seductive intrigue and subtle mind-possession. We invested in blood banks, bribed hospitals, and recruited thrill-seekers willing to "sell" their veins for a taste of the supernatural. Yet no mortal reservoir could ever match the rush of the hunt—the predator's thrill as it stalks through moonlit woods, heart pounding with anticipation.

To this day, we walk the line between monster and monarch, our curse as much a burden as a gift. And though time may cloak our history in shadows, the beast within still stirs, forever hungry for the next dance of death beneath the silvered sky.

"How is the progress coming?" Abigail's voice cut through the hush as she stepped into the chamber, hands folded over her stomach in that deceptively serene pose she favored.

I met her gaze, a small, confident smile tugging at my lips.

"I'm meeting her tonight."

She and Daniel needed no further explanation, every hunt we orchestrated was a family ritual, each step choreographed with cold precision. Abigail's pale eyes glinted with approval, and she inclined her head toward Daniel.

"Well done," she praised, lips parting to reveal those razor-sharp canines.

"Then let us not tarry," Mother commanded, her tone as relentless as sharpened steel. "End this damnation."

She lingered a moment, her hand resting lightly on Daniel's forearm—an unspoken benediction—then turned and strode away, each heel striking the stone corridor like a tolling bell. As her footsteps faded into the distance, I exhaled softly. Mother never played the games we did; her cruelty was decisive, her wrath precise.

The less she knew, the more she trusted us to see our plan through. Once Maeva's confidence was mine, and the secrets of Meridith's curse laid bare in her blood, then—and only then—would I bring Mother into the fold.

Tonight's rendezvous with Maeva set my pulse aflame. The beast within me stirred, muscles coiling beneath my skin like a spring. I had lured countless women before—soft words, tender touches, a kiss that tasted like honey and promises.

But with Maeva, the final act would be exquisite. I would draw her close beneath the moonlit arbor, my voice a velvet caress in her ear. Her pulse would drum beneath my fingertips as I pressed my lips to her throat, the promise of warmth and safety dissolving into pure, predatory hunger.

In one fluid motion, fangs would pierce silken skin—an intimate betrayal she would never see coming. Her blood, warm and copper-sweet, would flood my senses as I drank deeply, each heartbeat a gift I stole. Fingers digging into her waist to anchor us both, I'd taste the very essence of her life.

With each swallow, her strength would ebb, her limbs going limp in my arms. Her breath would falter, light in her eyes fading to gray as I pulled back, watching the final spark extinguish with a soft sigh. In that breathtaking moment, our curse would edge closer to an end—and her last heartbeat would echo mine forever.

Maeva was slight of frame, her shoulders not even close to mine, and yet I knew the blood coursing through her carried powers I could neither rouse nor restrain—no matter how much she tempted me with her innocence. Meridith's legacy lay dormant in her veins, waiting to shatter every lock I'd so carefully forged. My only safeguard would be patience: to entice her into an alliance without awakening that slumbering storm.

I paused at the edge of my desk and swept my gaze across the scattered photographs. Agents had slipped these stolen images among medical files and half-legible genealogy charts. Each portrait captured a different facet of her life—her curly hair tumbling over oversized hoodies as she hurried down the street, the bookstore's sign blurred in the background. I traced the delicate curve of her jaw, the thoughtful tilt of her head, reminding myself that this was no mere conquest. This was business. My family's salvation depended on her trust.

Tonight, as the sun bled pink and purple over the horizon and the moon claimed her throne, I felt the ancient hunger stir beneath my ribs. The forest around our fortress exhaled in chorus—owl calls, rustling underbrush, the soft footfalls of creatures born to darkness. Immortality had once felt like a gift; now it was a weight that twisted in my chest, a knife I carried day after endless day. I knew the peace of death would be a gift far kinder than the unending thirst.

My obsession with Meridith's descendants had nearly cost me my mind. Centuries of dead ends had hollowed my days, driving me toward an edge I no longer feared to cross. It was Daniel—my brother in blood and spirit—who pulled me back from that precipice. In his steady presence, I rediscovered a different kind of peace: a purpose beyond revenge and despair. He showed me that even in this cursed existence, we could forge our own meaning.

And so, with the night as my cloak, I prepared to meet Maeva Sinclair—not as predator, but as supplicant. For within her lay the final key to an age-old curse, and with that key, a chance—perhaps—for us all to find rest at last.

Chapter Seven

Maeva Sinclair

I slipped into the cab ten minutes too late, my stomach twisting as I rehearsed every worst-case scenario. In my apartment, I'd paced in circles—dozens of laps burned into the carpet—second-guessing my choice of dress, my wildly uncooperative hair, even the decision to leave the safety of my front door. Familiar trinkets and the gentle hush of my living room had felt infinitely more comforting than tonight's unknown.

By the time I hailed the cab, I'd anchored myself with every breathing technique my therapist ever taught me: five counts in through the nose, seven counts out through pursed lips. I repeated my mantra like a lifeline—Just a meal. Just a meal. You can do this.

The driver's headlights cut through the evening mist as we pulled up to the restaurant's valet stand. My heart pounded in my throat when the valet opened the door, crisp in his navy vest. I pressed a trembling hand to his arm for balance as I slipped out, the click of my heels echoing against the marble steps.

A flash of electric blue caught my eye before I even looked up—his jacket, brass-buttoned, his posture perfectly composed as he held the door open. My pulse stuttered as I heard the soft chime of the front doors sliding apart. Warm light and quiet laughter spilled out, beckoning me forward.

Clutching my clutch like a life raft, I inhaled one final, fortifying breath and stepped into the glow—ready, at last, to meet whatever awaited me inside.

I smoothed the satin of my little black dress—its thigh-high slit whispering against my skin, the deep V-neck framed by a panel of sheer black mesh that hinted at elegance without revealing too much. My fingers wove through curly tendrils tumbling over my shoulders, pressing any rogue fly-aways into place.

A warm tide of aromas washed over me: cardamom and cumin from simmering curries, the sweet promise of caramelized fruit, and a chorus of fresh herbs from nearby tables. My mouth watered as a passing waiter set down a sizzling cast-iron skillet, the crisp hiss of oil laced with garlic and chili. Each scrape of cutlery and low murmur of conversation wove into the restaurant's symphony—glasses chiming, soft laughter rippling through the candlelit room.

I drew in a slow breath, letting the scents ground me: tonight wasn't about fear or hesitation. It was simply a moment suspended between anticipation and delight—one I'd learned to savor, plate by fragrant plate.

A soft hush fell over me once I realized I wasn't the center of anyone's attention. I inhaled deeply, letting the heady mix of smoked paprika, fresh basil, and warm vanilla calm my racing thoughts. The insistent knot of worry in my chest loosened as I scanned the candlelit room for his familiar silhouette.

My eyes drifted from the polished oak bar to the shadowy alcoves where couples whispered over flutes of sparkling wine. I traced the arc of steam rising from sizzling plates, the glint of brass chandeliers, even the gleam of polished mirror panels—yet there was no flash of his frame anywhere, no strong stance waiting for me.

"Did I get stood up?" I whispered to myself, voice trembling in the warm glow.

I forced a slow count: one… two… three… then looked again. A prickling heat gathered in my cheeks as tears burned at the corners of my eyes.

That quiet inner voice—once a soft caution—hissed with bitterness: You shouldn't have tried. You're alone. I gripped the fabric of my clutch, nails tightening knuckles-white, determined not to let self-doubt coil any tighter around my heart.

I pivoted to retrace my steps—only to feel a firm hand close around my elbow.

"Leaving so soon? Could we at least sit down before you end our date?" His deep voice rumbled in my ear.

I whipped my head back and met his gaze—those dark eyes pinned me in place, and I was lost all over again.

"I'm sorry," I mumbled, voice trembling. "I looked everywhere and thought you'd stood me up."

A teasing smile curled his lips. "You? Never."

With the gentlest touch, he guided my hand under his arm and led me through the dining room. The hush that fell in his wake was tangible—chairs scraped back; forks paused in mid-air. His towering frame in that midnight-blue jacket was unmistakable; each step he took radiated confidence, and I felt its warmth seep into my own bones.

As we passed table after table, I caught stunned glances—some admiring, some resentful. My cheeks warmed under their scrutiny, but I held my head high, buoyed by his steady presence.

A young woman at the bar followed our progress with smoldering eyes and a sly smile, her glance burning into me so intently I swore we'd met before. But I shook off the distraction; I refused to betray how rattled I felt.

We slipped past the kitchen door, where waiters darted aside—silhouettes in crisp whites—almost as if they feared interrupting his path. The air here was thick with the scent of rosemary and roasting meat, punctuated by the clang of pots in the back.

At last, we came to an antique Victorian staircase tucked behind a paneled archway. The dark wooden steps ascended in a graceful curve, their varnish worn smooth by decades of footsteps. He paused at the base, extending his free hand.

"Shall we?" he asked, voice soft as moonlight.

My pulse thundered in my ears. With one last steadying breath, I placed my hand in his—warm, reassuring—and let him lead me upward into the unknown.

I pause at the foot of the staircase, drinking in the graceful curve of each worn step and the warm glow of sconces lining the walls. Taking a slow breath, I place a trembling hand on the polished banister and lift my foot to the first riser. His steady grip on my arm keeps me from faltering as we climb, the wood sighing under our weight with each careful step.

At the top, he finally releases me and swivels to face me, a mischievous glint in his dark eyes. "I wanted this to be perfect for you," he says, voice soft as velvet.

My throat tightens in confusion and wonder as he pushes open a heavy door. Before me lies a hidden chamber transformed into a vision of intimacy: a small wrought-iron table draped in black silk, its surface scattered with blood-red rose petals and flickering tea lights. Black metal chairs, their backs entwined with vine motifs, cradle plush maroon cushions. Low strands of twinkling lights drape overhead like captured stardust, while clusters of roses in aged pewter vases fill every corner with a heady, honeyed scent.

My breath catches. The room's rustic sweetness swirls through me, drawing tears that glisten at the corners of my eyes. He steps forward and draws my hand into his, guiding me across the threshold. My heels click against the wooden floor as I move, each heartbeat echoing in my chest like a drum.

"Did you do all this?" I whisper, my voice trembling.

"Every petal," he replies, brushing a loose curl behind my ear.

My pulse flutters like a hummingbird's wings. No one has ever orchestrated something so breathtaking just for me. Warmth blooms in my throat as tears spill free, my vision shimmering with emotion. He reaches out, gently brushing one from my cheek, and I feel the room's magic settle around us—a promise of something deep, tender, and unforgettable.

Two waiters appeared as if from the shadows, each bearing a crystal flute of champagne. They set the glasses before us and, in one smooth motion, pulled out our chairs—an unspoken invitation to begin the evening. I let my gaze wander once more around the room, committing every detail to memory before tucking my feet beneath the tablecloth and settling into my chair.

A soft smile played on my lips. The entire space felt tailored to me, and I couldn't help but feel unexpectedly lucky. I crossed my legs at the knee and let my fingers lace together in my lap, trying to tame the flutter in my stomach. Across from me, he leaned forward, arms resting on the tabletop, watching intently. His dark eyes moved over me, a silent caress against my skin, and I shifted in my seat, my pulse stuttering in response.

The hush between us grew heavy. I opened my mouth to speak, but my mind went blank—only the hum of candles and the faint pop of a cork somewhere in the distance filled the silence. A bead of sweat slipped along my hairline; my underarms tingled with clamminess. He leaned back, one arm draped casually on his thigh, the other still on the table. My fingers began to tap, then twist, as the alarms in my head sounded their warning.

Finally, his voice cut through my panic.

"Are you always this nervous?"

I swallowed hard and met his gaze. His eyes were soft; concern etched in the slight lift of his brow.

"How could you tell?" I laughed, a shaky attempt to diffuse my embarrassment.

"Your legs are making the table dance," he teased gently.

Heat rushed to my face as I glanced down and saw just how true his words were. The tablecloth fluttered with each bounce of my knees. I closed my eyes, inhaled deeply, and whispered,

"I'm sorry. I haven't been on a date in a very long time."

The confession hung in the air between us—vulnerable, honest—and in that moment, I felt the tension ease just enough to believe this night might be something more than I ever expected.

He drew in a slow breath, then leaned forward, resting both elbows on the table. His fingers laced together, and he held my gaze as if it were the only thing in the room. I straightened in my chair, sliding back slightly, trying to carve a little space for myself beneath the tablecloth.

"I don't get out much either," he admitted, his voice low with relief.

His admission was a revelation. I nodded, feeling the ice in my chest crack just enough to let warmth seep in.

"I—" I began, but he continued.

"I stick to what I know: home, my routines. I don't date, not truly, unless something—or someone—captures my interest." He lowered his chin, eyes never leaving mine, and offered a small, knowing smile that barely revealed the flash of his teeth.

Heat blossomed in my cheeks at the intensity of his attention. My chest prickled with sweat, and a subtle tremor worked its way through my limbs: a delicious, maddening anticipation. I shifted my legs, crossing them the other way, then uncrossing them—each movement drawing a sharper line of amusement on his face.

"Still nervous?" he teased, voice soft as silk.

"Not quite," I lied, though the tremor of my hand around the champagne flute said otherwise.

His laughter was quiet, a gentle ripple that settled into the air between us. Encouraged, I took another sip—then another—letting the bubbles keep pace with the flutter in my heart.

"So," I said, setting the flute down and leaning forward in turn, "tell me about yourself."

He leaned back, one arm draped casually over the back of the chair, the other resting on the table. The candlelight caught the angles of his face, and I could feel myself drowning in the quiet confidence he radiated.

My cheeks flushed as his shirt fell open, revealing the sculpted planes of his chest. The air between us grew thick with something more electric than candlelight. I cleared my throat, reminding myself why I'd come tonight.

"Tell me," I murmured, leaning back so I could meet his gaze again, "what drives you, Elias?"

He paused, fingers lingering over the last undone button, then closed his hand into a fist and leaned forward. The tension in his shoulders shifted, and his dark eyes glimmered with something vulnerable.

"I'm driven by legacy," he began, voice low and even. "By responsibility to a family name that spans centuries… and by the promise of something more—of finally finding someone who sees me, and not just the veneer of Knight."

I nodded, my heartbeat fluttering at the intensity in his gaze. This was more than small talk; it was a door opening between us.

"And you, Maeva?" he asked, tilting his head. "What do you seek in a place you call home?"

My breath trembled as I considered the question: honesty or charm? I chose honesty.

"I seek belonging," I admitted, my voice barely above a whisper. "Someone who understands that feeling lost can sometimes lead you exactly where you need to be."

He studied me for a moment, then reached across the table, brushing his fingertips against mine. The contact sent a warm spark through my veins.

"To belonging, then," he said softly. His thumb traced small circles on my knuckles as he raised his glass, and I mirrored the gesture—two fragile souls reaching across a sea of uncertainty, daring to find safe harbor in one another.

A soft laugh escaped me at his earnest response. I lifted my glass once more, willing my nerves to stay in check.

"My name is Maeva Sinclair," I said, swallowing. "I'm twenty-four. I moved here almost a year ago—initially for my college graduation trip—but I fell in love. I felt a pull to this place, like the universe was nudging me back. So, I waited until graduation and took the leap. It just felt… right." I paused to sip, watching his eyes reflect the candlelight like liquid glass.

He smiled—a slow, half-smile that warmed the space between us. "Maybe it was fate bringing us together," he said softly.

We drifted into easy conversation, trading stories of childhood, travels, and small victories we'd celebrated along the way. He listened as if each detail were precious, leaning in when I spoke and meeting my gaze with genuine curiosity. I couldn't shake the feeling that he already knew me—that he'd seen the real me long before tonight.

By the time our glasses were nearly empty, I realized I could talk with him for hours—about anything and everything—and still uncover new questions to ask, new corners of his world to explore. In his presence, the restlessness I'd carried for so long fell away, replaced by the thrilling sense of connection I'd only ever dreamed of finding.

The candles began to dim as the wickers ended near to the base of the glasses. I had talked more with him than I had with most people. He made me feel wanted and that I was the only person he wished to give his attention to. My heart skipped every time he looked into my eyes. He never wavered with his gaze from mine, always staring at me every time I said something. His deep dark eyes were so penetrating and fierce, I felt a sense of vulnerability like his eyes knew something about me that I did not.

Staring into someone's eyes made my anxiety flicker, it was not something that I tried to accomplish. I couldn't help but refocus on all the surrounding candles and lights and deflect from his gaze. I could feel the wall around my heart chip bit by bit every moment I sat with him.

There was something about him I couldn't quite place—an uncanny familiarity, as though our souls had brushed before this life. Perhaps fate had woven our paths together long ago.

A sudden shiver traced my spine, and the faint tang of burnt tobacco curled around my senses once more. I shifted in my seat, pressing my legs together beneath the tablecloth, desperately trying to steady the rapid flutter of my pulse. My fingertips curled into the fabric at the table's edge as warmth flooded my cheeks and chest, each breath coming shorter than the last.

His gaze held me in a silence that felt charged with every unspoken word. My heart hammered so loud I could hardly think, yet the world beyond our table seemed to fall away—only the soft glow of candles and the steady rhythm of his presence remained. In that suspended moment, I realized just how profoundly he had unsettled me … and how thrilling it was to let him.

The desire for him to take me on that table—right in front of the waiters and candles—flooded my thoughts. My nipples pebbled beneath the thin fabric, and my core throbbed at his grazing touch against my skin. I clenched my legs tightly in desperation, not wanting to embarrass myself.

I raised the crystal glass to my lips and drew in slow, deliberate sips. The ice clinked softly as it tumbled against the rim, each shard of cold kissing my mouth before the crisp water tumbled down my throat like a mountain stream. With every swallow, the dizzying haze of desire loosened its grip—my heartbeat slowed, the heat in my veins cooled, and the relentless ache that had consumed me began to ebb.

Around us, the candle flames flickered against the wrought-iron candelabra, casting dancing shadows on the black tablecloth. I blinked as clarity returned, the room's opulent details—the wine-red velvet chairs, the rose petals strewn at our feet—sharpening into focus. I lifted my eyes, surprised to find his dark gaze still fixed on me, calm and unwavering beneath the soft glow.

Confusion fluttered in my chest as the last wisps of lust dissolved, leaving behind a steady calm and the undeniable awareness of his presence.

"Would you like to come over?" His voice is sweet and seductive.

He slipped my hand into his and began to trace slow circles on my skin with his thumb. I lifted the glass again—this time the icy water shocked me fully awake—and the fog of desire lifted, leaving me acutely aware of what had just transpired. Anxiety crept back in, coiling around my thoughts as I tried to steady my racing heart.

"No," I said, my voice firmer than I intended.

My mind scrambled, words and emotions tumbling too quickly for me to sort. In that moment, I realized how little control I'd felt over my own body.

Before I could pull away, Elias tugged my hand toward him with surprising force. Panic flared in my chest; I tried to draw back, but he was stronger. My eyes widened, sweat prickling at my temples, as I froze—helpless under his grip—wondering what he would do next.

He tightened his grip and spoke with clipped authority, "You will come with me."

Pain and pleasure tangled as the pressure in his hand increased. A familiar haze washed over me, the sharp scent of tobacco mixing with something darker—desire. My fingers trembled; the water glass sat unreachable on the table, and the world narrowed to his commanding gaze and the strength in his arm.

A knot of panic coiled in my chest, begging me to pull free—yet beneath it, a softer impulse urged me to yield. My breath hitched as the tension in my muscles shifted, the anxiety that had gripped me moments ago melting into acquiescence.

Finally, I let my shoulders drop and whispered, "Okay."

His dark eyes lit with triumph, and he released my hand just enough to allow me to slip out of my chair. With a slow, satisfied smile, he murmured, "Good witch."

Elias sprang to his feet, shrugging into his jacket with swift, determined motions. He spoke, but his words blurred into the haze that still clouded my mind—witch? Why had he called me that? A jumble of thoughts fought for purchase as I stared at him, paralyzed. Wake up, Maeva! I willed myself to move.

"Get up," he barked, irritation threading his tone.

I forced my gaze back to him, yanked my purse from the table, and shoved myself to my feet—only to have my heel catch in the tablecloth. I yanked at the drape, trying to free my legs, but my other foot snagged as I kicked out. The entire setting slid toward me. I stumbled back into my chair, and the water glass toppled, dousing my dress and face in ice-cold liquid.

The shock of freezing water surged through me like a lightning strike, shattering the fog in my head. Pain and rage coiled in my gut. I slammed both hands onto the table, using the momentum to pull myself upright. Heat flared behind my eyes, and tears stung as they slid down my cheeks.

"I said no!" I screamed, venom in every syllable.

His irritation flickered into surprise at the force of my outburst. I felt a prickling energy in my fingertips, like shards of ice skittering across my skin. Yet I planted my hands firmly on the table, grounding myself in the fire of my own defiance.

My face was still hot with anger, I hadn't noticed I was leaning forward over the table—until a tingling heat in my fingers yanked my attention down. At my fingertips, a faint ribbon of blue light began to coil and dance, like smoke set aflame by moonlight. I froze, heart hammering, as the glow solidified into a small, intricate brand etched into my skin: a delicate knot of interlocking lines that pulsed with quiet life.

I'd never seen anything like it. The rest of the room blurred—Elias's sharp features, the flickering candles, even the polished silverware—fell away until only the brand and its soft azure glow remained in focus. A tremor ran through my hand, and the light flickered in response, as if recognizing my shock.

"What… what is that?" I whispered, voice tight with disbelief.

Across the table, Elias's confident composure fractured. His eyes widened, and he took an involuntary step back, the flicker of candlelight dancing across the beads of sweat at his temple. In that moment, I realized this glowing mark was more than a surprise—it was the first clear sign of something powerful stirring within me.

I sat up straight, leveling my gaze at my hand as I held it before my face. Curiosity banished the anger I'd felt moments ago. Across the table, Elias's eyes went wide, and he took a cautious step back. The candle flames flared orange and gold, burning brighter as if drawn to the pulsing light on my fingertip.

Beneath my skin, the tiny brand glowed with iridescent blue, its steady rhythm hypnotic. I barely noticed Elias inching away until the room seemed to heat around me, the air was thick with tension. He raised his hands in a placating gesture—palms open—sweat beading at his brow and darkening his shirt where droplets trickled down his chest.

I met his retreating figure with unwavering eyes, matching his apprehension with my own fierce focus. In that charged silence, I could feel the energy crackling between us, binding the space around our table in something electric and unknowable.

My skin felt the energy bouncing of the walls and flickering in the candles. I could feel the heat wrap around me. My body felt like I was pulsating waves of adrenaline into the air. "Daniel" Elias said with caution.

A tall, dark-haired man appeared beside the table and cupped my face with startling speed. His bright blue eyes—deep as ocean trenches—locked onto mine before I could even react.

"Calm down," he said in a sharp tone. "You're on a romantic date."

The anger that had coiled inside me unraveled instantly. I sank back into my chair, a soft smile spreading across my lips as the tension drained away. The haze lifted, and I embraced the warmth of this evening, the thrill of being here with Elias.

He slid his façade of attentive partner back into place, his dark eyes softening as he leaned forward. With deliberate grace, he reached across the candlelit table, curling his fingers around mine before drawing me into a gentle, lingering embrace—his other hand brushing a stray lock of hair from my forehead as if to reassure me every beat of his heart.

My heart fluttered at the warmth of his touch—every time Elias held my hand, I felt small and safe cradled in his powerful grasp. I longed to melt into his broad chest, to curl against the effortless strength he radiated. My slender fingers seemed woven perfectly into the web of his, as if we were always meant to fit together.

He leaned forward and brushed a soft kiss against the back of my hand. My pulse skipped—such a tender, old-world gesture felt miraculous in that moment. How could one man be so impeccable, so attentive? Elias was the embodiment of a perfect gentleman, and I was dizzy with gratitude that he had chosen me.

We drifted back into easy laughter and gentle conversation, each shared story stitching us closer. As the evening wound down, we mapped out our next rendezvous—his proposal sending a thrill of warmth coiling through my chest. I felt as if the night had spun into gold around us.

Outside, a bright yellow cab idled in the streetlight glow. I rose to leave, stepping forward to thank him for the most enchanting evening I could remember. In an instant, Elias reached out, cupping my face with both hands and drawing me in. His lips met mine with a soft urgency, and I leaned into the kiss, our breaths mingling.

His mouth was silk against mine—then flame. Our tongues danced in a playful duel, each caress bold and searching. I closed my eyes, surrendering to the heady swirl of his scent—tobacco and something richer, like dark chocolate—and pressed closer, molding myself against the solidity of his suit-clad form.

He was so much taller that I stood on tiptoe, arms winding around his waist beneath his jacket. My hands skimmed his back, fingertips tracing the ridges of muscle that flexed at my touch. A low growl rumbled from his chest, vibrating through me, driving me higher still.

When he finally broke the kiss, his breath warmed my cheek. His voice was a dark murmur in my ear "Sleep well, Maeva Sinclair."

I stayed pressed against him for a moment longer, reluctant to let go of the exquisite reality we had created. Then, reluctantly, I stepped back—heart full and trembling, already counting the hours until I could feel his arms around me again.

Chapter Eight

Elias Knight

I watched her cab vanish into the night, its taillights blinking out like distant embers. At the restaurant's threshold, I exhaled the breath I had been holding, uncoiling the tension in my shoulders. I loosened the top buttons of my shirt and tugged the collar free, letting the cool breeze trace across my chest and collarbone. My fingers raked through my hair, trying to smooth away the flicker of disgust that had risen in me moments ago, an unwelcome reminder of how dangerously close she had come to losing control.

A sudden chill curled up my spine like a living thing. Daniel materialized at my side, his silhouette framed by the restaurant's warm glow. Together, we watched the yellow cab shrink into the distance, swallowed by the street's shadows.

"Do you think she knows what she's capable of?" he asked, voice low and measured.

I rubbed my jaw; muscles still coiled with frustration. "Not yet. She is not aware of the force she has unleashed."

Daniel's brow furrowed. "Do you think she was… testing us?"

"Or toying with us," I murmured, eyes narrowing as I recalled the blue brand pulsing on her skin. "That glow upstairs wasn't an accident."

He gave a hard nod. "We may have awakened her magic."

Agitation sharpened my senses. My carefully crafted plan felt like it was slipping through my fingers—and I had no patience for setbacks. I turned back toward the restaurant's entrance, and my shoulders squared.

With a crisp tug, I straightened my collar and cracked my neck, the predator sharpening his focus.

A spark of excitement flared in my nostrils—tonight's game was far from over. Beneath the fading echo of her taxi's engine, I felt the familiar thrill of the hunt stir. It was time to press our advantage and see how Maeva Sinclair would respond when the true challenge began.

I let my gaze sweep over the crowd—none of them aware of the predator in their midst. Laughter and clinking glasses filled the air while their unsuspecting faces glowed in the warm lamplight. I sorted them out like cattle, spotting those with a hint of something worth tasting.

Then I found her at the bar. She toyed with a straw, eyes cast down, and when our gazes met, she lifted her head as if accepting a silent challenge.

Two can play this game, I thought, curiosity flickering through me.

She wore a bright-red dress with a daring neckline—bold, but not to my taste. I preferred deeper hues, richer tones, ones that spoke of old-world elegance rather than modern flash.

"Where are you going?" Daniel's voice rumbled at my shoulder. He had turned to watch me, dark eyes tracking my steps.

"I'm bored," I replied over my shoulder, voice low.

Without another word, I slipped off the banquette and crossed the room toward the bar, each stride measured and confident. The woman's eyes followed me, intrigued—and I knew she would be the perfect diversion.

I settled onto the stool beside her and ordered my usual—a neat Old Fashioned. As the bartender slid the glass across the polished wood, I let my attention linger on the stranger: the slight arch of her eyebrow, the soft curve of her lips. She sipped her drink; curiosity etched in every line of her posture.

I ordered my usual drink and settled beside my mark. Lowering my chin to meet her gaze, I leaned in and let my hand rest on her lap, just at the crease of her dress. Her eyes never left mine as my palm slid along her thigh, pressing more firmly at the inner curve before drifting downward. I could feel her pulse quicken as her heart raced to keep up.

Daniel moved in from behind her and placed his hands on her shoulders. He stroked her arms gently, the light touch sending shivers through her. Then he tilted her chin and brought her face close to his, pressing a soft kiss to her lips.

"You're ours tonight," he whispered before pulling away.

Her cheeks flushed with heat and excitement, and a soft giggle escaped her lips. I shifted so my legs straddled her, matching her rising anticipation. Her breath hitched, and her eyes fluttered in response to each new touch. Daniel tilted her head to one side and kissed her again, his lips tracing along her skin, while I continued to caress the inner curve of her thigh. She leaned into us, her body responding to the mounting tension. I leaned close and whispered in her ear, and her soft moans filled the air.

"Would you like to come have some fun with us?" I whispered to her.

She leveled her gaze on me, a wicked smile curving her lips as though she believed she still held the reins—unaware that from the moment her eyes first met mine, her desire had been set into motion. In reality, she had never stood a chance against the subtle pull we had woven around her.

Daniel flagged down a dark sedan, its leather seats gleaming beneath the streetlights. The driver—a silent silhouette—slid us in and eased away from the curb into the night's hush. The cab's interior smelled faintly of new vinyl and the sharp tang of city air seeping through the cracked window.

Her laughter bubbled up again, bright, and breathless, echoing off the curved ceiling. Without hesitation, her hands darted to the waistband of our trousers, fingers trembling with impatient excitement. The glow of the passing streetlamps danced over her flushed skin, and I felt the heat of her need as keenly as my own.

"Not yet," I murmured, voice low and teasing, sliding my hand over hers to forestall her eager touch. The word hung between us, a promise that the evening's true game was only just beginning.

As I withdrew her hand from mine, I pressed soft kisses along her wrist and up her forearm. She moaned in response just as Daniel cupped her breast over the dress, his fingers deftly twirling her hardening nipple through the fabric. He moved on to lick and nuzzle her neck, increasing the pressure until she arched her back and parted her legs, welcoming us both.

When we finally arrived at our estate—now called Dubois Manor—the drive had taken us beyond the city's edge into deep seclusion. A massive iron gate, each side forged as a raven's wing, loomed before us. Its dark silhouette cast a cage-like shadow on the gravel driveway. This château had once borne the name Knight Chateau, until our family's downfall forced its rebirth under a new title.

After our downfall, the estate remained under the care of Sophie Dubois—my mother's most trusted handmaiden—and her descendants for centuries, bound by an iron-clad agreement that guaranteed its protection until our return. Once a haven of peace and vitality, these walls have become our prison: a bleak, stone hell that both confines and tortures us. Yet despite my hatred for its cold embrace, I always find my way back home.

The gates groaned open at our approach, their wrought-iron wings parting to reveal a ribbon of gravel that crunched under our wheels. Along its length, oil-lit lanterns hung from wrought posts—each pool of amber light cutting through the surrounding gloom like sentinels guarding a secret. Beyond the glow, the woods pressed in so thickly that the path ahead vanished into shadow; only those born of the night—or clever enough to follow the faint undercurrent of wind through the pines—could ever hope to retrace its course.

At the driveway's terminus, the manor's façade loomed: an arching portal of black iron bands and rivets set into cold limestone. Above it, bartizans jutted from battered stone turrets, their crenellations draped in a tangle of emerald moss and twisted ivy. Gargoyles crouched at each corner, their slate-grey faces frozen in silent warning. Heavy iron grilles, patinated by rain and time, guarded the tall, narrow windows, while the scent of damp stone and centuries-old mortar clung to the air. This was no mere residence, it was a bulwark against every foe, a fortress that dared time itself to challenge its stone-cold resolve.

The gravel crunched under our feet as we made our way to the great entrance. She halted mid-step, eyes wide, drinking in the sight of our ancestral home. Her gaze traced the soaring pillars and sweeping archways that bore my family's crest, pausing at each tall window where dimly glowing candles peeked through tendrils of ivy and delicate, midnight-blooming flowers that had crept across the stone façade.

"It's absolutely stunning," she whispered, voice hushed with wonder.

She twirled on the spot, caught in the magic of the moment—a princess believing her prince had delivered her to a new castle, complete with every fairytale promise of romance and love. Yet behind the grandeur lurked the darker truth: in the shadows of these halls dwelled monsters whose minds were shaped by blood and power. And the moment she stepped beyond those doors, there would be no turning back—no escape from their world.

I let Daniel have his way with her first. He poured her a drink—a potent blend of his blood and whiskey. The women generally accepted such concoctions without question, eager for the heightened mood it promised. Once they consumed even a small amount of our blood, it was easy to influence them: the mixture in their system dulled their doubts and made them receptive to every suggestion we offered.

Her moans grew louder as Daniel's touch drove her higher pleasure. I sank into a blue-velvet Victorian parlor chair with gilded trim and poured myself a glass from my decanter. The warm, metallic taste slid down my throat, setting my pulse racing. I stretched out my legs and draped my arms over the chair's arms, my glass dangling from my fingertips. From the corner of my eye, I watched them, her calls of ecstasy stirring the beast that lurked within me.

My gaze locked onto the curve of her neck as she glanced at me, bottom lip caught between her teeth. Her hands tangled desperately in his hair, and ripples of pleasure arched her back. His lips roamed over her breasts as his fingers closed around each one, drawing her nipples into his mouth. She tugged at her dress, lifting it as he shifted between her legs. Her hands fumbled at his belt, desperate to free him, while she writhed beneath his weight. She parted her legs, silently urging him on as he adjusted himself against her soaked lingerie. Her hips began to move in time with him, the thin fabric doing little to contain their heat.

"Please," she whispered, voice trembling with need.

"Quit talking," Daniel commanded, voice low and steel-edged.

He rose into a seated position, the satin sheets rustling beneath him, and fixed her with a gaze so intense it felt like iron bands around her pupils. Every muscle in his jaw tightened as he stared, his dark eyes unblinking under the soft glow of the bedside lamp.

Her cheeks, still warm moments before, drained of color. Her lips, once parted in plea, closed in stunned silence as her head fell back against the plush pillows. The flutter of her lashes slowed, leaving her stare vacant and vulnerable.

I quickly tightened my grip on her neck blocking her airway from filling her lungs. Her moans turning into silent screams. Her eyes filled with terror burrowed deeply into mine as her face began to turn red. Her arms reached for my hands as she tried to release my grip. I tightened my hand harder against her esophagus forcing her face to turn a shade purple. Her mouth commanded shut by my grip, and her face petrified as her eyes scanned the room for help, hoping Daniel would come to her aide.

I lifted her body off the bed and brought her face inches from mine; the stench of fear washed over her face like a wave. Her face began to turn blue as I restricted her airway from any helpful breath. Her hands scratched down my arm in a panic, but she was unable to fight me off. I dropped her from my grip back onto the bed.

Daniel let out a loud laugh as he watched the woman try to twist and squirm off the bed. With a swift motion that she could not see, I grabbed her again by the neck and pinned her one last time. I could feel her blood rapidly course its way through her veins under the weight of my hand. I released and gripped her neck once more. I teased her with air with every chance that I let go. Controlling her life in my palm. I listened to the beautiful sound of the iron waterfall that flooded back into her veins from my release.

"Now, you were having all the fun. It's our turn now" I said with a sinister smile.

I smiled, baring every tooth—each a slender needle glinting in the dim candlelight. My jaw shifted unnaturally, elongating until my lower fangs stood fully exposed, ready to rend flesh as easily as parchment. Terror widened her eyes, and a silent gasp escaped her lips.

In one swift motion, I seized her and tilted her head back toward Daniel. His own smile split his face, revealing teeth just as vicious—rows of ivory daggers that gleamed like lanterns in the flickering light. His calm blue eyes had hollowed into smoldering embers, casting an otherworldly glow across the chamber.

She tried to scream, but her voice died in her throat as I leaned in. My fangs hovered at her pulse point, the space between predator and prey narrowing to a razor's edge. The torches guttered overhead, sending shadows dancing like specters against the stone walls. My fangs itched against her skin, but I held back, savoring the moment—the crackling anticipation, the pounding of her heart beneath my fingers.

A shriek tore from her lips as she clawed and kicked, desperate to break free. In an instant, Daniel's jaws closed around her shoulder, his teeth raking through skin and muscle. A geyser of blood spurted into his mouth, crimson droplets splattering across the bed. Horror widened her eyes as the life ebbed from her body. He tore the flesh from her bones in a single, brutal motion, leaving a ragged wound where her shoulder had been. Blood and sinew filled his mouth as he slowly chewed, a guttural moan of satisfaction rumbling from his chest.

I tilted her face toward me one last time and watched as terror bled into emptiness. Her spirit flickered and vanished—escaped from my grasp. In those moments, I felt nothing at all. Then I sank my teeth into her neck, tearing flesh as her blood trickled away. Her struggle slackened, once-fighting arms now lay lifeless on the sheets.

We both rose, mouths and shirts smeared with drying blood. As the adrenaline ebbed and the warmth settled, Daniel slipped silently from the room. I was left alone with her remains, tasked with hiding the evidence of my hunger.

Another victim lay in my bed. I gathered her remains and walked out to the balcony, where the moon hung low in the silent sky. Trees swayed in the night breeze as silver light danced across the lake below. I lingered for a moment, drinking in the stillness, then released her body into the water. Another sacrifice—to the lake, to our peace.

Chapter Nine

Daniel Black

The weeks since my meeting with Maeva crawled by each day heavier than the last as I watched our plan's edges fray. Elias moved within her orbit—shared coffees, lingering walks—always careful to avoid provoking the magic we had only just glimpsed. Meanwhile, I remained the ever-present sentinel, my surveillance teams ghosting behind her through crowded markets and shadowed lanes. Not once did Maeva glance over her shoulder; in her world, our threat was invisible.

At dawn, I stayed in bed longer than usual, drawn by the pale, liquid light pouring across my chambers. I sat propped against a mountain of silk pillows, the cream-and-tan flagstones beneath the rug catching every mote of dust that drifted in the sunbeams. My phone glowed in my hand as I flicked through encrypted reports: each message, each map notation, another piece of the intricate puzzle we were determined to solve.

Above me, a gilded chandelier—its metalwork twisting like vines—cradled half-burned white candles. The soft hiss of melting wax underscored the hush of the morning. Heavy velvet drapes, midnight-black and plush, framed the open balcony doors. Beyond them, the lake lay like a sheet of glass, reflecting the sky's first pink blush. A whisper of a breeze stirred the curtains, carrying the faint scent of dew-damp pines and distant water.

In that quiet sanctuary, I traced the plan's next moves on my screen, drawing in a slow breath. The world beyond these walls felt distant—yet every waking moment, every soft ripple on the lake, reminded me that time was slipping away. And soon, we would have to act.

An antique mahogany desk sat to the left of my bed, its surface buried beneath a chaotic sprawl of parchment and ledgers. Behind it stood a high-backed Victorian chair, its deep-green velvet worn threadbare at the arms from countless sleepless nights. In the center of the room, a broad hearth crackled, filling the air with the smoky sweetness of hickory. Flames danced around the charred logs, each pop and hiss echoing through the quiet space.

My bed rested on a raised ebony platform, draped in black silk sheets that gleamed like oil under the firelight. A towering velvet headboard loomed behind it, its surface soft enough to cradle my weary back. Two steps below, a thick black rug sprawled across the floor, its pattern—two ravens soaring above a pine-green forest—casting dark omens at my feet.

I scrolled through messages on my phone, trying to distract myself from the impatience gnawing at me over Elias's cautious approach. I set the device aside and closed my eyes, inhaling the familiar tang of smoke and ember. A distant memory surfaced—one of my last ties to humanity.

I had tasted my first victim behind the stables, the warm blood slick on my chin, flesh torn between my teeth. My mother had found me then— her horror silent, her tears pouring freely in the lamplight. She had knelt beside me without a cry, hand trembling as she asked what had happened. I could not explain why the hunger had taken me, why I had become the monster she had spent her life defending the innocent from. Watching her grief that night—the raw despair etched on her face—was a pain more searing than any mortal wound.

In the years since, I had learned to mask my thirst, to bury the worst of it beneath civility. But tonight, as the flames leapt and guttered, I felt the old fear flicker at the edges of my mind: a warning that some memories are best left buried in the dark.

I remember the weight of their faith long before my world shifted. My parents wore rosaries at their throats, murmuring the Lord's Prayer whenever I wandered too close—an act as natural to them as breathing. I knew I had to leave them, to shield them from the storm I would inevitably bring.

Once I was exposed—once the church discovered the monster I had become—they would be branded as demon-harborers, cast out or worse. So, I fled to Knight's home, a fortress of shadows where I could keep my secret safe and protect what remained of my family.

Elias sensed his humanity slipping away before I did. We had no foresight into how far our transformations would go, nor the cost. From time to time, I returned home, skulking through the village's back alleys to watch my family from afar. I yearned for my mother's warm embrace, my father's easy laugh—simple gestures I knew I could never reclaim.

Years passed. My reflection betrayed no age: skin unmarked by time, hair dark and abundant where grey should have taken hold. I discovered strengths beyond any mortal's: I could outrun the wind, bend will with a drop of my blood, and hunt through the night like a ghost in the forest. I honed my gifts relentlessly—shaping thoughts, bending visions, and converting every faint sound into clarity.

One evening, drawn by a whisper of memory, I crept back to the village. The church bell tolled a funeral dirge—my father's passing had brought mourners to my childhood home. Villagers drifted like shadows through the lantern-lit yard, their hushed condolences floating on the chill air.

That night, I slunk inside. My sister's house lay silent, her children's breathing soft in the next room. In the dim hearth-glow, I found her—my mother, fragile in her grief yet radiant in the candlelight.

I knelt beside her and took her hand in mine. "I love you," I whispered, voice thick with longing.

Her eyes, damp with tears, met mine with a knowing calm. "I knew you would come," she said, each word a gentle blade that cut straight to my heart.

I choked on the emotion. "How did you know?" The question broke free in a cracked whisper, betraying the child I once was.

She squeezed my hand soft and unafraid. "A mother's love doesn't fade, even in the darkest night. I felt you before I saw you."

I lifted her hand to my lips, pressing a gentle kiss to the soft, wrinkled skin mottled with age's liver spots. Her delicate smile lingered as her silver eyes fluttered closed, and I felt the slow falter of her heartbeat beneath my palm until, at last, the rhythm stilled in absolute silence.

In that moment, something inside me shattered. I couldn't tell whether it was a shard of my own long-buried humanity or the final thread of our family's curse snapping free—but whatever it was, it consumed me utterly.

Six centuries have passed since that night, and I can no longer summon the echoes of their laughter or the warmth of their faces; they've become blurred shapes in my memory, drifting further into shadow with each passing year.

This manor—my ancestral refuge—has also been my prison. When the village's wrath drove us into exile, Elias, Mother, and I scattered to the farthest corners of the world. We swore that after a century's absence we would return, allowing generations to forget the name Knight before reclaiming our home. And for hundreds of years, the plan held true.

But I grow weary of flight. I'm tired of the hunger that gnaws at my throat, of the monster I've become. Tonight, as the moon casts silver veins across these stone walls, I realize that true freedom may demand a final sacrifice. If peace is a gift reserved for the living, then I must decide whose life will buy my own.

Click… click… click. Her heels echoed off the marble floor, each measured step a reminder of the power she wielded. Abigail Knight—the mistress of these halls—glided toward me like a panther on the prowl, her breath steady, eyes gleaming for any sign of weakness.

"You may come in," I murmured. My voice was calm, but my heart still thudded in my chest.

The door swung open, and Abigail entered my sanctum. She paused, taking in the tapestry of papers, maps, and photographs spread across my antique mahogany desk. Even in repose, she commanded attention: strawberry blonde hair pulled into a regal chignon, alabaster skin unmarked by time, and an air of lethal grace that betrayed her monstrous nature.

Without a word, she crossed the room and swept up the black and white photo of Maeva—seated at a Parisian café, Raven's Grimoire casually propped beside her coffee cup. Her gaze flicked over the image, then to the scattered notes and maps tracing Meridith's bloodline.

"I assume you have a plan," she said plainly, voice cool as stone.

I exhaled, lifting the photograph from her hand and studying Maeva's curious smile. "I might," I admitted. "But it could require force. Maeva's powers erupted under extreme duress—it seems they're tied to her emotions, a defense mechanism triggered when she's overwhelmed."

Abigail settled into my Victorian chair, her long, pale legs crossing beneath the desk. She watched me, intrigued by the complexity of taming such magic. I continued, "She manipulated water to escape Elias's seduction, conjured gusts of air, even stoked the flames of her date. If I hadn't spiked her drink with my blood, we might never have regained control."

At my words, her jade-green eyes narrowed, the candlelight dancing on the sharp planes of her face. "Elemental magic, like Meridith's," she mused. "The grimoire should contain the enchantments for those spells."

"Interesting," I echoed, feeling the weight of destiny settle in my bones. Between us, the scattered clues and ancient pages felt charged with possibility—and peril—waiting for us to turn the next page. "When it finally revealed itself to Maeva, hopefully it will bring all the answers we need. That is my theory. The book could've awakened her powers once in her possession. But Maeva couldn't conjure up magic on her own without distress."

I exhaled sharply.

"We'll have to force it out," I said.

Abigail's spine stiffened as I set aside Maeva's photograph and lifted an iron-worn key from its hiding place—a secret brick concealed behind a faded portrait above the hearth. The key slid into the lock of my desk's hidden drawer, its rusted teeth catching briefly before the wood groaned open. Dust drifted from the crack, and I withdrew a sculpted ebony box etched with ancient sigils.

Abigail rose from her chair, the candlelight flickering over her expectant gaze as I placed the box on the desk. She leaned forward, hands flat against the desktop, eyes tracing the intricate carvings that pulsed with old magic.

"This belonged to Helen Willis," I explained. "A member of the Raven Coven who fancied herself Elias's queen. Naïve, she believed in his promises and helped him gather every artifact we needed to break the curse."

I paused, letting the silence fill the room. Helen had stolen Meridith's Grimoire and the cursed blade that killed my father—both protected by coven wards that barred all but true witches. Yet Helen, under Elias's manipulation, had slipped through every enchantment.

"The box's seal was forged by Helen's own magic—designed so only Elias could open it," I continued. "It withstands flame, steel, any force. But once Elias extracted the knowledge he sought, he betrayed her. Like so many before, she paid for her devotion with her life."

Abigail's eyes darkened at the tale, and she placed a gentle hand on the box's lid. "Then this is the key," she murmured, "to unlocking Maeva's power—and ending our bloodline's curse."

Young witches of the Raven Coven were Elias's favorite prey—at first, the disappearances were hushed and mysterious, but over time he began leaving their bodies for families to discover, a grim warning scrawled in blood.

Rebecca rose to lead the coven shortly after, her mastery of its magic the only thing that kept its secrets alive in a world that had nearly forgotten them.

Abigail's sharp gaze pinned me as she crossed her arms, beautiful hair cascading over her shoulders. "What are you planning?" she asked, voice soft but firm—her eyes challenging me to reveal how far I would go to save our family.

"I intend to force her powers into the open," I replied, voice low and resolute.

I glanced once more at the photographs of Maeva spread across my desk, each image a piece of the puzzle we needed to finish.

A fierce smile curved Abigail's lips, exposing needle-sharp canines. She turned away from the desk and strode toward the door, every movement regal and predatory.

"I have no doubt," she called over her shoulder before slipping into the corridor, her shadow billowing behind her coming to life.

Chapter Ten

Maeva Sinclair

Every free moment in my week revolved around Elias. Sometimes we'd curl up on my couch after dinner; other nights, we'd linger late at coffee shops until the baristas flicked off the lights. He was unfailingly kind—never rushing, always checking in to make sure I was comfortable. His gentle patience chipped away at my walls, and I fell harder for him each time.

Still, when it came to taking our closeness further, my heart would thunder in my chest, and a quiet voice in my mind would whisper, not yet. We found our own perfect in-between: soft kisses at the door, lingering touches on the stairs, hands clasped in the dark before sleep. I'd tease myself— "Tonight might be the night," I'd think—only to feel that old fear coil in my gut, urging me to hold back.

And every morning afterward, I'd wake in his arms, safe and warm, and wonder why I couldn't trust myself to take the next step. The ache between us was so sweet it hurt: a promise of something deeper, held just out of reach by my own restless heart.

Each morning I'd wake tangled in his sheets, my heart pounding with regret. Here was a man who treated me like a treasure—fully clothed in my bed, never once pressuring me beyond my comfort—yet I'd let my anxiety win every time. I knew he'd explored these intimacies before; I hadn't. And still, I yearned to try. His steady presence, the warmth of his arms, the soft brush of his lips on mine—it all whispered that I could lean into this safety. But when the moment came, I'd pull away, crippled by nerves. And by night's end, I'd mourn the chance I'd let slip away, longing for the courage to meet him halfway.

We began with gentle kisses, my lips trailing him until I found the courage to climb onto his broad chest. Straddling his hips, I felt the heat of his body beneath me. His scent—burning tobacco and something dark—wrapped around me, and when his tongue met mine, it deepened my desire like a whispered promise.

His hands came to my waist, strong and insistent, guiding my motion even as I moved against him. Every brush of fabric and press of skin sent a thrilling pulse through me, reminding me how close we stood to the edge of something unspoken yet irresistible.

I'd kiss him aggressively, and he'd return it with equal force. He'd lean in to meet me, tangling his fingers in my hair and pulling me closer. His urgency to consume my mouth and body only fueled my own burning desire for him. I couldn't help feeling compelled to give him everything I had—like a gravitational pull beyond my control.

I'd start at his lips and trail kisses down to his chest and stomach, wanting to taste every inch of him. With each touch, his muscles rippled beneath my lips, contracting against me, and I loved the way he moaned with every lick. My hands would caress his abdomen, memorizing the subtle rises and falls of each muscle as my tongue slid along the ridges— lingering in the V-shaped line that drew me irresistibly lower.

I loved to tease him at the waistband, gently flicking my tongue just beneath the elastic. He was always patient—I never had to force his pants undone. He knew I'd eventually slip my fingers under the fly and unzip him, exposing his length. As soon as I cupped him through the fabric, his hands would clench the pillows beside him and pull them to his face in anticipation.

His length was too big for one hand—I needed both to fully grasp him. It was so thick that my fingers couldn't meet, so I wrapped each hand around him and stroked, twisting gently up and down as my lips closed around the tip. My tongue swirled over the vein that pulsed beneath his skin, and the wet heat of my mouth drew salty-sweet moans from him. Saliva dripped down his shaft, adding slickness to every stroke. When my jaw ached, I let go and trailed soft licks along both sides, pausing to suck each of his balls into my mouth and savor their smooth weight before diving back onto his cock again.

Sometimes I couldn't quite take him all the way in without strain, and I'd gag lightly when he thrust into my mouth. Saliva would spill from my lips as he rocked his hips, urging me on. When he came, I swallowed every drop and gently wiped my mouth clean.

Then, with a swift move, he'd flip me onto my back and peel away my panties. Hovering over me, he'd suck at my core, his tongue tracing blissful patterns while his fingers entered me slowly, matching the rhythm of his mouth. I'd see stars from the pure intensity of it.

His strong arms would lift my legs above his shoulders; his hands forced the back of my thighs back towards my abdomen and my knees close to my chest. All I could do was moan with pleasure and spread my legs for this man. He would lap at my core and then tease his tongue at my opening until I begged for him to put his tongue in for me. Then, he would drive his tongue in and out deep into my core as I screamed out in pleasure.

My eyes blackened and all I could see was the galaxy in my eyes. My legs shook as my hands would run through his hair in between my legs. My apex covered his lips and chin as he continued to please me, forcing me to convulse as I arched my back to his every touch.

When we weren't at home, he would always pick me up in one of his nice cars and we'd drive around talking, park in random spots, and make out in his car like high schoolers avoiding the police. I wanted to breathe him in every chance that I got. The desire I had for him was unlike anything that I have experienced, and I wanted more of it.

Sometimes when I woke, I half-expected the dawn to dissolve his memory like morning mist—like he'd been nothing more than a beautiful dream I'd outgrown. Instead, his laughter still echoed through my thoughts, richer than any nighttime fantasy. Each sunrise felt like a baptism into a new reality where he existed, and every ordinary moment in his company glittered with an intensity I'd never known.

Lori saw the change before I could articulate it. She'd watch me drift off mid-conversation, eyes distant, as if I were catching echoes of a private joy.

"He's taken too much of your time, I don't trust him," she'd warned, brow furrowed. She couldn't explain it—just that something about him felt unsettling. I brushed it aside as protectiveness after all, he never pressured me, never rushed me. He was the picture of patience, gently coaxing me out of my anxieties, making me feel safe enough to imagine closer things.

Tonight, we'd planned to toast under the amber halo of our favorite pub's lights. But at the last minute, his text arrived: "Stuck at the office. Raincheck?" I ought to have shrugged it off—one night alone couldn't mean much. Instead, a cold tendril of fear wrapped around my spine.

My heart thudded so hard I was certain he'd heard it through the phone. I found myself spiraling through every canceled plan, every unanswered text, convinced he was finally tired of me. The familiar comfort of solitude turned jagged, and the room felt suddenly too quiet, too large—an empty stage where his absence was the only performance.

My mind spun with worst-case scenarios, each one more unbearable than the last. Tears pricked at the corners of my eyes as my pulse thundered in my temples, each beat drowning out the distant hum of the city beyond my window. A clammy cold sweat formed at my hairline, and I could almost taste the metallic tang of fear on my tongue. I forced my breath to deepen—slow, steady inhales and exhales—yet the knot in my chest only tightened, my emotions boiling over like water on a too-hot stove.

As panic coursed through me, the room itself seemed to heat up. The air pressed against my skin like a suffocating blanket; every surface felt suddenly sunbaked. I could feel droplets of sweat tracing down my spine, gathering at the small of my back, sticky and insistent. I ran a shaky hand over my forearm, and the moisture clung to my skin, cold and unsettling. My heart raced on—urgent, relentless—while the apartment's normally comforting shadows seemed to close in, reminding me that tonight, some distance lay between us, and I had no idea why.

"What the hell…" I whispered, scrambling for my thermometer. My palms were slick with sweat as I gripped the doorframe for support. Hot beads ran down my hairline and stung my eyes. The apartment felt like an oven—stifling, oppressive—and no matter how hard I tried to steady my breathing, my heart galloped in my chest.

Elias had canceled at the last minute. The empty space beside me was suddenly cavernous, and panic slithered through my veins. I sank to my knees, tears spilling down my face as a fresh wave of abandonment crashed over me. My fingers tingled with warmth, and I sobbed uncontrollably, each gasp of air more desperate than the last.

I pressed my forehead into my trembling hands, willing my breath to slow, but my thoughts spun out of control: He doesn't care. I'm not enough. The heat overwhelmed me again, pinning my chest in a vise. I was utterly alone, drowning in an anxiety that refused to let me go.

A hard knock rapped against the door. My breath caught in my throat—had I imagined it? I stayed on the floor, listening. Then again: knock, knock—louder this time.

Heart pounding, I pushed to my feet and crept forward, every step light against the hardwood. With trembling fingers, I peered through the peephole. A tall man filled the frame: broad shoulders, strong neck, clad in a charcoal-gray button-down that hugged his lean muscles. Panic flared in my chest, and I stumbled backward onto the floor.

"C-Can I help you?" My voice came out in a strangled whisper. I brushed damp strands of hair from my forehead, the room suddenly became too warm, my heart racing.

He paused before speaking, his voice low and steady. "I'm Daniel—Elias's brother. He asked me to come and escort you to his home."

Relief flooded me. My knees felt weak as if the floor might give way—but in that moment, hope bloomed. I rose, my hands still shaking, and unlatched the door. Peeking out, I found myself face-to-face with the answer I'd longed for: a way back to him.

My hair hung in messy tendrils over my shoulders, each strand damp with tears I could no longer hold back. My eyes were rimmed with red; my face flushed from exhaustion and heartbreak. I met Daniel's gaze as he stood in my doorway—tall, dark-haired, with those same deep-blue eyes that felt both familiar and unsettling. My breath caught in my throat.

"You can come in," I managed, voice still tight with sobs. "I just need to grab a few things."

He offered me a small, understanding smile and stepped inside. A cold draft trailed the living room, taking in the space with careful, almost clinical attention—eyes drifting to the rumpled couch, the scattered books on my coffee table, the single lamp that fought back the shadows. My heart thudded in my chest, unnerved by the quiet scrutiny.

I hurried through my bedroom, tossing a small duffel onto the bed—an extra sweater, my phone charger, a water bottle. When I returned, I found Daniel leaning against the wall, arms crossed. His once-gentle smile had hardened into something more reserved, unreadable. I paused in front of him, searching for those ocean-blue eyes.

Daniel's disdain for bedroom chatter was legendary—he found the symphony of a racing heartbeat far more intoxicating than any whispered word. With each labored breath she drew, the pulse at her throat gave a tangible proof of life—and power—flowing through her veins. In the hush that followed, the only sound was the muted patter of her pulse and the soft sigh of the sheets settling around them.

I looked back at my desk, where photographs of Maeva lay scattered among notes and maps tracking every branch of Meridith's bloodline. I flipped through the documents, hunting for any clue I had overlooked.

The grimoire was now in Maeva's hands, and—unfortunately—her powers had manifested. Why hadn't her therapy notes mentioned anything about abilities? The book itself must have awakened them. Frustration coiled inside me; Meridith had been exceptionally cunning when she set this curse in motion.

I rubbed my temples with my free hand as my thoughts jumbled. A distant moan snapped me back to the present. At my desk, I watched Daniel's head lower as he tended to her needs, his concentration absolute. She cried out again, and my irritation flared. I drained the last of my drink, set the glass down with a sharp clink, and strode toward the bed where their tryst sprawled out before me.

Daniel generously sucked and lapped at her core as she reached for me to join them between her cries of pleasure. I bent over the bed on one knee and wrapped my hand around her throat, forcing her to look at me. Her hot breath, rising from the warmth of her chest, blew across my face. Her body teetered on the edge of release, her legs trembling in desperate anticipation, muscles convulsing beneath my palm.

"Are you having fun?" I asked, my tone dripping with sarcasm.

She inhaled sharply, her chest rising and falling as she arched her back even further.

"My turn," I chuckled.

He looked…different from Elias—still handsome, but more distant, more guarded. And in that instant, I realized this wasn't the easy reunion I'd imagined.

"Ready?" he asked, voice low.

I nodded, swallowing hard against the lump in my throat. As we stepped out together into the hallway, I couldn't shake the feeling that I was trading one version of him for something altogether more complicated.

I slung my bag over one shoulder and squared my stance.

"I'm ready," I said, voice a notch too sharp.

Daniel stayed silent, arms folded across his chest, the fabric of his shirt stretched taut over broad pectorals. He looked me up and down, brow furrowed as if appraising a puzzle, he wasn't sure he wanted to solve.

To break the tension, I lifted a hand. "I'm Maeva," I offered awkwardly.

He glanced at my outstretched palm, hesitated for a heartbeat, then placed his large hand in mine. We shook once, twice—until the strap of my bag slipped from my shoulder and yanked my arm down. Still clasped together, I leaned to catch the bag, our hands twisting so that mine landed palm-down atop his. I yanked my hand back with a nervous laugh.

Daniel didn't let go. He tilted his head; gaze locked onto our joined hands. My chest tightened at the awkward closeness.

"Everything okay?" I asked, forcing a smile.

He blinked, shook his head as though waking from a daze, then ran a hand over his face, pressing the bridge of his nose. He exhaled deeply, voice low and taut.

"Where did you get that?"

"Get what?" I frowned, dropping my bag to the floor with a thud.

Daniel's eyes snapped back to mine. "The mark on your finger."

I stared down at my hand as if I'd never seen it before, flipping it palm-up and palm-down. He reached out, gripped my ring finger between his thumb and forefinger, and guided it under my nose.

"That mark," he repeated, voice unnervingly steady.

I looked—really looked—at the intricate sigil etched into my skin, and my pulse thundered in my ears.

"I don't know," I whispered, staring down at my finger.

The mark was pale—almost the same color as my skin—and until now I would never have noticed it. Three parallel lines ran the length of my finger, each terminating in a small triangle: the one nearest my nail pointed upward; its counterpart by my knuckle pointed downward. A fine line that stretched from my knuckle to my nail with intricate designs that vined over my finger.

Panic rose in my chest. How had I missed this until now? I combed my eyes over every inch of my hands and forearms, rubbing at my skin as though a closer look would erase my oversight. Sweat trickled down my spine; my heart slammed against my ribs; shame and anxiety wove together until I felt aflame.

Daniel appeared at my side with a glass of ice water. I took a trembling sip; the cold liquid soothed the scrape of panic in my throat and steadied my racing pulse. As the anxiety receded, I felt the truth of that raven sigil settle like a warning against my skin—one I could no longer ignore.

I picked my bag up from the floor and stood perfectly still, ready to follow him to Elias. My eyes swept over the living room one last time to make sure everything was as I'd left it, but my thoughts kept drifting back to the mark on my finger—and the panic I'd nearly succumbed to. I could still feel that knot of dread pulsing beneath my ribs.

Daniel inhaled deeply, his gaze settling on mine. "I used to know someone with that exact mark."

His eyes shimmered red for an instant—those familiar blue orbs now tinged with old pain and regret. I didn't dare speak; I could see he needed a moment to steel himself. He closed his eyes, exhaled, and when he opened them again, the sorrow had vanished. He straightened, the muscles in his shoulders shifting into place, and his expression hardened with resolve.

"I'm so—" I began, voice cracking.

He cut me off, his tone sharp as a flint. "You will not speak of anything that happened here. We're going to my home, and once we arrive, you will do exactly as you're told."

My face drained of emotion. The pity and pain vanished, leaving only an empty, unblinking stare.

Chapter Eleven

Daniel Black

I slammed my foot down on the accelerator, the engine's growl echoing the fury that twisted in my gut. Night air whipped through the cracked window, carrying the scent of wet asphalt and pine—nothing I could sink my teeth into. My knuckles went white on the wheel as the road blurred beneath me, each passing tree a phantom flicker of what I'd rather hunt.

My pulse drummed in my ears, drowning out the world but for the single, insistent craving that ruled my veins. Even as the speedometer climbed, I felt the bars of my own restraint tighten. Sharp fangs pressed against the inside of my lip, hungry for more than just the bitter tang of night air.

I stole a sidelong glance at her—Maeva—sitting pristine beside me. The silver wash of moonlight painted her features in cool relief: high cheekbones, a straight nose, and lips so still they might have been carved from alabaster. Her hands, folded delicately in her lap, bore that impossibly perfect sigil—a raven's wing unfurled in ink-dark lines that seemed to pulse on her skin.

I traced the emblem in my mind, then lifted my gaze to her face. Even now, as she sat motionless and silent, she radiated a dangerous, magnetic beauty. I knew that beauty well—it mirrored the calm before a storm, the serene mask a beast wears just before it strikes. My own monster writhed behind my ribs, restless as a chained wolf pacing its cage, claws scraping steel with each thought of what lurked beneath this quiet.

But Maeva's power lay dormant tonight, coiled like a great bear in hibernation, its deep breaths barely stirring the underbrush of her blood.

Her pulse tapped like distant drumbeats against her slender wrist, her veins carrying magic as steady and relentless as a mountain river.

Each time I met her gaze, a hollow ache blossomed in my chest—a longing no spell could ever satiate. I craved not only the power she wielded but the woman who wielded it: the soft lilt of her laughter, the warmth of her smile.

Those quiet afternoons in Makenzie's study—poring over her crippling anxiety, her depleting confidence, her dreams—wove a gentle bond between us, one I carried long after the candles burned low. My own beast stirred at the thought, craving more than blood—craving the sharp sweetness of connection, the possibility that beneath our curses we might find something human, something real.

I forced my eyes back to the road—a ribbon of asphalt glinting under moonglow—and gripped the wheel tighter. The wind whispered past the open window, carrying only the promise of home—and the ghosts we could never leave behind.

Her steady breathing beside me offered a quiet solace I'd scarcely allowed myself to imagine. The woman who once lived in perpetual angst now sat so calm, her heart beating in gentle rhythm with the engine's hum. I knew there was no turning back once her power was unleashed; this was the moment I'd been waiting centuries to reach. I craved the peace that lay just beyond the horizon, a final rest from the curse that bound us both.

As the trees thinned and moonlit fog crept over the mountain pass— soft tendrils wrapping each branch in silvery mist—I felt the familiar riddle stir at the edge of my mind:

"A curse set takes blood and love.

A curse broken takes heart and peace."

—✦ ⋆ ◇ ★ ✦—

Dim torch-lit flames flickered in the darkness, casting Maeva's gaunt silhouette in a restless dance against the cold, damp stones. Each drip from the walls sounded like a muted heartbeat, echoing her own hollow rhythms as she waited. A sweet breeze, carried in through the barred window from the lake beyond, drifted across her—an almost-tender reminder of freedom she could taste but not claim. Rusted chains swayed overhead, their hollow clinks promising only more torment.

Maeva sat slumped in the ancient wooden chair, back pressed to unforgiving stone, her small frame wrapped in exhaustion. Strands of brown hair fell into her eyes, hiding the fierce longing burning behind them—the desperate ache to be anywhere but here. Every shift set her iron cuffs rattling, each echo a bitter taunt. The runes carved into the metal glowed faintly, holding her power at bay, sealing her hope in a cage of cold magic.

I watched from the shadows, arms folded, one boot pressed against the opposite knee. The firelight framed me in half-darkness, but even here, Maeva's gaze found me—steady, yearning, wounded. Her wrists, her feet, even the very air around her seemed to stretch toward me, as if praying for rescue. I felt the pull in my chest, the fierce want to close the distance, to shatter her chains, to carry her away from this place of stone and sorrow.

In that moment, the cell felt impossibly small, the walls growing tighter around us both. Yet her silent plea reached out, a fragile thread of longing pulling at my resolve.

Its words brushed against my cheek like a lover's caress, reminding me that every sacrifice I'd made had led here. Ahead, the road wound through the shadows, and with each mile I felt the weight of my centuries-old burden begin to lift.

"I need some information from you," I said sharply.

I stepped from the shadows, my silhouette swallowing the meager torchlight as I approached her. My hands curled into fists, buried in the pockets of my pants. With long, deliberate strides, I closed the distance until my tall frame loomed over her petite form, cutting off the fragile glow that half-lit her skin. Maeva lifted her head, hair tumbling back in tangled waves to reveal eyes as hollow as night—empty of expectation, yet somehow alive with the flicker of that single dancing flame in her pupils. In that moment, every ounce of my resolve coiled tighter around the desperate promise in her gaze.

"Okay" she stated plainly.

I knew the taste of my blood in her system would break down her defenses, but I wanted to be certain. I'd slipped just a drop into the water in her apartment earlier, forcing her walls to steel themselves under a sudden wave of panic—sparking the small mercy of keeping her calm, for now.

Still, I needed answers. Blood carries every memory—every hidden truth—and I had to coax her free. This wasn't a guessing game; it was a contest of wills and knowledge.

I knelt before her; our eyes locked in the smoky torchlight. Gently, I lifted her wrist to my mouth. The iron cuffs clanged softly as I leaned in, the sweet, metallic tang of fear and life mingling on her skin. My canines slid forward, ivory blades glinting. When they pierced her flesh, Maeva let out a sharp hiss, the sound swallowed by the chamber's damp silence.

Warm blood welled from the wound, flooding into my mouth. Instantly, her life unspooled in my mind: childhood laughter, teenage heartbreak, every triumph, and sorrow swept through me in a roaring torrent. Each memory was bright and vivid, searing through my veins like molten fire.

I released her wrist and staggered back, gasping for air. The deluge of her memories pressed against my temple, heavy as stone. My breathing came in ragged heaves as I fought to reclaim my own mind.

Maeva's wrist drooped limply in my hand; dark droplets fell to the cold stone floor in a small, shining pool at her feet. I swallowed hard, anchoring myself against the onrush of her past—and prepared myself for whatever truths still lay buried within her.

I met her blank stare for a moment longer, then—without warning—forced my grip on her wrist and bit down again, harder this time. I pressed my teeth into her flesh and sifted through her memories until I found what I needed. In an instant, Meridith's face blossomed before me: her pale skin, the determination in her eyes, the moment she chose her fate.

I yanked back so violently that I stumbled onto the cold stone floor. Gravel dug into my elbows and coarse dirt stained my shirt in dark patches. A white-hot pain bloomed at my temples as centuries back of Meridith's life battered my mind. Every flash of her past throbbed behind my eyes, threatening to shatter my sanity.

Gasping, I staggered to my feet and pushed myself away from Maeva's chair. I pivoted, leaning against the damp wall, and lifted my chin to steady my breath. Slow, deliberate inhalations helped quench the storm raging in my skull. As the vertigo eased, I faced Maeva again. Her eyes—still wide and unblinking—held only questions and fear.

I took a steadying breath and forced my attention back to the terrified girl before me, not the ancestor whose memories still echoed in my mind. Carefully, I wrapped her wrist in a clean strip of cloth, staunching the bleeding. The fog I'd clouded her mind with should now be lifting—her hazy confusion giving way to clarity.

Her eyes snapped up to mine, widening at the unfamiliar room and the weight of the rusted chains locking her wrists to the chair arms. A strangled sob escaped her throat as she realized she could not run. Her panic surged: each rattle of the iron sent fresh tears coursing down her cheeks, smearing saltwater stains across her blouse.

I stood back, arms folded, watching her struggle for purchase in the worn wooden seat. She shook it violently, the wood protesting beneath her weight. Her voice cracked and trembled with raw terror, heart hammering in her ears as she gasped for breath between frantic, pleading cries of "P-Please let me go" she cried out to me.

I leaned in, resting my palms on the worn oak arms of her chair. My face hovered mere inches from hers, our gazes locked eye to eye in the flickering torchlight.

"I want to play a game of honesty, Maeva," I whispered, voice low, almost tender. "I will ask you a question—and you will answer truthfully. If you do not…" My lips curved into a thin, cruel smile. "…I will force the truth from you."

She swallowed, the raw scrape of her breath echoing in the stale air. Her voice trembled to life. "Ask me what? I— I don't know anything."

"Actually, Miss Sinclair," I replied softly, stepping back out of her reach, "you already have all the answers."

I folded my arms across my chest, leaning against the edge of the rickety table. "A curse to be set demands blood and love; to be broken, it requires heart and peace." What do you know of it?"

She closed her eyes as though to summon courage. When she spoke, her voice was barely more than a breath. "Ugh… nothing."

I tapped my teeth together in mock disappointment. "Tsk, tsk"—the sound echoed against the stone walls— "see? I warned you about lying."

Fear flared in her eyes—crimson reflections of the torch's flame. Hot tears welled, trembling on her lashes. She strove to catch her breath. "W— wait, please," she begged.

I moved back to stand directly before her, patiently silent. Around us, the cell's shadows deepened. She fought for words, as though rifling through a locked chest of memories. At last, she cried out, voice cracking, "I don't know what it means!"

My patience snapped. "What about the book you bought from the bookstore?"

Her head jerked up in disbelief. "I—I keep it in my bag. How do you know about that?" Confusion blurred her features.

I hissed, "What have you seen in that book?"

"Nothing, its blank," she whispered, eyes confused.

I let out an exasperated breath. "It's not a book, Maeva—it's a grimoire."

Stepping to the table, I slid her canvas satchel toward me, its strap scraping across the rough wood. With deliberate calm I withdrew the ancient volume and set it open before her. Then I took a single step back, watching, waiting for her to meet its dark promise.

"Tell me what you see," I snarled.

Her gaze snapped down to the open grimoire. Chains clinked with every tremulous turn of her slender wrist as she flipped through page after blank page.

"Nothing," she whispered, voice hollow.

My patience shattered like brittle glass. Fury swelled in my chest— an animal's rage straining at its bonds. I stepped back into the shadows, easing the final sigils on my mind's cage, letting the beast surge free. Torchlight danced over my face as my jaw shifted and ivory fangs slid forth—too long, too perfect, too hungry for mercy.

"What do you know about monsters?" I growled, voice low and primal.

Her head jerked up, eyes wide. Her chains rattled again as her pulse thundered beneath trembling skin. She tried to scramble to her feet—but the iron cuffs bit into her flesh, and she collapsed back into the chair with a sob, hair plastered to her sweat-slick temples.

I vanished into the darker corners of the cell, my silhouette flickering at the edge of her vision. Only two pale lantern-glints betrayed my position as I watched her panic. She hunted the darkness with frantic eyes, breath coming in desperate, stuttering gasps.

"Tell me, witch," I whispered from somewhere behind her, "what do you know of monsters?"

Her head whirled, heart pounding so loud I could hear it in the echoing against the stone. Her fingers clawed at her sleeves, tears carving bright tracks down her dirt-streaked cheeks.

With a thunderous growl, I stalked forward—slow, deliberate steps that shook the wooden floor. Each footfall drove home the truth she refused to face there was no escape from me now. The only sound in the cell was her ragged breathing and the distant drip of moisture from the walls.

When I was mere inches away, I paused—and the cell grew colder still. Her eyes, brimming with terror, locked on mine. My claws flexed at my sides, hungry for the warmth of her blood.

I leaned down; hands braced on the arms of her chair so my face hovered level with hers. A soft whimper slipped past her lips as my teeth ghosted against the hollow of her throat. I drank in her scent—the tang of sweat, a whisper of lavender—and let the moment stretch, savoring her fear. Then, with a sudden flick, I sank my canines into her flesh. Her cry cracked against the stone walls, sharp enough to warn me off—just barely—but never enough to sate me. Before her gasp could fade, I melted back into shadow.

Her hand flew to her neck, pressing the wound closed as tears welled in her eyes.

"Tell me what you know," I hissed, circling her like a panther.

"I—I know nothing!" she choked out, voice raw.

I emerged again, seizing her wrist in one inky-black claw. My fangs punctured her vein, and hot blood glinted on my lips—sweet as the finest wine. She flailed, but her chains bit deep into her flesh and anchored her helplessly in place. Her sobs reverberated through the cell.

Slipping once more into darkness, I watched her tremble, eyes rimmed red, trying to shrink into the chair. My own mouth curved into a cruel smile, teeth bared in the dim torchlight. My eyes, black as midnight, shone with anticipation.

"Tell me what y—" I began, voice low and menacing.

"I said nothing!" she shrieked, voice breaking on the final word.

Maeva slammed her fist against the chair, the echo ringing off stone. Her other hand pressed to her chest, and her boot struck the flagstone floor so hard a vortex of blue energy tore through the room. The oak table snapped in half like twigs under that surge, its splintered pieces clattering across the cold floor. Another shockwave slammed into me, cracking my ribs against the wall. Dust and debris whipped into the air in a choking storm.

The torches guttered and died; smoke curled through the darkness, carrying the acrid tang of scorched wood. Maeva sat, still as a statue amid the chaos, eyes blazing cerulean. The swirling wind buffeted her hair off her face, whipping it back in perfect arcs. Each gust threatened to rip me from my feet, but I clung to the cracked stone.

In the roiling shadows, her blue eyes were the only light—bright, unblinking, merciless. A sliver of doubt quivered in my mind: had I underestimated her?

Then the door splintered inward. Abigail burst through, half the iron frame dangling from its hinges. Her eyes were pitch black; her fangs gleamed in the gloom. She snarled at Maeva's whirlwind, advancing on trembling legs.

Maeva rose, chains still clinking at her wrists. She met Abigail's approach like a tigress on the hunt—ready, contained only by her bonds. With a thunderous stomp, electric pulses crept up the ancient chains and suddenly cracked the locks. The ancient locking sigils etched into the wall—sigils meant to suppress her power—cracked and crumbled away.

The binding enchantments, our anchor of safety, lay broken at Maeva's feet. And in the sudden, stunned silence, only one truth remained: she was free.

She clenched the broken chains in both hands. Blue arcs of lightning crackled from fingertip to link, and in an instant the iron splintered away like brittle glass. The fragments tumbled to the floor in dull clinks.

Maeva's Raven mark flared to electric blue, mirrored by the storm of power dancing over her skin. Freed at last, she rose to her full height. The wind howled around her in a miniature tornado, tugging at her hair and clothing. Lightning flared at her fingertips, each spark illuminating the furious calm in her eyes.

She lowered her chin, gaze locked on Abigail and me, waiting.

Darkness filled every corner of the ruined cell, but Maeva herself shone like a star—terrifying, radiant. I'd never seen such raw power woven into such striking beauty. Unstable. Unstoppable. And somehow, utterly magnetic—even as I braced for the storm she would unleash.

"We need to get close enough to stop her" I yelled to Abigail.

"She'll tear this place apart before we even touch her," Abigail warned, her voice swallowed by the howling gale.

"Now" I roared, steeling myself against the swirling vortex.

We lunged forward in unison—Abigail charging straight into the eye of the storm, me sweeping wide to draw Maeva's focus. But even her mother's roar of wind clawed at us, threatening to hurl us off our feet. My pants whipped about my legs like living tendrils, and Abigail's heels barely found purchase on the slick stone.

Before we reached her, Maeva's hands flared with electric blue light. She thrust her palms outward, and the air split with thunder. Jagged bolts of crackling energy leapt across the room, painting the walls in brilliant, cobalt arcs. Each strike hit us like molten steel: Abigail was lifted off her feet, her hair fanning out in a halo of sparks, and I felt my ribs jar as if struck by a battering ram.

In a heartbeat, we were both swept up in the tempest of her power. The currents of wind and lightning wove together, spiraling us through the air. My body slammed into the ancient stones with bone-rattling force—centuries-old mortar splintering beneath the impact. Dust and debris exploded around me in a choking cloud.

When the whirlwind finally spent itself, Maeva stood at the center, her silhouette framed by drifting motes of light and shadow. Her eyes—brighter than any star—held both mercy and devastation.

Chapter Twelve

Elias Knight

I called Maeva but went straight to voicemail. It was unlike her to let calls go unanswered, she was always eager for my attention. Her voice hitched every time she picked up the phone. As our relationship deepened, so did her devotion. I had once told her that I would love her to be available whenever I needed her. She happily obliged every request. Her eagerness made her easy to control, as I tugged at her heartstrings without resistance. There was nothing that she wouldn't do for me.

After three unanswered rings, I decided to surprise her at her apartment. My annoyance with her grew stronger when she decided to not listen and pick up for me. This only fueled my eagerness to see her in person.

I needed her to do what I told her without hesitation. I didn't have time to coax her into always being at my disposal, even though she was happy to do that herself. Her crippling anxiety and self- doubt worked hand in hand with what I needed her to be for me. It made it easier to manipulate her feelings, rather than talk her into it.

I flung my phone onto the car floor. Anger thundered in my chest at her deliberate silence. The thought of her ignoring me when I specifically told her I needed her whenever I asked. I slammed on the gas, irritation taking hold of my emotions. My hands burned white hot against the leather wheel.

I walked through the halls of her complex, marching down the hallway to her door. My hands were in the fists at my side. My anger seeped through my eyes.

There was an old tan carpet that lined the hallways with gold patterned designs that had faded down the middle from consistent strides. Deep-green doors with faded gold numbers lined the corridor; I ignored them, focused on her number.

I turned the corner making my way to her door when magic pulsed ahead. I halted, closed my eyes, and tuned in to its familiar tingle. I stopped in my tracks; I tried to recognize the familiar residual tingle in the air. I tilted my chin down and took a deep breath as I focused my heightened senses on the magic. I closed my eyes as I stood in the hallway. Nostrils flared as motes of magic drifted like fireflies around me.

I stride slowly towards her door, focusing my senses on the surroundings. When I reached her doorway, I finally recognized a scent. Daniel. I inhaled again; sure, the enchantment belonged to him. It was her magic that I could feel dancing in the atmosphere. I relaxed my shoulders as they dropped down from the tensed position. My mind eased knowing the fact that my brother was the cause of my uncertainty.

I cracked my neck and ran my fingers through my hair as I resumed my role as Maeva's beloved like a mask and knocked three times on her door. No answer. My forced smile dropped; irritation crept back in. I knocked again this time harder. No answer. I tilted my chin down and closed my eyes. I targeted my hearing to her apartment for any clues as to why she wasn't answering the door. No movement in her home. Rage consumed my mind as I dug my phone out of my pocket to call Daniel. Each call went straight to voicemail.

"Dammit" I hissed.

I got back to my car and with fury I drove home to meet him. My foot slammed down on the gas pedal to the floor of the car as I weaved in and out of traffic not caring who was in my way. The animal tightly clawed at my insides dying to be let out. My patience for games slowly died down to pure bitterness of Maeva and her inconvenience of making me chase her.

Sweat formed in my hands as I continuously rolled my palms over the steering wheel. Adrenaline coursed through my veins as I came to the dark winged gates of the manor's grounds. My car swerved and hurled gravel from my tires like a wave of rocks, I quickly slammed on my brakes and skidded across the gravel driveway. I flung my car door open towards the massive iron wrought doors and stepped onto the manor's grounds.

Immediately I succumbed to a large force of magic that hit my chest, and I dropped down onto one knee. I held onto my door as the power surged through me like a lightning bolt sent specifically for me. The massive wave of power pulsed through the grounds of the manor leading into the woods. A force so heavy like a rush of wind sprinted from the manor trying to escape. The car shook back and forth from the strength of power. The trees that stretched across the sky shook from the violent magic.

It had been a long time since I had felt magic at this magnitude. My body quivered from the energy that expelled through me. I tried to regain my composure; I tried to find the strength in my legs. My chest was heavy from the weight of magic slamming against it. My legs limped as I tried to catch my breath. I forced myself up from the ground. My arm was still against the car door, bearing all my weight as I tried to regain my strength.

A deep growl formed in my throat; the beast recognized a threat nearby. My eyes shifted completely to black, and my needle-sharp fangs sprouted out from their restlessness. The beast slowly was let out of the cage waiting for prey to appear. Finally, my strength came back, and I pushed through the heavy iron doors. The magic still floated in the air; the energy pulsated throughout the manor.

I Adjusted my senses to the familiarity of my own home. I closed my eyes and took a deep breath of the familiar scent of musk and cedar. The dance of dust settled across their claimed surfaces while damp stones filled the large rooms. Musty rugs laid across the floor throwing dust and dirt in the air as you walked over. The scent of home, except, a familiar aroma of Maeva's scent was in it. My eyes widened; the rush of adrenaline flooded my veins.

Anger coursed throughout my body like a heat flash. I could feel the hairs on my neck stand from such aggression. Sweat beaded on my skin as I rushed through the large stone castle quickly. My eyes narrowing to every corner that passed. The air was heavy with the scent of the woman that caused such a force of magic. Like a predator following the scent of its prey, I reached the stairs leading to the bottom of the manor.

It had been centuries since I have stepped foot down there. Memories of tortured victims, their flesh covered the grounds, playing with their life for amusement. I could still hear their cries echo within the walls of their confinement. Their shadows hovered across the dark corners of the darkness.

I knew then the reason why Daniel brought her here. I raced down the stairs to the darkest corner of the bottom floor. My feet kicked up dirt and small droplets of stale water with my strides. When I approached, I heard Abigail and Daniel try to yell over the sound of the storm, I rushed to the broken door and the strongest wind threw me back against the damp stone walls. I quickly recovered and began to try and make my way into the room.

That's when I saw her. A Sinclair witch. Her bright blue eyes surged with magic at the center of the dark room. Her fingertips sparking with bright blue power like a lightning storm on a summer night. Her magic was powerful and untamed, even watching her made someone like me take a moment to second guess my own agenda.

I searched for my family through the dirt and wind that circled the room. Both tried to make their way to her without getting hurt. It wasn't going to work. She was too powerful for us to take on.

"Daniel!" I yelled out.

We both locked our eyes as I tried to reach for him. My arms and legs shook with all my strength not to give in to force that cyclone around her. My clothes tried to betray me as they kept pulling into the storm. My slick hair now pulled in every direction as the wind forced it to move without cause.

I grabbed onto his hand as he pulled me towards his direction against the wall. Abigail's back against the cold stone with her palms faced down. Her hair in disarray and her eyes had dilated black pupils that were no longer encased with white. She was waiting for the right moment to strike like a spider patiently waiting for the fly in its web. Her teeth protruded out ready and eager to land a deadly latch onto her Maeva. Saliva ran across her cheeks, the storm pulling the droplets across her face.

The room is pitched black except for the bright power of blue striking the darkness back. The power in her fingers lit the room with each spark and then darkness again until another. The blue light ricocheted against walls as the shadow of our bodies gave away our position with every flare. I looked at Daniel and with a nod of approval, I took a step into the storm. It was the only choice I had, or her magic would have torn this foundation apart.

The wind was fierce. Dust and dirt flying around encasing their master. I reached out my hand to her hoping she would recognize me.

"Maeva?" I said with my hand blocking the debris that scraped across my face.

Tiny peddles landed on my face as the wind dragged their sharp edges through my flesh. Droplets of blood formed as the wind took the beads away. It left a trail of crimson in its path.

I needed to get her attention. I wasn't even sure this was the same woman anymore. Doubt filled my mind as I stepped closer to her. My entire plan was about to be ruined, as of now. I needed to put an end to this magical violence.

"Maeva, baby it's me Elias" another step closer.

"Elias?" a small cry of relief slipped from her lips.

"I'm here love" I reached my hand towards her.

She gently stretched her hand and settled into mine. I pulled her tightly into me and embraced her as she sank into my body.

The sparks faded and her eyes returned to her normal brown. Her soft gaze melted through the fierce exterior. Her magic receded back under her skin, once again dormant. The thunderous wind died down and the cloud of debris fell back to its place on the cold ground. The room was once dark again.

I ran my fingers through her hair and gently caressed her long soft curls between each stroke. Our breath and heartbeats joined together in unison. Her scent filled my nostrils.

She exhaled a deep sigh of relief when I kissed her forehead with confirmation that I was here. Then a small flame ignited from behind me, Daniel's lighter flickered in the darkness, barely glowing against the sharpen blackness of the room. He reached up towards the smoldering torch that was once illuminating the room and reignited the wick.

A blaze from each torch burned bright, commanded the darkness back into the corners. Daniel and my eyes met again, this time with anger seeded within my gaze. He does not waver from mine. This was not supposed to happen. Her magic was untamed and if we ruined our chances, she was never going to trust us. I couldn't risk that, not for everything that I had worked so hard for.

My anger flared at Daniel. My eyes seethed with hatred and malice. My mind focused so much on Daniel when I did not notice that Abigail was standing next to Maeva.

Suddenly, she reached and grabbed her by the back of her neck. Her strength pulled Maeva quickly from my embrace and within a second, she is thrown against the stone floor with her hand tightened around her throat.

Abigail's eyes were as black as the darkest night. Her razor teeth fully extended from her mouth. Her jaw dislocated to an unnatural drop of more needled ivory teeth. Abigail finally had the opportunity to kill her prey; Maeva was frozen with terror at the sight of a true monster.

"A pretty girl, with pretty tricks" she hissed.

Small droplets of saliva dripped onto Maeva's face. Abigail tightened her grip again. It would take nothing for her to snap her neck within her grasp. Maeva's face began turning red as her breath shallowed. Her legs kicked beneath the monster on top of her. Her hands fought against Abigail's grip on her, trying to pry her strength back for a small breath of air.

"Enough, we need her" I growled.

Both their gazes met mine as I stood over them. For a small moment I allowed her torture with fear and my amusement to rest. The mistress released her throat and stood peering down at Maeva as she laid on the cold ground. Her hands braced her throat as she began to breathe in deeply.

The stale cold air of mold and desperation filled her lungs. I stood over her and watched life come back to her one breath at a time. Her face that held terror of a monster she had only read about now revealed. The fear in her eyes at the words I spoke. I knew there was no going back after this.

Her magic was now awake. Plan B.

Chapter Thirteen

Maeva Sinclair

Fear was my only companion in this cell. The concrete slab they called a bed pressed cold and unyielding against my back—an unbreakable reminder that I could never escape. Every night I replayed that evening in a merciless loop: the knife's razor-hot whisper at my throat, the gleam of cursed black eyes. I thought I'd buried those memories long ago—locked them away beneath layers of denial—but the curse of my power refused to stay buried.

My thoughts spiraled, a cyclone of shame and dread. Anxiety struck my chest like a falling boulder, crushing breath from my lungs. My eyes stung with tears I couldn't hold back. I curled into a ball, forehead pressed against the stone, as hot saltwater dripped onto my knees. Darkness pressed in from all sides, the walls inching closer until hope vanished.

Then—footsteps. Heavy, methodical, echoing down the concrete stairwell. Once, Elias's stride would've made my heart soar; now it was a hammer pounding shame and fear into my skull. The steps stopped outside my door. I squeezed my eyes shut, letting the last tear fall at his appearance. His shadow fell across the slit of light—and with it, the final spark of hope died.

"Maeva, baby" he said with a small grin.

I lifted my head and met his gaze, my heart fluttering against my ribs like a bird desperate for freedom. Even now, torchlight danced across his face—illuminating the strong line of his jaw I once traced with my fingertips—while the other half remained shrouded in darkness, the part I never truly knew.

My chest tightened, torn between the ache of longing for the man he pretended to be and the icy fear of the monster he'd revealed himself to be. Every flicker of flame in his eyes pulled me closer despite every warning in my bones, and I couldn't decide whether I wanted to touch him or tear down the walls that held us apart and murder him.

My gaze locked onto him, every ounce of fury blazing in my eyes. The memory of my grief twisted into molten anger, coiling through my veins as his venomous deceit slithered through my thoughts. His familiar scent—once comforting—now hit me like waves crashing against jagged rocks, each breath a stab of betrayal. I'd believed in the beauty of his promises, a silken web so artfully woven it ensnared my heart—but now that illusion lay in ashes, replaced by raw, unfiltered rage. I stood there in silence, the space between us crackling with tension. My fingers dug into the cold iron bars, knuckles whitening, as he lifted his chin and took another deliberate step closer—every movement a reminder that the man I once loved was gone, and before me stood only the monster who'd shattered me.

"I know exactly what you're thinking," I snapped, leaning into the bars until the iron bit into my palms. "And believe me, I'm far stronger than you."

He smirked, the torchlight dancing off his fanged teeth. "You didn't strike me as all that powerful the other night. Why don't you step inside the cell? We'll put that to the test."

A tremor of anger lent me courage—I almost wanted to claw out his eyes, even knowing he could crush me like a twig. Magic throbbed under my skin, hungry to be unleashed, yet I couldn't draw on it. Not here.

"Maybe another time," he said, his voice low and measured.

A mocking gleam lit my eyes. "I'll wager if I unleashed my magic—"

He cut me off, tapping the rune-carved ceiling overhead. "—You can't. This cell's been warded specifically against witches."

He paused, the challenge momentarily wrinkling my confident mask. Beyond that, I sensed the hunger for power still swirling just beneath the surface—waiting.

He stepped back and swept his hand upward, drawing my gaze to the ceiling. Every stone was etched with glowing sigils—interlocking circles, sharp runes, and twisting glyphs that pulsed with pale light. Each symbol hummed with suppressed power, a chorus of ancient bindings that coiled around the chamber like iron chains.

My pulse hammered in my ears as I traced the patterns: a ward to mute my voice, a seal to stifle my blood's magic, a lock to cage the very force that was my birthright. I pressed my palm against the damp wall, fingertips grazing the cool grooves, and felt the weight of its rejection: this prison was not merely for bodies but built for ones like me alone.

A crushing wave of hopelessness washed over me, dragging every spark of defiance beneath its dark surface.

Terror coiled through my veins like ice water. My heart thundered so violently I thought it might burst my ribs. Breath caught in frantic gasps as one trembling hand slipped from the bars to press against my heaving stomach. Pain and despair crashed over me in relentless waves, each one stronger than the last, and my legs gave way beneath me. Panic clawed at my throat—was this truly my tomb? Would I ever taste fresh air again? Dread flooded every fiber of my being, burying me beneath an avalanche of hopeless thoughts. It felt as though my own mind was entombing me alive, each thought a shovelful of earth packing me tighter until I could barely breathe. I bowed my head and pressed my forehead against the cold iron bars, my voice cracking into the silence.

"What do you want from me, Elias?"

He leaned back against the stone wall, arms casually crossed over his chest, the torchlight dancing in his dark eyes.

"I need your help with something," he said, voice steady but bearing an unspoken edge.

A fresh wave of anger flared through me, hot and bitter. "What could I possibly help you with?" I snapped, my gaze sharp enough to cut through steel.

He pushed off the wall and closed the distance between us in two long strides—far too close. The air around him seemed to hum. He dropped his voice to a whisper, low enough that only I could hear.

"I need your magic to solve a problem."

I staggered back, my pulse thundering in my ears.

"What—my magic?" I rasped, swallowing hard against the ache in my throat. I hadn't summoned a single spell since that night. The memory of that pain still burned beneath my skin—why would I ever unleash it again?

He stepped forward, urgency sharpening his features. "If you help me, Maeva," he said, voice low, "I swear I'll let you go."

Those words—once a promise of safety—twisted like a knife in my chest. His dark eyes bore into mine, desperation flickering there, the same haunted look I'd once trusted with my very soul.

"How do I know you won't break your word?" I found myself whispering, terror and defiance warring in my chest.

He placed a hand over his heart, the motion so earnest it stole my breath. The torchlight glinted off the silver cuff at his wrist. "I always keep my word," he vowed.

His vow hung in the stale air like a noose—play by his rules or remain trapped forever. I didn't believe him—not for a second—but it was the only chance I had to feel the sky on my face again.

I drew in a shaky breath and nodded. "Fine."

A slow smile curved his lips, lighting his eyes. "Perfect."

Even in the dim torchlight, his fangs slid free—needle-sharp and hungry for blood. And yet I had just struck a bargain with the very evil they promised.

My shoulders slumped under the weight of exhaustion. I took a weary step toward the cold slab when suddenly his hand shot through the bars and clamped around mine.

I froze. Terror exploded in my chest as I looked up into his eyes—pupils elongating into vertical slits, the predator within staring at me.

The sudden shift rooted me to the spot. I yanked, but his grip through the bars was ironclad. Cold sweat gathered on my brow as his glare pinioned me. Terror rippled through my limbs—my knees threatened to give way. His hand clenched tighter, crushing my fingers against the iron. A white-hot lance of pain shot up my arm. My skin reddened under the pressure; I could almost feel my bones crack.

"I'm begging you—Elias, my hand," I choked out, tears blurring my vision.

He leaned closer, voiced a venomous whisper. "That fucking mark."

My heart lurched. "What mark?" I rasped, panic tightening my chest.

I screamed as tears streamed down my face, the pain almost blinding. He finally released my hand, and I clutched it to my chest. Stumbling back, I hit the floor hard and slid against the cold stone wall, curling up as far as I could. The chill air of the cell brushed my hair, but it did nothing to numb the agony.

Across the room, his eyes never wavered—still locked onto me like a hunter sizing up prey. A low growl rumbled in his throat. He drew a slow breath, cracking his neck deliberately, then tugged at his suit jacket until it sat just right. His other hand raked through his hair in a gesture of fierce impatience. Even as he composed himself, I knew this respite was only temporary. The storm behind those calm movements was far from over.

"That is very interesting," he said, that fake grin curving his lips.

My heart pounded as he shifted from monster to man—predatory hunter one moment, impeccably dressed gentleman the next.

Fear surged through me, and I pressed my injured hand to my chest, tears springing as pain flared up my arm.

Moments dragged into what felt like hours as we simply stared. I couldn't summon words, only quiet whimpers. He remained motionless by the door, hands in his pockets, scrutinizing me with a half-smile. A chuckle slipped past him as he tilted his chin upward amused, while I saw nothing to laugh at.

"And here I thought you were just a pathetic little girl who couldn't go a day without breathing techniques" he sneered.

His words stabbed me like a blade, twisting deep in my chest. He'd weaponized my own anxiety against me, and I felt hollowed out, incapable even of a retort. A familiar heat flared—pure, scorching anger. I refused to let him belittle me. I'd carried this smallness all my life; I wouldn't let him deepen that wound.

"I might not last a day," I said, voice steady, "but you needed a fortified cell just to hold me."

His smile faltered—and I allowed a small one of my own to surface. He was right: I was vulnerable. But he needed something strong enough to contain me, or this entire place would have crumbled.

"You're right. I had help from someone much stronger than you." He said firmly.

Without another word, he turned and strode toward the stairs. Torches guttered and snuffed out in his wake as he marched down the corridor. He climbed the steps, each footfall echoing, until a final slam and the click of the lock left me alone once more. My chest tightened at the hollow silence—trapped, abandoned, with only the faint glow of dying torchlight for company.

Chapter Fourteen

Maeva Sinclair

Moonlight poured through the narrow window, its silver rays tracing the carved sigils on the stones—reminders that I was still their prisoner. Outside, the full moon hovered above the treetops like a watchful guardian, its perfect glow softened by the embracing darkness. I fixated on its surface, memorizing every crater and blemish as though they held secrets. Below, wind-swept pines swayed in time with the gentle rise and fall of the lake's mirrored surface. The stars shimmered on the water in a thousand iridescent sparks, and for the first time in days, I felt a hush settle over my racing heart.

The stone slab beneath me felt as frigid as the lake's breeze. Heavy iron chains at each corner rattled against the walls with every gust, a metal reminder of my captivity. Thin sheets and a lumpy pillow offered no shelter from the bitter air; they were little more than mocking whispers of comfort.

All I could crave was warmth—any spark to stop my bones from shaking until they ached. I drew the blanket up to my chin, tucking it around my neck, and burrowed into the pillow as best I could, desperate to keep the cold slab from stealing the heat of my scalp.

"Here." A soft male voice echoed through the hall.

I sprang upright, the thin blanket slipping from my shoulders as I vaulted off the slab. The pillow tumbled behind me, landing with a dusty thud on the cold dirt floor. At the gate's bars, Daniel stood framed by torchlight—his crisp coat collar catching the glow, dark eyes widening in surprise as he registered my sudden movement.

Every muscle in his lean frame was tense, yet he raised one hand slowly, palm outward, fingers splayed in a silent plea for calm. My pulse thundered as sweat bead on my brow; the sharp scent of damp stone and metal filled my nostrils.

Heart hammering, I pressed back against the wall, blanket forgotten, as his unexpected arrival sent a fresh wave of fear crashing through me.

"I brought you a couple more blankets and another pillow" he said.

Daniel raised the bundle—blankets and pillow—in one hand, tilting his chin with a small, earnest nod. He slid the soft wool through the bars, catching the torchlight and making them glow like a promise of warmth. My heart thundered so loud I thought he might hear it from the other side.

Nightmares of that terrible evening still haunted me—his face twisted in command as I unleashed my magic. Now, breath hitched in my throat, I watched the man who'd tortured me offer comfort. My skin prickled where his gaze met mine.

Yet the blankets waited. Summoning a shuddering breath, I pushed myself up from the cold floor and took a hesitant step forward, careful not to show how torn I was between fear and the desperate need to feel warmth once more.

I yanked the blankets toward me, tugging them free of his outstretched hand—only to catch a whiff of charred flesh. I glanced down in horror as Daniel's fingers sizzled, skin blackening and peeling back in savage curls. Blistered bubbles of pus surfaced and popped, the acrid smoke curling into the cell.

My stomach lurched, bile rising. I clutched the blankets to my chest and stumbled backward, knuckles scraping the stone wall. He retracted his hand, bringing it to his face as if to wipe away the horror—only to watch the burns vanish. Intact, unscarred skin remained. He flexed his fingers, then casually slid his hand into his pocket, leaving me trembling in the flickering torchlight, unsure if I'd truly seen what I'd just witnessed or if it were yet another cruel trick.

"How the hell did you just—?" My voice cracked as I struggled to form the question, every word laced with disbelief and fear.

""This cell was built so magic can't breach its sigils," he said, voice steady.

"It's for your protection as much as ours," he added, reaching toward the runes overhead.

My breath trembled. "This is insane."

He stepped closer, eyes gentle now. "You'd be amazed at the strength you possess, Maeva Sinclair."

His words hung in the cool air, a promise and a warning wrapped in one.

I pressed my back against the wall, mind racing. Me—dangerous? I couldn't even face a day without teetering on the brink of a breakdown. Yet here he was, weaving bedtime-fairy-tale nonsense into my reality: magic, sigils, monsters.

I was supposed to believe I was the witch straight out of a children's story. He straightened, a faint smirk curling his lips. Without another word, he turned—and left me alone in the darkness once more.

"Thank you," I whispered, clutching the blankets and pillow so tightly I could barely breathe. Beneath their coarse weight, a smoky haze of hickory curled into the cell—warmth and home, yet utterly impossible here. My chest tightened, and I slid down the slab until I sat against the cold stone. The scent flooded my senses, pulling me from the edge of panic into a fragile calm.

Beyond the bars, he froze. His broad back tensed, every muscle visible under his shirt. I held my breath as he turned, the torchlight slicing across his profile—sharp, unreadable. Our eyes met in that glinting half-shadow, and for a heartbeat the world narrowed to that silent exchange.

His lips quirked into a faint, almost predatory smile.

"You're welcome," he whispered.

I dared not move or speak, the blankets a flimsy shield between me and the ones that are using me. The cell's chill pressed in, but so did the unspoken promise—and the threat—in his words. My heart thundered with both relief and dread: this small comfort came at a price I wasn't ready to pay for yet.

Chapter Fifteen

Maeva Sinclair

I curled into a tight ball on the hard slab; blankets twisted around me. My eyes felt scorched from days of tears and restless nights. Time had blurred into one endless darkness, but I knew it was late—too late to fight the exhaustion any longer. My limbs trembled from constant anxiety, every muscle screaming for rest. As my eyelids fluttered shut, the weight of the cell pressed in, and I wondered how long I could survive this prison of mind and stone.

Despite everything, these new donations were as close to comfort as I'd get in this prison—and I wasn't about to complain. A cool breeze slipped through the bars, brushing my cheeks and tangling my hair. I wrapped the thick blankets Daniel had provided tightly around my shoulders, leaving only my face exposed to the night air.

Beneath them lay an unexpected gift: a tanned animal hide. Dark brown with coarse black fur and white-striped edges, it sprawled across the slab like a forgotten memory. I buried myself in it and felt something I hadn't in days: warmth.

For a moment, I was back on those childhood camping trips—dozing beneath the stars, wrapped in my parents' greatcoats, while crickets whispered in the grass outside my tent. In this cell of stone and shadow, that memory was a lifeline, carrying me toward sleep despite the fear waiting in the dark.

Childhood memories surfaced, flooding me with a bittersweet ache. My eyes burned as tears—not from fear this time, but from longing— trickled down my cheeks. The whisper of hickory in the air warmed my aching bones in a way I hadn't known was possible, and a gentle calm settled over my racing mind.

For the first time in days, the hide felt like armor: a barrier against the prison's cold and the suffocating weight of magic. I hugged my knees to my chest and curled into my nightly ball, the soft fur against my skin lulling me toward sleep.

In that cocoon of blankets and memory, I finally let go—and surrendered to the fragile peace of slumber.

Warm sunlight warmed my face, and shifting cloud shadows danced across my skin. The chill of the night was already a fading memory. Golden beams filtered through the leafy canopy above, spotlighting drifting motes of pollen like glimmering specks in a lazy ballet. Dragonflies darted overhead, their wings catching the sun in fleeting flashes of emerald and sapphire.

I lifted a hand to shade my eyes—and found myself seated in a riot of blossoms. A living tapestry of scarlet poppies, fuchsia lilies, and violet irises bloomed at my feet, their colors so vivid they seemed painted onto the earth. I leaned forward and cupped a single bud, marveling at its dew-dappled petals. A cluster of bees hummed around me, their velvet bodies alighting on each flower in a dance of gentle purpose as they gathered nectar.

Beneath me, the grass rolled like waves—each blade swaying in harmony with the breeze. The air was rich with the scent of wild mint and honeyed blossoms, and even the soft hum of distant birdsong felt like a lullaby. This wasn't the cold stone of my cell—it was a dreamscape of warmth and life. My heart twinged with longing and sorrow, knowing it wasn't real. Yet for a moment, I surrendered to its beauty, allowing the dream to hold me in its gentle embrace.

I closed my eyes, letting the symphony of the forest wash over me—rustling leaves, distant birdsong, the soft hum of insects. I needed to be certain the purpose that brought me here was near, not some elusive phantom I'd have to chase.

Then, like a ribbon of sunlight through the canopy, sweet laughter wounds its way through the trees. I snapped my eyes open, scanning the riot of blooms and ferns. Nothing. Heart pounding, I spun again, searching for each moss-cloaked trunk, each carpet of flowers. Still no one.

A low male voice cut through the giggle—warm, teasing. I followed it, footsteps light on winding roots. I hopped the thick brown tendrils that snaked across the forest floor, each step bringing me closer. The laughter returned—this time mingled voices, male and female—dancing just beyond sight.

My pulse quickened, and I quickened my pace. The incline steepened, and I pressed my hand to the rough bark of a towering oak for support. My legs trembled with the unexpected exertion, every muscle alive with anticipation. The voices drew nearer, their laughter bright as bells, and I realized whatever magic had summoned me here was not hidden—it was waiting, just ahead.

My breath was shallow and short; I was trying my hardest to catch it. Filled my lungs with deep inhales of fresh air. I learned my back up against a very large tree to provide support, I felt like I was going to pass out from exhaustion. I tilted my chin up to the sky and let the sun kiss my cheeks once more. My eyes squinted shut enjoying the freedom of the sun when light moaning softly landed on my ears. I snapped back to attention and opened my eyes waiting for another sound to follow.

My ears pricked at the sound, and I froze—another moan, this time dangerously closed and placed behind me. Heart hammering, I pressed my back against the broad trunk of the ancient oak, hands splayed on its rough bark for balance. Every gasp and rustle from the unseen couple made my skin crawl with embarrassment and something darker—curiosity.

I shifted sideways, careful not to crack a twig, inching around the tree's flank. A tangle of clothing lay strewn on the grass—browns and creams tossed aside as if discarded in haste. Once-vibrant blades beneath it were flattened and wilted, crushed by heated bodies.

Then I saw them: two figures entwined, moving in a blur of urgency. Their breaths came in ragged gasps, lips parted in wet, urgent sounds that echoed through the hush of the woods. Hands roamed feverishly across bare skin, as if mapping every curve and plane, searching for release. My cheeks burned. I should have turned and fled—but I was rooted in place, caught between the desire to look away and the pull of raw, pulsing life laid bare before me.

My cheeks flushed crimson as I realized the couple was making love in the heart of the forest. Their soft moans ignited a warmth deep in my chest, spreading down to my thighs until I felt damp beneath my clothes.

Embarrassed, I pivoted around the tree, pressing my back against its rough bark. My breath came in shallow gasps as their rhythm washed over me. I grounded myself by gripping the trunk with one hand, inhaling slowly to tame the heat racing through my body—yet I couldn't tear my eyes away. Curiosity won over decorum, and I risked another glance.

My core was pulsating, and I wanted to watch. The desire to feel a man want me like that, felt like a rush of white-hot hunger that started from my chest and settled in my center. I turned back around from the tree and saw the man on top of the woman thrusting himself deeper into her. Her legs spread just enough for him to fit and crossed behind his hips. With each deep thrust her body rocked back and forth with every tandem movement. His right hand was planted firmly at the side of her head, his large muscles straining and flexing as he held himself aloft. His toned triceps and shoulder muscles bulged under the weight of his body pressed against hers. With his left hand, he gripped her hips as she arched her back and rolled her body beneath him.

Her breast hardened as they receive a kiss from him between each thrust. In an instant he quickly removed himself from her and flipped her over onto her stomach. He began to grab onto her waist with both hands and pulled her ass towards him. His thrusts were harder and deeper this time. His moaning and grunting began to claim the forest. He reached with one hand and forced her back to arch deeper towards the ground. Her arms stretched out grasping on the crumbled grass in front of her while she screamed with pleasure to the ground.

When the woman lifted her head. Her beautiful blonde hair lain frantic around her face and shoulders. Her body shook violently from his force into her body. She pushed her hand from around her face and forced her hair to one side.

My breath caught as her face came into view—Rebecca, the same woman who'd screamed those vicious insults at Meridith by the fire. Heat flushed through me, but I forced myself to look away and pull my hand from my pants. Shock and anger coursed through my veins: what was she doing here, and why had I been drawn into that hidden corner of the forest?

My mind flashed back to her tirade, the way she'd stood before everyone and slung those cruel insults at Meridith. What was Rebecca doing here? And who was the man with her—this flawless stranger who seemed bent on shadowing her every move?

I forced myself to look more closely: broad shoulders dipped into a slim waist, the curve of his back muscles shifting with each breath. Even in this unexpected clearing, his posture spoke of confidence and strength.

My pulse quickened—not from desire, but from the single, urgent question burning in my mind: who were these two, and what game were they playing in the heart of the forest? His skin glowed with a warm bronze hue; every contour of muscle defined as if sculpted by a master. Broad shoulders tapered into powerful biceps and forearms, each sinew taut beneath the surface. His core—abdominal muscles carved like stone—flowed seamlessly into strong, sculpted obliques.

When he settled his large hands on her waist, they fit her curves perfectly, the contrast of his strength and her form undeniable.

His hair was a dark, lustrous brown that blended seamlessly with his sun-kissed skin. Thick waves tumbled over his shoulders, the ends brushing against his collarbones and obscuring his eyes in shadow. Each strand caught the light as he moved, giving the impression of a living curtain that both concealed and hinted at the intensity beneath. With the end near, he quickly readjusted his position to thrust harder and deeper into her as he chased his own pleasure. Their moans echoed into my ears as they both screamed out with ending pleasure.

They tumbled back against the soft forest floor, laughter mingling with ragged breaths. He lay on his back, chest rising and falling in slow, satisfied rhythms. One arm rested across his forehead, shielding his eyes from the dappled sunlight. Under his other arm she nestled against him, her body curving perfectly to his side.

She lifted her head and pressed gentle, warm kisses along his collarbone and the slope of his chest, her eyes alight with affection. He reached up to stroke her hair, fingers tangling in bright, sunlit strands, and for a moment the world around them—the vibrant blooms, the whispering breeze—faded away, leaving only the soft rhythm of their shared warmth.

She traced a fingertip along his collarbone, gaze soft.

"I wish we had more moments like these," she murmured, smiling.

He closed his eyes at the warmth in her voice. "Mm," he replied, voice low and content.

Her hand curled around his thumb brushing his palm. "One day, I will make you king—and stand by your side as your queen."

He opened one eye, arching a brow with playful amusement. "Really? And when will this day be?"

She leaned in, breath warm against his ear. "I've found it," she whispered, voice rich with promise.

His head snapped up in surprise, her smile lighting every freckle on her cheeks—and then I saw him. Elias, strolling into my dream as if he owned it. My stomach knotted into molten lead, bile rising hot in my throat. I pressed my palm to the rough bark, bracing myself against the shock.

A scorching wave of emotion slammed into my chest, crushing the breath from me. How was he here? What was this nightmare's purpose? My pulse thundered so loudly I could barely think; questions boiled in my mind like water on the verge of overflow.

Yet my feet betrayed me, carrying me forward without warning, as though drawn by some unseen force.

Then a sudden chill crawled up my spine, and the vibrant forest blurred into freezing gray. A damp musk filled my nostrils, and the faint slap of waves against a shore whispered in my ears.

Colors bled and bled—emeralds to ash, blossoms to dust—until all I could see was the black iron of my cell. I clutched the tree trunk, heart pounding,

I pressed my palms and forearms into the rough bark, digging my fingernails so deep that I tasted iron on my tongue. Pain bloomed in my fingers, but I clung to the tree as if it were my only tether to this strange reverie. Every heartbeat thundered in my ears while I forced myself to stay—to unravel whatever secrets this dream might hold.

I pressed my back harder against the rough stone wall, then swung my legs over the edge of the slab and planted my feet on the cold floor. My fingers still throbbed from the splinters—their sting a grim reminder of my desperation to stay in that dream's last grasp.

The cell was silent except for the distant drip of water and the soft whisper of wind through the barred window. I drew the blanket down from my mouth, exhaling a plume of white as the frigid air filled my lungs. My cheek brushed the rough wool, and I shivered, wrapping the layers tighter around my shoulders.

With eyes still closed, I felt him—the imperceptible shift in the air, a presence like ice against my spine. He was there, just beyond my sight: patient, watchful. In that oppressive silence, his vigilance was almost comforting, a promise that I wasn't entirely abandoned to these walls.

Slowly, I tilted my head toward the direction of the cell door, listening for breath or movement. Nothing but the soft echo of my own heart.

Finally, I found the courage to peep open one eye. Torchlight flickered against the far wall, illuminating a tall, shadowed figure—him— leaning just out of reach. I swallowed hard, throat tight, and lowered the blanket just enough to speak without choking.

"If you're going to watch," I rasped, forcing my voice through the clutch of fear in my throat, "the least you can do is talk."

Silence swallowed the cell—thick, suffocating. Every drop of water echoed like a tolling bell.

My pulse hammered until my ears rang.

At last, Daniel's voice cut the dark: "Fine"

I steeled myself against the chill.

"The game of honesty?"

A soft scrape on stone—he was moving closer. Shadows shifted; the bars between us grew colder. "Information for information?" I probed, each word deliberate.

"Mm," he whispered, exhaling fog.

"We're searching for answers… answers one of us holds, the other needs."

His boots scraped nearer. I felt the weight of his gaze, even without seeing him.

"True," he said, voice low and unwavering.

My chest constricted. "If I help, what's in it for me?" The words hung on a ragged breath.

"You can stay alive."

My stomach was lurched. I tasted bile. "But Elias—"

His laughter, cold and hollow, cut me off. "Do I look like Elias?"

I shut my jaw against tears and anger, the lines of my cell pressing in. Yet beneath the dread flickered hope—dangerous, desperate hope. Clenching my fists around my blankets, I forced out a nod.

"Then let's begin," Daniel murmured, and the bars rattled as he stepped back into the shadows—ready to start the first move of our deadly truth game.

Chapter Sixteen

Daniel Black

I leaned into the chill of the stone, the torchlight flickering across her delicate form like a spotlight. Each breath she drew under the blankets felt impossibly intimate—her chest rising and falling, the soft rustle of fabric against skin. The scent of her hair, wild and dark, drifted over the bars, a heady mix of night air and something uniquely hers.

My pulse thundered in my throat as I watched her shift, eyelashes brushing her cheeks. In that motion, the curve of her neck—so vulnerable and inviting—took my breath away. I flexed my fingers against the iron, longing to close the few inches between us, to trace that graceful line from shoulder down her arm.

The silence crackled with forged electricity. My jaw went dry; each heartbeat was a drum in the stillness. I could almost feel the heat radiating from her, a silent promise of warmth against my frozen skin. My throat constricted as desire coiled tight in my chest, a living thing demanding release.

When her lids fluttered open, our gazes locked—hers wide with uncertainty, mine raw with need. The space between us pulsed, each second stretching into an eternity of unspoken longing. My breath caught. I tasted the iron tang of the bars as I edged closer, every step silent, every nerve alight.

Then her voice, a soft tremor, broke through the haze. "I'm ready."

The single declaration set my blood ablaze. The world narrowed to that moment—the promise in her tone, the echo of her heartbeat against my own, and the electric pull that neither chains nor silence could deny.

"What do you want to know?" I asked her firmly.

Her eyes went wide, terror glinting in their depths.

"What kind of monster are you?" she whispered, voice trembling.

I tilted my head, narrowing my gaze until it felt like iron. She wanted honesty, I would give it to her.

"Books, legends, myths—they're full of monsters: demons, vampires, skin-walkers. Whatever society invents this century," I said, a sarcastic edge cutting through the air.

Her stare sharpened—she knew I'd evaded the truth, but it was the only answer I had. I'd lived long enough to know the names they slapped on us.

I leaned forward, heart quickening as I studied her—so small and fierce, with those wide eyes full of wonder and fear.

"What do you know about magic?"

"Only what I see in movies."

I let a hint of a smile soften my tone. "Interesting."

Her brow furrowed. "What is?"

I straightened, genuinely impressed by her demeanor.

"You come from a powerful coven—witches whose bloodlines run deep, centuries old. It's remarkable, really. I'm surprised your family didn't teach you… or your mother before you."

Her breath caught, chest rising and falling as she absorbed my words. In that moment, I saw not just fear, but the spark of something stronger— pride, potential, a legacy waiting to be claimed.

Her color drained from her cheeks, panic flickering in her wide eyes as my words landed. She swallowed hard, drawing a shaky breath, forcing herself to stay present. I could almost see her anxiety teetering on the edge—like a glass filled to the brim, ready to shatter under the slightest knock. Yet she steadied herself, chin lifting with quiet resolve. Even in her fear, there was something remarkable about her strength—fragile, yes, but undeniably there.

She lifted her hand, palm away, revealing the faint brand on her skin—The Raven Coven. Anxiety rippled across her features as she stared at it.

I inhaled slowly, stepping closer until the sigils in the ceiling seemed to pulse in response. The cell's darkness, once my refuge, fell away, and the air crackled with the magic trapped in those runes. Heat prickled on my arms as I leaned forward.

"That," I said, voice low and steady, "is the mark of the Raven Coven."

Her breath caught, and the color drained her face. She dropped her hand to her thigh, then lifted it again, fingertips brushing the brand as if it might vanish. Each gentle pass of her thumb over the etched lines betrayed her shock—and a flicker of awe.

The silence stretched between us, charged with her unspoken questions. In that moment, I saw not just fear in her eyes, but something deeper: belonging. And I knew this revelation would change everything.

"It must have appeared when you first tapped into your powers," I said, dark satisfaction warming my voice.

Her fingertips hovered above the raven brand, trembling as she absorbed the weight of the revelation. I continued, stepping so close that the sigils overhead seemed to echo my words with heat.

"The Raven Coven brands each initiate. When your soul binds to its magic, the mark awakens. You'd never needed it—your power slept too hard. But this… is the original brand, older than my own time. We believed it was lost, faded with each generation of elders. We searched for centuries for a descendant of the one who wore its sigil, and until now… no one bore the mark."

Silence fell like a shroud. In the flickering torchlight, I watched her face pale, the raven's lines shimmering faintly under her skin—a promise of power and prophecy neither of us could yet fully understand.

She swallowed hard, dread pooling in her wide eyes. "What happened?"

I let the question hang, then met her gaze with steady resolve.

"One of the coven's most powerful sister—bound by love and ambition—betrayed the Circle. She craved the throne with her lover: to be queen and king. So, she turned on her sisters, slaughtering every woman who refused to swear fealty to their union. One of those victims was your ancestor, Meridith."

Her breath hitched, the candlelight catching tears in her lashes.

"That's—why you need me? Because I'm her descendant, you think I can help you?

I nodded, the weight of centuries pressing down between us. "Yes."

She looked away, fingertips tracing the raven brand. Outside, the sigils in the ceiling pulsed as if in answer. In that moment, our fates intertwined—and the true game of honesty began.

A heavy silence hung between us, broken only by the distant drip of water. Maeva's gaze flickered back to the raven brand on her hand, a flicker of pity in her eyes as she drew a shuddering breath.

"What do you want with me, Daniel?" she asked, voice brittle, forehead resting on folded arms against the bars.

I straightened, casting sharp angles across my face.

"Your blood holds the key," I said, tone laced with contempt.

"Meridith's memories run in your veins—her triumphs, her betrayals, her final, desperate acts. You're the only one who can unlock them and break this damned curse."

Her shoulders hunched, and she lifted her head, eyes brimming with tears.

"And after that… what happens to you?"

I let out a harsh, humorless chuckle.

"Why do you even ask?" I spat, disdain cutting through the cold air.

"This curse has bound me for centuries—stripped me of life, love, every shred of humanity. If it kills me instead of setting me free, so be it. Better to end this wretched existence than drag another soul through its horrors."

She recoiled, pressing her fingers to the raven's lines.

I turned away, jaw clenched, but then a flicker of something—desperation—softened my tone. I took a step closer; my voice was low.

"Please," I pleaded, each word a jagged edge.

"I've sacrificed everything for this. I need you to help me finish what was started. Only you can bring this to an end."

Her eyes widened at the shift—from scorn to raw imploration.

"Help me," I begged, reaching toward the bars.

"Prove you're strong enough to break free of fear. I can't do this alone."

In that moment, the disdain fell away, replaced by a desperate hope that her answer might finally shatter the centuries-old chain.

Our eyes locked, and in that gaze a silent accord passed between us. She hesitated, chest rising as she drew a rattling breath, but offered no answer. I pressed my back harder against the stone, every muscle coiled in anticipation.

She dropped her gaze to the floor, eyelashes brushing her cheeks as she inhaled again, gathering courage. I wanted—and needed—more from her, but I held my tongue, waiting for the questions that never came.

Something deep in me ached: pity, longing, hope. I wanted to tear down these walls, cast aside the iron bars, and stand beside her, free to wield her power openly. I imagined her magic roaring through her fingertips without constraint, reshaping our fate, not as a prisoner, but as a queen of her own destiny—a force as immense as the storm she'd once unleashed.

"Maeva," I whispered, voice rough with urgency. My words trembled on the edge of confession.

"Please."

In that moment, the cell's oppressive chill felt less certain—because in her silence lay the first spark of the future we could forge together.

I had to stop my mind from unraveling for her, couldn't do it. I felt myself teetering on that edge, where compassion threatened to pull me off balance, but I knew that if I fell, I'd never be the man she'd want—my monstrous self would swallow whatever remained. So, I forced myself to step back, locking that ache away alongside the beast in my chest. With a final, deliberate motion, I shut the door on both my mercy and our fragile understanding—leaving her, and the hope of change, on the other side of cold iron bars.

Her voice trembled as tears welled in her dark eyes.

"What happens if I can't help you? What if you don't find what you're looking for?"

I leaned forward; my voice was cold as iron.

"Then I will bleed you dry until you give me the answers I need." My gaze sharpened.

"I've already tasted your blood, Maeva—once in Mr. Makenzie's office, and again down here in this cell. I know exactly who you are and every memory you hold."

Her pupils dilated in shock, the memory of that first assault flashing across her face. She collapsed into herself, trembling violently as her mind raced to connect the dots from then until now.

"That was you?" she gasped, voice barely more than a whisper.

A slow, cruel smile curved my lips.

"How did I—" I paused, letting the fear settle deeper.

"It's an illusion. The moment you taste my blood; I can weave whatever you need to see. You felt safe with your therapist? Well, I sent him on a permanent vacation six feet under—and repurposed his office with my people. That tea you trusted so much…"

I let the words hang in the air, watching her shudder as the full betrayal dawned on her. I let the silence stretch, watching her piece it together as realization shattered her calm. My lips curved into a faint, almost sympathetic smile. I'd slipped into another guise so she wouldn't see me coming—another man entirely in her mind. Yet every step I guided, every carefully laid clue, had led her here, shackled by trust and tears for Elias.

I settled back against the cold stone, arms crossed, as she finally broke. Her sobs echoed in the cell: harsh sniffles punctuating the hush. Blankets twisted around her, little shields against the cold and her own grief. Dark strands of hair clung to tear streaked cheeks, each salty drop crystallizing at her jaw.

Despite the cruelty of it all, a small ache stirred in me. She'd sacrificed everything for a lie—one I'd nurtured, piece by cruel piece. Yet as her racked shoulders shook, I could not deny the fierce, raw honesty in her pain.

The game had turned, and I found myself caught in its most dangerous turn: witnessing the broken heart of the only woman brave enough to hold me to my word I watched her tremble against the stone— arms wrapped tight as if she could hold herself together by sheer will. Her breaths came in ragged gasps, each sniffle a jagged edge against the silence. Tears and cold snot streaked down her face, her pain raw and unfiltered.

She was my pawn, trapped by choices neither of us fully made. Empathy died in that cold cell; here, there was only business. Yet, as I looked at her curled form, something inside me yearned to reach out—to bridge the iron bars and offer more than cruel necessity.

Life had taught me one lesson over centuries: it doesn't care. Seasons change, the sun stills, and new victims fall in its light.

With that truth heavy in my bones, I turned away. One last, lingering glance at her—small, broken, desperate for a warmth I couldn't give—and then I walked back toward the door. I left her there in the damp darkness, her own tears the only solace.

"Wait, one more thing" a raspy voice in the black called out.

Her voice was so small in the darkness it nearly broke me. I hesitated, the door's iron cold against my palm, but turned back one last time.

"Rebecca…" I began, voice thick with something I hadn't meant to feel.

"She was once a part of the coven. But her ambition burned too bright."

My gaze flicked to the floor, where her sobs blurred into the shadows.

"When the coven refused to bow to her and her love, she unleashed her fury. She slit throats in moonlight, sanctified betrayal with blood, and left Meridith's body broken as a warning."

I swallowed, the words tasting of ash. "Rebecca happened," I repeated, each syllable a benediction and a curse. "And with her, the covenant I believed in died."

Silence wrapped us again, only her ragged breaths filling the void. In that moment, I longed to step back through the bars, to gather her in my arms and vanish this nightmare. But I was no hero—and the cage between us remained.

I closed the heavy door with a final, echoing thud, leaving her silhouette swallowed by darkness. My footsteps echoed down the corridor until I reached my chamber, where I collapsed into the leather chair. My body felt like a boulder sinking into the depths—the impact stole the breath from my lungs.

My thoughts crashed into my skull like storm-driven waves against jagged cliffs. Exhaustion draped me over like a shroud, but sleep was a distant promise I couldn't claim—my mind refused to quiet.

That riddle kept hammering at my senses:

"A curse set, takes blood and love, a curse broken, takes heart and peace."

I knew she alone held its meaning, buried in that pitch-black cell. My elbow pressed into the armrest, and I bowed my head against my hand, fighting the whirlwind in my mind. Rest was impossible—until I found her and unlocked the secret that might cost us both our peace.

I didn't hear Abigail enter until the flicker of her silhouette crossed the firelight. My breaths rattled in my chest like broken bellows, each inhale stabbing me with the ache of failure. I forced myself to meet her glare, but my voice caught in my throat. Her spidery fingers curled at her sides, nails gleaming like obsidian daggers in the hearth's glow. She stalked forward, each step measured, predatory—an elegant wolf circling its wounded prey.

"Well?" she snapped, the single word echoing in the cramped room.

I exhaled; embers cracked between us. "She's got the original mark," I confessed, leaning back in my chair.

"The brand of the original Coven appeared."

For a heartbeat, Abigail's composure shattered. Her breath hitched, and her eyes flew wide as she stared at me, incredulous.

"What?" she whispered, voice half-lost in the roar of the flames.

"That… that mark hasn't been seen for centuries!" She took a stumbling step back, fingers clutching at her throat.

"Impossible."

"All too real," I said, watching her face blanch. "It revealed itself the moment she unleashed her power."

Abigail's knees wobbled. She reached out, as if to touch the air, then recoiled, shaking her head. "If that brand is back..." Her voice trailed away, fear and astonishment warring in her eyes.

Before she could recover, the door banged open and Elias strode in, his silhouette sharp against the corridor's torchlight. The curve of his jaw caught flames, and for an instant I saw the old hunger gleam in his eyes.

Abigail whirled on him, disbelief, and fury blazing.

"Did you know?" she hissed. "You knew that mark could return?"

Elias's lips curved in a slow, chilling smile. "I suspected," he admitted, voice low. "But I never expected it to surface on her."

The crackling hearth and the pounding of my heart were the only sounds as we all registered the impossible truth: the true Raven magic had awakened again.

Elias's eyes blazed as he stepped closer, voice sharp enough to cut the silence.

"Rebecca changed the coven's sigil when she became their leader. She killed everyone who didn't stand with her. How is it that she has the original Raven mark?"

I leaned forward, voice dropping to a bare whisper that carried through the charged air.

"I killed Meridith myself."

Abigail's eyes narrowed into slits; malice sharpened in her tone.

"If she truly bears that ancient mark, then Meridith must've hidden a descendant, right?" she spat. "We killed every last soul tied to her bloodline. How in all hell did one slip through?"

Her words hung in the smoke-choked air, the unspoken accusation echoing like a challenge. In silence, the three of us realized the depth of the betrayal: somewhere, Meridith's secret blood had survived—and now threatened to unravel everything we'd built.

Their stares bored into me, sharp as spears, each calculating the next move in this deadly game. I sat frozen, eyes fixed on the dancing embers, the weight of my centuries pressing on every bone.

"It doesn't matter how she bears that mark," I said at last, voice rough with exhaustion. "What matters is she has it. We need her to unlock Meridith's grimoire and end this." I drew in a ragged breath. "Her powers are now awake—and they will shield her when it deems it necessary. She may not summon them at will, but any threat we pose will trigger her magic. We must change our approach: she goes free, under guard, and we guide her steps. One wrong move, and her magic will turn on us."

"Figure this out. I will be back."

Elias's command hung in the air long after his footsteps faded down the corridor.

The door clicked shut behind him, and the sudden silence pressed in on me. My thoughts felt sluggish, as though wading through tar.

A single, relentless impulse throbbed in my chest: I needed to return to her cell. To see Maeva again—even if I could only stand on the other side of cold iron.

My heart pounded with the memory of her wide, frightened eyes and the soft tremor in her voice. I could almost feel the heat of her sorrow, the faint pulse of magics I'd woken. Every fiber of me yearned to rush back, to speak one more time—to close that impossible distance between us.

But logic reared its head, brutal and unyielding. We had a plan. A curse to break. The fragile truce we'd forged couldn't survive impulsive mercy. I shoved the thought of her—of her tears and that raven brand—deep into the shadowed recesses of my mind, alongside all my other sins.

I leaned forward until my face hovered just above the tiny flame dancing in the hearth. Its flicker cast quivering shapes across my reflection, and for a moment I felt divided: the man who would see her safe, and the monster bound to this dark purpose.

As the flame guttered, I let the darkness reclaim me, steeling myself for the choices to come.

Abigail's posture softened, the edge of her predatory poise giving way to something almost maternal.

"Well," she said, voice low and careful.

"She is a woman. Perhaps I can reach her in a way you cannot."

Mistress straightened her spine and smoothed the folds of her petticoat; even in this dim light she carried herself like a queen surveying her court.

I looked to Abigail, curiosity prickling at the base of my skull. Abigail did not trifle nor toy—if she offered this, she must have a plan sharper than any blade.

"She trusts gentleness," Abigail continued, stepping closer to where I sat.

"If I speak to her as one woman to another—share simple kindness—I might break through her fear."

I studied her: the way her shoulders relaxed, the sincerity warming her voice. Whatever Abigail intended, it was our best chance to guide Maeva willingly. And so, despite the tangle of doubt in my chest, I nodded.

"Do it," I said quietly.

"But tread carefully—one wrong move, and her magic will turn on."

Abigail's lips curved in a purposeful smile.

"I know," she answered.

Then, without another word, she swept past me, ready to weave her delicate web and bring Maeva into her trap.

Chapter Seventeen

Mistress Abigail

The torches along the corridor sputtered as I descended the spiral stairs, their wavering flames casting skeletal shadows against the damp stone. Outside, the morning mist pressed against the tall windows, turning the world beyond smudged gray shapes. The manor's cold breath curled through every arch and pillar, vines dripping with dew that glittered in the dim light.

Each footfall echoed against the flagstones beneath my heels, a metronome counting down to her cell. The fog outside pooled at the base of blackened pillars, creeping like a living thing across the courtyard, slipping under doors, and curling around my ankles as I passed. Even the great lake lay hushed and steely, its surface locked in that same mournful gray.

At last, I reached her door. The torchlight danced across the iron bars, illuminating her small, frail form curled on the hard stone. The blankets wrapped her like a cocoon—thin shields against the chill—but did little to hide the hollow of her cheeks or the tremor in her sleep.

Poor child, I thought, and felt a cold twinge twist in my chest. Yet I would not be fooled by innocence. I knew what she was—descended from Meridith, the witch who had cleaved our family with blood. I remembered my boy's confession, the weight of centuries pressing on them as they admitted their sin. And I knew how deeply that betrayal had wounded us all.

My hand hovered for a heartbeat at the latch. The ghost of my husband's laughter—his life's warmth—had once filled these halls. Now it was replaced by this stillness and her soft breathing, a reminder that I had lost everything to the very curse she carried. It wasn't Meridith's hand alone, but the legacy she wove that ensnared me: a web spun long ago, now bearing down on the next generation.

I pressed my palm to the cold iron, steeling myself. Today, I would draw closer to her pain—learn what she knew and finally claim the peace that had eluded me for centuries.

With a measured exhale, I opened the door—ready to face the descendant of our destruction.

"Hello again, Maeva." I greeted, the corner of my mouth tilting into a gentle, almost tender smile.

I planted my feet firmly on the cold stone, fingers laced loosely at my waist as I watched her. She stirred beneath her threadbare blankets, every slow movement a testament to her fragile strength. When she forced herself upright, her effort was heartbreaking to behold.

Her eyes—once bright with fear, were now hollowed and bloodshot, rims crusted with salt and tears. The dark circles beneath them smudged into the pale hollows of her cheeks like bruises. Strands of her dark hair clung to her forehead and cheeks, knotted from days of neglect. Flecks of dirt clung to her skin, smudged across her arms and beneath her nails like evidence of her confinement.

She wobbled on unsteady legs, blanket slipping from her shoulders as she reached for balance. I took a single, deliberate step forward, the torchlight catching the steel in my eyes. Despite her fury and fear, I felt a flicker of something else— pity, perhaps, or an ache of responsibility.

Her gaze flicked to the bars, then back to me, uncertainty, and a spark of defiance warring in her eyes. I remained still, silent but present— an unspoken offer of truce, if only she dared accept it.

The blankets pooled at her feet like a spent rag, revealing skin and tattered clothes steeped in neglect. Yet her eyes—sharp, unbroken—met mine through the bars. Her brows drew together in fury, and though exhaustion etched dark shadows beneath her lashes, the fire in her gaze rivaled any flame.

Even the cell's protective sigils trembled at her presence, their heat paling against the intensity she radiated. I swallowed hard, every instinct screaming caution. Her power was raw and unpredictable—nothing like the coven's tempered witchcraft—it would lash out without warning. I squared my shoulders and softened my voice.

"Would you like to come with me for breakfast… and a walk?"

Her eyes narrowed, disbelief flickering across her features. Arms crossed over her chest; she stepped close enough that I could almost feel the heat behind her gaze. My teeth itched beneath my lips, tiny droplets of blood whispering against my tongue as my pulse thundered in my ears.

"I'll go with you," she said, voice cold as steel, "but if you try anything—"

"I won't," I promised, every word laced with sincerity I hadn't felt in centuries.

Reaching into my coat, I drew forth a heavy iron key, its surface etched with the same arcane sigils that burned across the cell's stones. I fitted it into the lock and turned. It caught on ancient gears, then released with a resonant click.

Immediately, the runes lining the bars glowed a furious red, pulsing in time with my heartbeat, before fading back to iron.

With a soft groan, the cell door swung inward. Maeva's breath caught, awe and wariness battling in her eyes as she beheld the magic unfolding before her. I stepped aside, gesturing through the threshold.

"After you," I said, voice gentle, "let's get that breakfast."

She paused—a queen emerging from her prison—then slipped across the threshold with deliberate grace. As she joined me in the corridor, I felt the tug of something dangerous and magnificent at my side: the power of the Raven's legacy, awakened at last.

I found Maeva at the back of the manor in the old kitchen, steam curling around her like a promise of warmth. I'd insisted she wash away the grime of her cell first, leaving only clean skin and damp hair as she took her seat at the table.

The table itself was a testament to time: six slabs of oak joined so seamlessly they looked hewn from a single ancient tree, their dark stain worn away in places to reveal the pale heartwood beneath. It sat off to one side of the room, its heavy feet planted firm on flagstones mottled with age.

To our left, a vast fireplace yawned up the wall. The stones—ranging from rich chocolate to sun-bleached sand—arched in a perfect semicircle, crowned by a flat lintel that disappeared into the shadowed ceiling. Inside, iron bars held a great cast-iron pot; beneath them, neatly stacked logs promised supper. Bundles of brittle herbs and faded flowers dangled from hooks along the hearth's frame, their fragrance still faints in the chill air.

Shelves on either side sagged under the weight of dust-coated kettles and pots, while bowls and plates lay undisturbed for years, their surfaces mottled by time and neglect. Even the drinking cups, rimmed in cobwebs, caught stray beams of light like tiny, dusty diamonds.

I filled a delicate teacup from the kettle's spout, letting the hot water plunge over a sprig of lavender and chamomile. The steam spiraled up, carrying the soothing scent straight to Maeva. Her shoulders, so often tense, finally relaxed; she closed her eyes and inhaled, a breath of relief escaping her lips.

"You're safe here," I murmured, offering the cup to her.

She accepted it with a small nod, fingers brushing mine for an instant. We sat in companionable silence as she sipped, the warmth spreading through her like a soft balm.

When she set the cup down, Maeva rose and moved through the room with curiosity shining in her eyes. She touched the iron bars, traced the worn grain of the table, and ran her fingers along the dusty shelves.

I set the grimoire before her, its familiar leather spine creaking in the silent kitchen. Maeva's gaze snapped back to the table, her world narrowing to that binding. Her pupils dilated, and I saw her pulse flutter at her throat—each heartbeat pounding a staccato warning.

In that hush, the air thickened with magic, the book's presence humming like a live wire. I knew this power belonged to her alone—and that only she could awaken what lay hidden in those blank pages.

"I was hoping you might give it another try," I said softly.

Maeva's eyes flicked up, sharp with defiance.

"I can't read it—if that's what you want."

She seized the grimoire and slammed it open. Blank pages stared back at us like a taunt. She riffled through page after page, her fingers tapping in growing frustration.

"See?" she snapped, closing the book with a thud. "Nothing."

The silence afterward was heavy—pregnant with unspoken need. I watched her chest rise and fall, the faint tremor of her shoulders betraying how deeply she wanted the words to appear. And I knew it wasn't her fault, the book—it was the lock waiting for its key.

I rose smoothly from my chair, folding her plate and cup into my hands as though clearing the remnants of a cordial meal. The grimoire's open pages lay between us, a void of arcane promise. Maeva's entire focus remained locked on its blank parchment.

As I reached to set the China on a nearby sideboard, I let my grip slacken "accidentally." The cup slipped, clattering against the stone floor in a tangle of porcelain shards. Steam from the smashed herb tea curled aloud as the cup's handle clinked against the hearth's cold, blackened bricks.

"Christ," I murmured, voice thick with contrition, stepping forward to scoop up the fragments. Maeva's eyes widened, her chest tightening as if the sound itself had struck her. Panic flitted across her face. She knelt too, jacket pooling around her knees, and reached blindly to help.

In that instant, her palm caught on a jagged edge. A thin ribbon of blood welled up immediately, tracing a path from her palm to the floor. The coppery scent of freshly split flesh hit her like a blow.

"Ah—!" she gasped, recoiling involuntarily. Her hand shook violently, the wound pulsing brightly. She pressed quivering lips together, eyes brimming with tears.

"Hold still," I whispered, pressing a towel against the cut. The coarse wool soaked up the blood almost instantly. She whimpered, shoulders rising and falling in shallow, frightened gasps.

Her pupils darted between the towel and my face, dread eclipsing the stovepipe flicker of the hearth. Every muscle in her small frame trembled. I felt a flicker at our shared trance—the grimoire's magic humming to life, drawn by her offering.

She stared down at that blood, horror etched into every line of her body. Outside, the manor's ancient stones groaned in the dawn mist, and for a heartbeat, the empty pages seemed to tremble—waiting for the key they'd long denied.

I snatched the towel and pressed it against her palm. Her eyes went wide with terror, breaths coming in sharp, uneven gulps as warm droplets traced a trembling line down her arm. My own chest tightened at the metallic tang in the air.

Her fingers flexed against mine, pale and shaking, as she stared at the red ribbon unfurling across her skin.

"It— it won't stop," she whispered, voice cracking.

I gripped her forearms and hauled her to her feet. She staggered, legs unsteady, eyes darting from my face to the blossom of blood. A wet trail glistened in the hearth's light, from her wrist to elbow.

"Hold on," I urged, wrapping another napkin around her hand and binding it with deliberate pressure. She let out a small, strangled sob, knees buckling before my arms caught her.

"Oh my god, Maeva, let me help you," I said, voice thick with urgency.

My fingers shook as I adjusted the cloth, heart pounding with guilt and something darker—an instinctive pull toward the life pulsing through her veins. Her wide, fearful eyes met mine, and for a moment.

"Here—take a seat. Let's get you patched up." I guided her back to the oak chair, voice soft but firm.

She sank onto the battered wood, I settled into my own seat across from her, the grimoire resting untouched between us—a silent witness to our fragile moment. The flickering firelight cast dancing shadows over her pallid skin.

After a breath, I reached across the table and gently peeled back the blood-soaked napkin. The cut, though shallow, was ragged—a thin gash across her palm that bled stubbornly. Tiny beads of blood clung to the fine hairs on her wrist.

Her breath hitched and her hand shook in mine. She glanced at the wound, then at me—eyes wide, pupils darkened by fear. I pressed my thumb over the edge of the gash, applying steady pressure.

Blood welled again, fresh rivulets snaking down her palm until droplets fell onto the grimoire's blank page. Maeva and I both froze, watching in horrified fascination as each crimson bead spread like ink in water.

Instinctively, I pressed the napkin back over her cut, squeezing until the bleeding slowed. But my eyes stayed locked on the page. The blood seeped into the grain of the parchment, weaving itself through invisible lines—then, as if guided by some unseen hand, letters bled into view.

Before our eyes, the page transformed. Tiny black letters emerged as if borne on a gentle current—each character unfurling like a whisper on water. Maeva and I leaned in, breaths suspended, as lines of curling script crawled across the parchment.

Then images formed between the words: a twisting staircase, a raven's wing, a moonlit lake. The ink itself seemed alive, swirling into place in sinuous ribbons that froze into precise shapes.

Across the page, entire passages appeared in a hand older than time, the letters etched with subtle flourishes that caught the torchlight

Line after line, page after page, the empty grimoire brimmed over. Words scratched out their own blanks as though correcting centuries of silence. Symbols that once lay dormant flared into being—mystic runes that danced in the glow of her awakening magic.

Maeva's lips parted in astonishment, her trembling hand hovering above the living text. The book that had once been silent now sang with her heritage—and with every revelation, the promise of untold power shimmered between us.

I settled back into my chair as Maeva drew the grimoire closer, her fingers tracing the newly revealed lines. With each page she flipped, the air shimmered around us—tiny motes of luminescent dust rising in her wake, whispering of half-remembered spells.

Her Raven mark flared to life, a beacon of electric blue that pulsed in time with her heartbeat. Wherever her fingertip brushed the words, the letters glowed in response, as though the ink itself recognized its rightful heir. Swirling glyphs at the page corners unfurled into vision, offering brief glimpses of arcane sigils and long-forgotten rites.

Her eyes, wide and unwavering, glowed with a newfound purpose. In that moment, it was undeniable: she was not just Meridith's descendant—she was the living member of the Raven Coven.

As the final page revealed its sigils, Maeva closed the book with deliberate calm, her gaze lifting to meet mine with a steady confidence I had never witnessed. The grimoire's words had found their voice in her blood

My pulse thundered in my ears as Maeva's eyes darted over the newly inked lines. Each syllable she murmured was a step deeper into the coven's secrets—secrets I had chased through centuries of empty echoes. Now, they spread before her like a living tapestry, and I felt both triumph and terror coiling in my chest.

I returned to the kettle; hands unsteady as I poured fresh boiling water over dried chamomile. Each hiss of steam felt louder than the last, echoing the frantic hammer of my pulse. I forced my face into the mask of a concerned host, gently sliding the new teacup toward her—every motion calibrated to soothe rather than betray the predator beneath.

But beneath my calm, a storm raged. The lingering scent of her blood hung heavily in the air, setting my teeth on edge. My ravenous ache pulsed like a fist against my ribs, a reminder that her magic—and her life—were both poison and salvation to me.

As the tea steeped, I felt each second stretch taut with risk: one misplaced glance, one tremor of her mark's electric blue glow, and the power she'd unlocked could obliterate the fragile peace I'd fought centuries to reclaim. My eagerness curdled into dread; impatience warped into fear.

When I finally lifted the teacup, my hand shook so fiercely the porcelain threatened to crack. My throat tightened—hot with unshed bloodlust—and I braced myself for the moment she might look up, her eyes aflame with the unbridled force of the Raven Coven at her command.

I felt the weight of my options press in around me: seize the grimoire now and lock her away again or end her quickly and harvest every drop of blood until its secrets bled dry. My pulse thundered as those thoughts collided in my skull.

I closed my eyes, inhaling the sharp tang of her magic still clinging to the air. My fingers curled around the teacup's handle so tightly the porcelain bit into my palm. Behind a deliberate calm, my teeth ground back the hunger that flared at the memory of her cut, the way her blood had answered the book's silent call.

But there were other moves to make—subtler, more cunning—before I could unleash my true intent. So, I forced my shoulders down, masking the storm roiling beneath my coat. Patience, I reminded myself, swallowing the growl in my throat. The coven's curse would not be undone by violence alone; it required every piece of the puzzle she held.

"How about that walk now?" I offered, voice smooth.

Maeva blinked, breaking from the grimoire's spell. Reluctantly, she snapped the leather straps across its cover, sealing away my future in its pages. She cradled the heavy tome against her chest and rose.

Together, we slipped out through the carriage doors onto the frost-damp stones of the courtyard, then onto the winding path leading into the woods. Gravel crunched beneath our boots; overhead, the skeletal branches of ancient oaks tapped softly in the gusty wind. Above us, ragged clouds drifted in gunmetal swaths, the early light slashed silver across the fog-blanketed forest floor. Moss-dark trunks loomed like silent sentinels; their crowns lost to the mist.

I halted mid-step, turning to her. In the grey half-light, her hair caught stray glimmers of dawn, and her chest rose and fell with eager, unguarded breaths of cold air. She looked free—but nothing could be farther from the truth.

Here, among the ancient trees, she remained precisely where I wanted her: in my playground, on a leash of her own making. As she traced a finger along the grimoire's bound edge, I saw the flicker of both wonder and dread in her eyes—and I knew that, eventually, she would do exactly what I needed.

"Make the fog go away," I ordered, voice hard as granite.

Maeva swallowed and laughed nervously, glancing at the swirling mist.

"I— I can't do that."

"You have magic," I snapped, stepping forward until my shadow fell across her path. "And you carry a book brimming with it. Dispel it."

Her lip trembled, tears gathering at the corners of her eyes.

"You don't understand," she whispered, voice cracking. "I'm not what you think."

Her chest rose in ragged gasps; each inhale cut off by panic. Her fingers tightened around the grimoire's spine, knuckles paling. The fog curled around us like living smoke, tendrils brushing our coats.

"You're not a sad little girl, Maeva," I said, voice low and unyielding. "You're a witch—with power coursing through your veins. Stop pretending like you're nothing."

Her shoulders hunched, tears spilling freely now as she stared at the ground. The fog swirled at our feet, mocking her doubt. I took another step closer, the gravel crunching under my heel.

My chest heaved as I drew in a ragged breath. Then, without warning, I changed. My lips peeled back in a rictus snarl, revealing row upon row of gleaming row of ivory fangs—each tooth elongated into a razor-sharp dagger. My jaw popped forward, extending until the cold night air burned my exposed gums. With a sickening crack, my irises bled into inky blackness, swallowing the pale blue of their former light.

In that instant, my fingertips burst forth into cruel blackened talons, curved and honed like predator's hooks. My nails lengthened so quickly they split the skin at my cuticles, dripping dark rivulets onto the gravel at Maeva's feet.

She froze, terror etching every line of her face as she stumbled back. The first pale glow of dawn caught on my claws, throwing jagged, inhuman shadows across the path. With each breath, a deep, guttural growl rumbled from my chest, as if some wild beast had been unleashed beneath the skin. Her eyes darted from my fangs to those talons, wide as saucers, and I saw in them the stark, unfiltered truth: she was face–to–face with the monster I'd always been.

The fog swirled around us, as if recoiling from my transformation, and Maeva's eyes widened in disbelief. There, under the skeletal canopies of the oaks, the monster within me stood bare—and she knew I was no longer the woman who had offered her tea.

Maeva's heel dug into the gravel as she scrambled backward, arms flailing for purchase against the slick moss at the path's edge. I advanced in deliberate, silent strides—each step closer a promise of inevitable capture.

"Get up," I snarled, my voice a rumble of thunder that shook the mist from the trees.

She shook her head, tears carving rivulets down her cheeks. The grimoire lay abandoned at her feet; its leather cover spattered with dew and diet.. She reached for it, fingers trembling—only to recoil when her knuckles brushed the cold, wet leather.

Panic seized her. With a strangled sob she pushed herself to her feet, hands pressed against her chest as if to hold her heart in place. Her hair clung to her face, damp with dew and fear. I wrapped my fingers around her throat, lifting her until her boots barely brushed the gravel. Her frantic kicks sent shards of stone skittering across the path. I maintained the chokehold, feeling her pulse pounding beneath my fingertips as blood welled around the claws I'd pressed into her skin.

Her screams rattled the trees, each exhalation a desperate gasp for air. I pulled her face closer—so close that beads of sweat spattered across my cheek from her frantic breathing. My talons dug deeper, drawing hot rivulets down her neck, but I held still, every ounce of my strength focused on that single grip.

I watched the last spark of life flutter behind her lids. Her body hung limp in my iron grip—every heartbeat a fading echo. The fog swirled at our feet as the forest fell silent, waiting.

For a heartbeat, I held her there—skin pale as moonlight, lips-tinged violet. Slowly, ever so slowly, I tightened my grip. Her head lolled against my knuckles, her pulse a mere whisper beneath my fingers. Time stretched thin, each second a knife's edge.

Her body jolted, spine arching as if struck by lightning itself. Her eyes flew open—brilliant blue, crackling with electric fire. Instinctively she reached for me, her fingers wrapping around my wrist in a vice-tight grip, and I stumbled back, releasing her so she could drop to the ground.

In an instant, her hair stood on end, each strand dancing with static as flickers of sapphire light leapt along the tips. The very air around us stung with energy: her fingertips snapped with crackling pops, sending tiny arcs of electricity dancing across the gravel.

A sudden heat bloomed at my feet as a wind began to swirl, rising in furious gusts that whipped leaves into frenzied spirals. The fog roiled, drawn into the whirlpool of power she'd unleashed. Branches overhead groaned as if in warning, and the path itself seemed to quake under the onslaught of her awakening magic.

She stood, chest heaving, every inch of her crackling with elemental force. Each breath she drew sent sparks arching into the air. In the surge of wind and light, I realized the true depth of what I'd provoked—and the terrible cost of underestimating the witch before me.

The clouds above us blackened in an instant, rolling in like a tide of ink. Thunder shook the canopy overhead as leaves and wisps of my hair whipped across my vision, caught in Maeva's burgeoning gale.

I forced my claws back into mere fingers, my fangs receding with a fluid snap, until once more I stood in the guise of Mistress Abigail—regal, composed, her predatory edges softened by the last glimmer of daylight. I straightened my spine, smoothed my skirts, then lifted both hands, palms outward in a gesture of truce.

"I am not going to harm you," I called over the rising wind, voice strained but earnest.

"I only sought to show you how powerful you truly are."

Her chest heaved in the electric storm she'd conjured. Sparks still danced along her fingertips, casting eerie blue halos on the gnarled roots at her feet. For a heartbeat, she stood motionless—one foot planted on the swirling earth, the other poised to flee or fight.

Maeva's storm-wrought breaths rattled in the sudden calm. Her bright blue eyes, still flecked with lingering sparks, tracked my every movement as I held my arms aloft in a vow of peace.

Then I caught the flash of empty straps at her side, the grimoire was gone. My heart lurched. In the chaos of her flight, she must have dropped it somewhere in this leaf-littered glade.

I spun on my heel, feet rooted to the ground, scanning the swirling detritus of twigs and torn petals. Panic seized me—without that book, the key to unraveling the centuries-old curse would vanish with the morning dew.

"Maeva," I called, voice tight with urgency. "We have to find your grimoire—now."

Her lips parted, but she said nothing. The charged air between us snapped with unspoken guilt. I took a careful step toward her, wary of reigniting her elemental wrath, yet desperate enough to risk it.

"It's the only way to understand your magic," I added softly, "to end this."

She stared at me, defiance, and fear warring in the depths of her gaze. Above us, the forest stood hushed, as if holding its breath. Somewhere beneath the discarded leaves, the grimoire waited—its silent pages the lifeline of both our futures.

Heavy footsteps thundered through the undergrowth, shaking loose dead leaves at our feet. Through the gnarled oaks, Elias's broad silhouette emerged first—his shoulders squared, eyes ablaze with hatred as he took in the crackling spark still dancing on Maeva's fingertips. Behind him, Daniel advanced, iron cuffs gleaming in his hand like a hunter's noose.

My hands dropped to my sides, palms open in a placating gesture, though my heart pounded against my ribs. Elias's gaze snapped from Maeva to me, his jaw flexing in silent fury. He was poised to strike, predator's stance—claws at the ready.

I stepped forward, my voice calm but urgent.

"Stop," I called. My words hit the silent clearing like a flare. Elias froze—barely—and Daniel faltered in his flank, shifting the heavy cuffs as if questioning the hunt.

Maeva remained rooted where I'd left her, chest heaving, eyes locked on me with a tumult of fear and defiance. Her fingertips still crackled with lingering electricity, the forest's mist swirling around her like a living cloak.

Elias melted into the dappled shadows, moving with a predator's grace as he flanked Maeva. His steps were soft as moss; every footfall rehearsed on the castle grounds' silent watch.

At the same moment, Maeva's fingers curled into fists at her sides—and the forest answered. A vortex of earth erupted around us, hurling pebbles and twigs like shrapnel. Roots tore free, scattering dirt; branches whipped against our legs, throwing all three of us off balance.

The wind roared in our ears, a furious gale birthed from her untrained power. Through the maelstrom, Maeva stood unmoved, eyes blazing emerald with unspent force. Every atom of that swirling tempest seemed to orbit her will, her gaze locked fiercely on her attacker.

Elias crept into position behind a moss-clad boulder, every movement silent as a stalking wolf. Maeva's fists clenched before her, summoning the next gale—dirt and leaves whipped around us in frantic spirals.

Suddenly, Elias's arm whipped forward. A fist-sized rock soared through the air like a dark comet. Maeva's eyes narrowed… then widened in surprise as she snatched it out of the wind, palm flat, rock frozen mid-flight. Her glare met Elias's across the whirlwind—scolding, unyielding.

In that heartbeat of astonishment, I surged forward. Daniel darted from the opposite flank, cuffs gleaming cold in his hand. Maeva whirled to face me, storm-lit hair whipping around her, but it was too late. Daniel snapped one cuff onto her wrist, its sigils flaring red against her skin. Maeva's footwork stalled as he spun her, then clicked the second cuff into place—binding her other wrist.

Instantly, the swirling wind around her stuttered and died. Leaves drifted to the earth; the forest held its breath. Maeva's charge drained from her limbs, and she collapsed to the ground, wrists bound, her blue-white magic extinguished. Her eyes, once electric with power, flickered back to a muted brown—beautiful, exhausted, terrified.

I knelt beside her, heart hammering. Was this the timid Maeva I thought… or something older, deeper, lurking just beneath her skin? The broken windstorm whispered its answer: the fire of the Raven coven still glowed within her, even shackled.

Chapter Eighteen

Lori Whittens

It had been nearly a week since I'd heard from Maeva. Normally our evenings were punctuated by at least a quick text—or one of our habit-forming late-night calls—but this time, nothing. My messages went unanswered. It gnawed at me, especially knowing she'd been in Elias's orbit increasingly lately.

I took the stairs down from the train station, nerves jangling with every step. By the time I reached her building, dusk was already settling in. At the lobby's polished desk, I offered a tight smile to Mark, the concierge—small, silver-haired, and always quick with a nod.

"Evening, Mark," I said, shifting the strap of my bag. "Have you seen Maeva this week?"

His green eyes met mine over the rim of his glasses. "Not since Tuesday, I'm afraid. Busy week for her." He rifled through a stack of envelopes. "Speaking of busy, you want to grab her mail? She's got a heap this time—bills, catalogs, you name it."

I didn't hesitate. "Sure, I can do that."

He handed me a neatly bundled bundle. The weight of her unopened letters felt heavier than I expected. As the elevator doors slid open behind me, I tucked the mail under my arm and squared my shoulders. Whatever was keeping Maeva silent these past days, I was determined to find out— beginning at her own front door.

The elevator doors slid shut behind me with a soft click that echoed unnaturally in the silence. I stood frozen for a moment, the hairs on my arms bristling as a cold prickle traced down my spine. Each breath felt shallow, as though the very air had thickened with unspoken danger.

I stepped forward, every footfall muffled yet magnified in my ears—thump… thump… thump—like a warning drum. The hallway lights flickered once, then steadied, casting long, wavering shadows that seemed to dance in the corner of my vision. My pulse hammered in my temples, and I swallowed hard, suddenly aware of how exposed I felt.

A faint breeze stirred, though the windows were locked tight, carrying with it a whisper of something—danger, regret, power? I couldn't place it, only that it set my nerves jangling. Door after door stood in silent vigil, their nameplates austere.

Maeva's lay at the far end, the wood grain darker somehow, as though it were absorbing the tension around it. My breath caught in my throat as I drew closer, each step measured, every sense screaming to turn and run—yet I could not. The corridor stretched interminably between us, charged with that strange aura, pulling me forward toward uncertainty

A rancid wave of decay and mold slammed into my lungs. My chest heaved, ribs straining as bile rose in my throat. Tears stung my eyes, blurring the hallway lights into ghostly halos. I doubled over, my palm pressed against the cold wall, Tendrils of nausea coiling in my stomach.

Before I could steady myself, an invisible force crushed me from behind—an iron weight across my shoulders—sending me crashing to my knees. My shirt soaked through with tears, my face burning with humiliation and dread. I gasped for breath, each cough wracking my body like a dry thunderclap.

Then—silence. Except it wasn't empty. A shiver skated down my spine as I realized I wasn't alone. There, just beyond sight, someone watched me. My heart thundered. I lifted my head, eyes darting down the deserted corridor—each door a dark promise—yet no one moved.

The stench clung to the air, but now it carried something else: the faint click of breath, the soft scrape of a footstep that shouldn't be there. Panic bloomed in my chest as I pressed myself flat against the wall, palms slicked. My throat tightened. Whoever—or whatever—was here, it had waited for me.

Summoning every ounce of strength, I lunged toward Maeva's door—only to be hurled sideways like a ragdoll. My legs flailed uncontrollably, and my back slammed against the unforgiving concrete wall with a sickening crack. My skull snapped off the surface, stars exploding behind my eyes, and then I hit the floor in a jarring thud.

A hot trickle pooled at the base of my skull, slick and dark, spreading into a growing stain on the hallway's grimy concrete. Dazed, I blinked through slits of vision—each flash of light hammering at my wounds—until, at last, I saw it: Maeva's door, tauntingly close, its brass nameplate gleaming like an unreachable promise.

Pain radiated through my side, every breath a shard of glass, but despite the blood and the ache, hope flared in my chest. I had nearly made it.

"Leave." My voice rang out, low and resolute.

The shadow shivered—an amorphous ripple of inky darkness sliding between me and Maeva's door. Edges flickered like a living void.

Summoning every ounce of will, I slammed my hands together—once, twice—each clap sending waves of glowing ember through the stale corridor air. On the third clap, molten light roared from my palms in a fierce column, striking the shadow with a hiss of steam and a shower of sparks.

The darkness recoiled, fracturing into thin, writhing tendrils beneath the wall sconces glow. With a final, guttering wail, it evaporated, leaving only the scent of ozone and a whisper of smoke curling from the charred concrete.

I dropped into a crouch, muscles trembling, pain radiating from where I'd first struck the wall. Yet around me, the oppressive charge had drained away—the hallway now quiet, mundane once more. I rose slowly, testing my shoulders, my breath coming easier. The path to that door lay open—no barrier now to deny me entrance.

That blast wasn't ordinary wards or basic charms—it was pure, raw force. No mundane witch ever wielded that kind of power—especially not against one of their own.

I rapped on her door until my knuckles stung—once, twice, again and again—each hollow thud echoing down the silent hallway. No answer. My heart thudded in my chest; panic curled in my stomach.

"Maeva!" I shouted, voice cracking. Still nothing.

Exasperated, I slammed my palm against the doorknob and channeled a surge of raw magic into the lock. My fingers burned as fiery orange light snaked into the mechanism. With a metallic click and a flash of embers, the door swung open.

A cold stillness greeted me inside—no laughter, no late–night teacups clinking, no soft sighs drifting from her bedroom. Instead, shadows pooled in every corner, as if the darkness itself had claimed this space. A sickening dread settled over me.

I stumbled in, footsteps loud against the hardwood. Doors stood half–ajar or thrown wide, revealing empty rooms: her coat hanging untouched on the hook, her sneakers by the closet, the coffee mug on the counter crusted with last week's dregs. On the kitchen table, a plate of half–eaten toast had gone cold—crumbs long since scattered by time, not hands.

My chest tightened. She was gone. And if she needed me—if she was in danger—every second I wasted searching an empty apartment that was a second too late

Chapter Nineteen

Maeva Sinclair

Another night swallowed me in its familiar gloom. I still hadn't come to terms with this strange new power coursing through my veins—it felt less like magic and more like a warm embrace tightening around my heart. When the grimoire was near, I tasted that power on my tongue, electric and alive, but back in this cell I felt only despair. Every scrap of confidence I'd managed to gather slipped through my fingers, leaving me raw and exposed.

Abigail refused to let me keep the book with me behind these bars—sigils or not, she said it was too dangerous. She doesn't trust me, and her distrust bites at my resolve. I replay every fragment of my dreams, even the terrifying one with Elias, searching for clues in each flicker of memory. But pieces are missing, and this puzzle—the riddle of my own blood—is still incomplete.

I press my forehead against the cold wall and close my eyes. The faint hum of the torches overhead does nothing to chase away the questions swirling in my mind. What did Daniel see when he tasted my blood? Why does Abigail fear me so? And, above all, where do I belong in this tangled web of curses and covens?

A white-hot fury coiled in my veins, each heartbeat hammering like a drum. Muscles clenched until my limbs felt as rigid as iron bars. The realization—they'd tricked me, used me—stoked a blazing hatred for this family. Yet beneath that rage, another emotion stirred: something darker, more potent.

A swarm of tiny sparks danced beneath my skin. My fingers tingled as if a thousand spiders skittered their legs across my palms. I closed my eyes, inhaling sharply, and there it was: raw power, pulsing just under the surface, desperate to break free.

It felt like a dam on the brink of collapse, holding back a furious river of energy. And for the first time, I understood that I wasn't merely their pawn—I was a force they couldn't contain.

The sparks beneath my skin trembled, desperate to burst into flame—but the sigils bound me too tightly. Frustration roared in my veins, each tiny tingle a reminder of the power just out of reach.

I craned my head toward the ceiling, where the red-glowing runes pulsed in time with my heartbeat. They were carved for one purpose: to keep me caged. My gaze snapped back to my hands, where the Raven Coven brand smoldered on my finger—proof I was different, bound to something ancient and unstoppable.

In that moment, clarity washed over me. I didn't need pills to steady my breathing—I needed freedom. I needed to stand on my own, to unleash the magic that quivered at my fingertips. As that realization settled into my bones, the tension in my body began to loosen. My shoulders dropped, the rigid knot in my chest unraveled, and a single, fierce thought took root: I would break these chains.

A surge of confidence washed over me like a breaker crashing onto the shore. The jagged fragments of doubt that had splintered my mind began knitting themselves whole again. Heat pooled behind my eyes, and each heartbeat thundered, "You are stronger than they know."

I pressed my palms into the cold stone, feeling the hollow echo of possibility beneath my touch. They may have trapped my body, but my mind was mine alone—sharp, relentless, ready to turn their own magic against them. Now, all I needed was a plan to outwit those who thought they'd caged a frightened girl, not a Raven.

I would claw my way free. I'd spent too many nights shivering against these stone walls—every heartbeat reminding me how deeply I'd been betrayed. But the grimoire was mine alone, bound by my blood and my blood alone. They're cursed it for a reason, and I'd rather let the walls collapse around me than lend them my magic.

My thoughts tumbled over themselves, each scrap of memory a lifeline. I recalled the flicker of flame that danced from a whispered phrase, the soft hiss of wind summoned by a breath—tiny spells I'd just barely glimpsed. My fingers ached to trace the leather binding; my blood thirsted to stain the pages and awaken their secrets.

The heavy door groaned open—and he was there. Daniel's broad frame filled the threshold before he crossed the hall in five silent strides. The lingering scent of hickory on him made anxiety rise in my throat, but I pushed it down and let my fury flare instead.

I clamped both hands around the iron bars, white-knuckled, waiting. Each tightening of my grip sent jolts up my forearms. No magic, just raw human defiance.

He stopped inches away, one hand casually buried in his pocket, the other—my blood-stained grimoire—held aloft between us. Flickering torchlight sculpted his features into shifting shadows: lethal, controlled, infuriatingly handsome.

My heart slammed against my ribs. I tasted copper on my tongue. I didn't need magic to feel the shock of power coursing through me at his nearness—this man was danger incarnate. But I forced myself to meet his gaze, to let my anger burn where my fear might have been.

"Miss Sinclair," he said softly, voice low enough that only I could hear. Then, without another word, he let the book drop onto the stone floor between us, its leather cover thudding in the silence.

I stared at it—my lifeline—knowing that taking it back would be the first step toward breaking free… or slipping deeper into their cruel game.

His eyes flicked up from the grimoire to mine, the torchlight catching the sharp line of his jaw. He slid one hand free from his pocket.

"I need something from you," he said, his voice like steel wrapped in silk.

I let my gaze drift over the cracked leather, then back to his face, a slow, teasing smile curving my lips.

"I need something from you, too," I whispered, letting the words hang between us like a dare.

For a moment, he froze—those storm-dark eyes widening just enough for me to see the flicker of surprise. Then the corners of his mouth quirked upward, revealing just a hint of those bright, predatory teeth. The air crackled with unspoken tension: his need for my magic, my need for the grimoire, and the dangerous pull between us neither of us would admit.

My breath caught at the tremor in his voice. The flicker of torchlight danced across his desperate eyes as he kicked the grimoire towards me.

"If I let you out," he pleaded, voice cracking on the last word, "will you help me?"

A jolt of hope pierced my chest—and with it, the sharp sting of distrust. My fingers itched to snatch the book and run, but I hesitated. He was counting on me.

"I… I don't know," I whispered, the weight of my own captivity pressing down on me. Every second felt like a lifetime.

He took a trembling step closer, the desperation in his gaze raw enough to break stone. "Maeva," he rasped, the single syllable loaded with every promise and threat he'd ever made, "please."

My heart thundered. Freedom lay just beyond these bars—his freedom depended on me, and mine on him.

"I'll look," I finally choked out, voice suffused with my own longing and fear.

"But you—"

He reached out; his fingers shook as they brushed mine. "Open the door," I begged, eyes blazing.

Hope and dread collided in my gut. I pressed my palm to the cold iron, inhaled his scent, and whispered back, "I'll help you…if you set me free."

The lock turned with a soft click—and in that moment, I realized just how desperately we both needed each other.

He eased the iron door open and slipped out first, the torchlight flickering off the scars on his jacket. My heart pounded so loud I was sure he'd hear it as I followed, bare feet silent on the cold stone. The corridor narrowed to a low archway—its rough-hewn ceiling so close I nearly bumped my head—and opened into a cramped chamber.

At its center stood a battered oak desk, scarred by decades of ink and candle wax. Two straight-backed chairs—one on either side—looked like they'd long ago surrendered any hope of comfort. Murky shadows pooled in each corner, only reluctantly chased back by the wavering torches set into iron brackets. Dampness clung to the air; every breath tasted faintly of mildew.

He paused just inside the door, throwing one broad shoulder back for me to enter. His silhouette filled the frame, and for a moment I worried there wasn't room for both of us. But he simply leaned against the lintel, hands splayed against the stone, as if staking his claim on the narrow space. I stepped in, brushing past him, my fingers grazing his abdomen— and felt the tension coil tighter in my chest.

"We're in a closet," I muttered, arching a brow at the cramped chamber.

"How presumptuous of you," he shot back, his sarcasm slicing the silence like a knife.

I glared at him from across the desk and sank into the creaking chair. His broad frame swallowed half the lantern-lit room, the flickering shadows clinging to his coat sleeves. Drops of sweat formed at my temples, but I forced my breathing steady—this was new territory, this raw pulse of magic thrumming beneath my skin. The grimoire at my side seemed to hum with the same restless energy.

He leaned forward, elbows on the desk, and the faint scent of ink and old leather drifted between us. My heart hammered as I realized I wasn't just reading—this was a negotiation, and my power was both the bargaining chip and the weapon. I swallowed.

"I need you to find something for me," he said, voice low enough that I felt it more than heard it. His gaze bore into mine, an unspoken challenge.

Magic stirred beneath my skin, an electric hum that sent goosebumps racing along my arms. Holding the old grimoire in my lap set my pulse thundering—its leather cover seemed to pulse in time with my heartbeat. I could feel the power slithering through my veins, a whisper at first, then a growing roar, as though the book itself recognized me and was calling out, demanding release.

Every breath I took tasted of possibility and peril, the same chaos of longing and fear coiling tight in my chest. For the first time, I understood how deadly beautiful my own magic could be—and how dangerously close I was to unleash it.

He leveled me with a slow, deliberate look, his spine straightening as he peered down the bridge of his nose. The torchlight danced across his strong jawline, casting sharp shadows that made his cheekbones and throat seem carved from marble. His eyes, softened by the flicker, held mine with an intensity that made my pulse drum in my ears. The fabric of his shirt stretched taut over his broad shoulders, outlining every muscle beneath—proof that there was nothing left to the imagination.

I felt his gaze on me, drinking in my own reaction: the flutter of my lashes, the quick hitch of my breath. If I weren't already anchored to this chair, I'd be on my knees without a second thought. Between us, the ancient grimoire lay like a fragile bridge of possibility—its spine directly in my path, throbbing with the promise of power. My heart pounded at the sight of it so close; my fingers itched, as though they could taste the magic that seeped from its pages. The silence, thicker than any iron door, every second stretched and pulsed with unspoken desire.

Daniel's voice was soft, almost a caress in the dim light.

"Abigail told me what happened. Could you do it again?"

Heat flared up my spine at the question—so close to freedom, with every answer I craved lying open on that table. I lifted my chin, letting my defiance show.

"How do I know I won't just hurt you?" I challenged, my voice chilling the space between us. He leaned forward, elbows on the tabletop, eyes glittering in the torchlight.

"If you do," he breathed, "then so be it."

His words weren't a threat—they were a confession. And with the grimoire's power humming beneath my fingertips, I realized: this was the only way out.

I wasn't sure what to expect from Daniel—he was nothing like Elias, inscrutable in that low torchlight. Yet there was a steadiness with him, a rare honesty in his blue eyes that made me wonder if he truly meant what he promised. Trusting him felt impossible—too many times I'd been used—but still I reached for the grimoire.

My fingers closed around the worn leather strap, the weight of its centuries-old magic pulsing beneath my touch. I slid the buckle free and opened the first page. On the surface, it was blank—but I knew the real spells lay hidden just beneath, waiting for my blood to awaken them.

My pulse thundered in my ears. "I need a knife or something," I managed, voice trembling.

He didn't hesitate. With a gentle stillness that did nothing to calm the storm in my veins, he slipped his hand beneath mine and pried my palm open.

Immediately, I felt the surge—white-hot magic pounding through my bones, igniting sparks along my skin. Tiny cobalt flickers danced across the flesh of my palm, crackling with raw potential. My breath caught in my throat as my fingers tingled, the power desperate to escape.

Daniel's thumb pressed gently to the center of my hand, dampening the spark for a heartbeat. His gaze locked on mine—steady, intimate, unflinching—holding me in place even as the magic trembled beneath us both. I was frozen, caught between fear and something darker, something electric. Outside, the torches guttered, as if drawing back in awe.

Daniel's teeth part my skin in a precise, almost reverent bite. Hot pain explodes where his canines puncture my wrist, and crimson rivulets spill between us, hissing as they meet the table's scarred wood. The sparks erupt around my arm in a wild corona—electric blue light dancing across my veins, illuminating the dark closet like a stormy sky.

My breath comes in ragged gasps as I grip the edge of the table, knuckles whitening. Daniel's other hand presses firmly against my forearm, anchoring me, his thumb gently sweeping the blood toward the puncture. His eyes never leave mine, steady and fathomless, as if he's reading every heartbeat.

With deliberate slowness, Daniel withdraws, lips stained scarlet. He lifts my wrist, turning it so that my palm faces upward. Across the grain of the wood, an iridescent script shimmers into being—runes and incantations long hidden, now crawling like living things across the page.

The air crackles with raw possibilities. Only our two breaths remain, ragged with shock and wonder: his, steady and heavy with triumph. And as the final letters settle into place.

The moment his pupils shift to inky voids, a chill ripple through me—his eyes, once warm, now a starless sky. He releases my wrist, and life's lifeblood arcs in slow crimson rivulets across the grimoire's newly inked pages. My blood beads at each rune, as if the book itself thirsts for every drop.

I stare—heart hammering—at the way Daniel's chest heaves, each breath a thunderclap in the cramped pantry-closet. He leans back, head bowed, as if the weight of what he's just done pulls at his very spine. His shoulders rise and fall in measured rhythm; the fabric of his shirt stretches over tight muscles that betray both exertion and restraint.

Finally, he tips his head up, eyes still smoldering ebony. An unspoken question passes between us: what have we set in motion? The air crackles, alive with the promise—and danger—of the magics now unlocked. Every rune on the page pulses faintly, echoing the beat of our shared, uneasy exhilaration.

I lean forward, my heart pounding. "What do you see?"

Daniel's gaze flickers, and for a heartbeat his own color returns—blue—before plunging back into darkness. He studies me, as if weighing my soul. Finally, he speaks, voice low and measured:

"Everything you've done. Every step you've taken since you opened this book."

"Her memories flow in your blood. I saw her first triumphs—how she discovered her power.

My breath catches. "You mean… Meridith's?"

A slow nod.

"I see them in my dreams," I whisper, voice barely more than wind. "Sometimes I'm there living in another time. I watch scenes play out, then shift as though I've flipped channels on a broken film reel. Moments of her life bleed into one another, but they don't always feel like her memories. They feel distorted fragments stitched together from stories that don't belong to the same person."

I lowered my gaze to the grimoire, rivulets of blood snaking across its blank parchment until the ink began to bloom—words unfurling like ripples across a still pond. My breath caught, and I instinctively pressed my other hand to my chest, trying to staunch that stubborn trickle from my wrist.

Daniel rose from his seat, the soft scrape of wood against stone echoing in the narrow closet. He circled the table with deliberate calm, each step measured as he came to stand at my side. Then he knelt and produced a strip of coarse linen.

His fingers, warm and certain, cradled my wrist. I watched his jaw tighten in concentration as he folded the cloth neatly, binding the puncture with gentle precision. When his gaze met mine, it held a flicker of concern that sent an unexpected warmth through my chest—an unsettling mix of gratitude and something deeper I couldn't name.

I looked up as he settled back into his seat, the linen still pressed against my wrist. His brow knit in genuine confusion.

"What?" he asked, voice low.

I swallowed, the warmth from his touch still lingering beneath my skin. Leaning back, I pressed the cloth more firmly in place, trying to mask the fluttering in my chest.

"Nothing," I snapped, my voice sharper than I intended.

He studied me for a long moment, the torchlight catching the edges of his worry before he turned his attention back to the grimoire. I flexed my fingers beneath the bandage, savoring the soft comfort even as my throat tightened with the reminder of why I was here.

"You don't have to be kind to me," I said, forcing my tone cold and clipped. "I know I'm only useful for what I can reveal."

His head tilted slightly—a gesture so small it was almost imperceptible—yet it spoke volumes. For a heartbeat, the distance between us felt small, as though the thin strip of linen could barely contain the magic and something more, something unforeseen, simmering between us.

"I know, can you see anything that pertains to the curse?" he cleared his throat.

I pulled the old leather-bound book closer to me; I scanned the pages searching for anything that could possibly lead to a curse and monsters. I flipped back and forth making sure I wasn't missing any information. Her writing contained so much knowledge, it took up every space of the paper, it was hard for me to piece together. Herbal medicines and midwife situations were not exactly helpful to the cause. I continued to search when I finally found a small note a curse set in blood.

I lifted my eyes to meet Daniel's gaze, he was peering down into the book, reading what was written. He took a deep breath in, and his shoulders sank. He placed his elbows on the table while holding his head. A moment of relief washed over him. I searched over the pages and found another note spoken with love.

The scattered pages felt deliberately jumbled snippets of incantations half-written, recipes for tinctures smeared with age, and fragments of her own handwriting laced through it all like a secret code. One leaf might list "henbane root, steep at midnight," while the next picks up two dozen lines later with "—only under a waning moon," leaving gaps that taunted me. My eyes swam over the faded ink and hasty cross-outs, trying to stitch together Meredith's intent.

Leaning back in my chair, I pressed my palms into my temples, jolted by the thrum of my own frustration. It was like trying to solve a puzzle with half the pieces missing—and the knowledge that every fragment here mattered kept me from giving up. I closed my eyes for a moment, tasting the phantom tang of her blood on the edges of my mind, and braced myself to dive back in.

I rubbed my eyes and shook my head. "It makes zero sense," I admitted, voice tight. The pages still swirled in my vision—half-spoken spells, bloodstained margins, broken sentences begging for that missing connective thread.

Daniel's lips pressed into a thin line. He leaned back, crossing his broad arms over his chest, the fabric of his shirt stretching across powerful pectorals "A curse set takes blood and love—a curse broken takes heart and peace." he repeated, voice low and grave,

His words settled between us like a promise and a threat all at once. My throat tightened—how was I supposed to untangle centuries-old magic when even these cryptic riddles refused to yield their secrets?

I glanced back down at the open grimoire, its once-blank pages now alive with Meredith's fragmented story. Each line felt like a door half-ajar, daring me to push it open… if only I could find the key.

"You're a witch and her descendant—can't you figure it out?" Daniel snapped, blue eyes flashing with impatience.

My chest tightened. "And you're a vampire who's walked this earth for centuries—couldn't you have already figured it out?" I shot back, my voice sharp as steel.

He ran a hand through his hair, frustration, and regret flickering across his features.

"The curse is what binds us, makes us monsters. It's all we've ever known."

Silence stretched between us like a drawn blade. I pressed my fingertips to the page—Meredith's jagged handwriting blurred into meaning I could almost grasp.

I echoed the phrase again, letting each word roll over my tongue like a foreign incantation:

"A curse set takes blood and love—a curse broken takes heart and peace."

The syllables felt heavy in my mouth, as if they carried a weight far greater than their simple forms. I pressed my palms flat against the grimoire's open pages, fingertips brushing the damp streaks of my own blood. The leather binding warmed beneath my touch, pulsing in time with my frantic pulse.

Leaning forward, I dropped my forehead to my folded arms on the table. My temples throbbed in sync with the slow drip–drip–drip of blood onto the wood. The room's torches guttered in the evening draft, sending shadows skittering across the walls.

I closed my eyes and whispered the riddle again, this time more slowly, as though each word might unlock a hidden door in my mind:

"A curse set takes blood—and love…" My chest tightened at the memory of Elias's betrayal.

"… a curse broken takes heart—and peace." I felt the promise of peace slip through my fingers like smoke.

Exhaling on a tremor of breath, I lifted my head and met Daniel's expectant gaze. The firelight caught the frustration etched in his scarred features. My temples still pulsed, but beneath the ache a spark of resolve kindled.

"Heart and peace," I murmured, voice trembling with both fear and something like hope. "That has to be the key."

A bolt of power exploded through me, a molten current coursing hot and bright through every vein. My skin felt as though it had been plunged into searing water—heat rippling up from my core until my limbs threatened to ignite.

My eyes snapped open, pupils flashing electric blue as the magic enveloped me. The grimoire's pages beneath my outstretched arms caught in a flare of azure flame, the air around me crackling. I was welded to the chair—every muscle locked, every thought dissolved in a tempest of pain.

Tears streamed down my face, hissing into steam the instant they hit my cheeks. My head snapped back on its own, spine arching as though drawn by unseen wires. My mind fractured—each heartbeat a hammer blow of panic and terror against the fragile shell of my consciousness.

Then suddenly, the inferno eased. The flames winked out. My body went limp, and I slipped into a vast, echoing silence: a trance deeper than any sleep. In that stillness, the riddle whispered itself into my blood: "A curse set takes blood and love; a curse broken takes heart and peace."

And I knew—this power was the key I'd been seeking.

Chapter Twenty

Maeva Sinclair

Snowflakes drifted down in slow spirals, each one a tiny crystal ballerina performing against the growing dusk. A chill wind swept them across the clearing, scattering white diamonds over latched fences and frozen earth. Underfoot, the snow lay soft and unbroken, save for my footprints tracing a narrow path toward the cottage.

To my right, a neat stack of chopped wood stood guard by a rough-hewn stump—its surface rimmed with frosting, an old iron axe leaning against it like a silent sentinel. Beyond, a low wooden fence framed rows of winter-shrouded vegetables: stout stalks and weary leaves bowed beneath their snowy quilt. Between the rows, the soil—once rich and dark—lay hidden, its promise of spring yet undiscovered.

Above me, skeletal branches trembled with fresh powder, the occasional cascade of loose flakes whispering in the hush. The sky bled from steel gray at the horizon into deep indigo overhead, where the first shy stars glittered. Each spark felt impatient, as if the night itself could barely wait to spill its velvet cloak across the world.

Ahead, the cottage rose—a humble silhouette against the twilight. Its steep straw-thatched roof, layered thick as a winter cloak, bristled with frost. Smoke curled in a thin, pale thread from the chimney, promising warmth within. A single lantern hung by the heavy wooden door, its glow a beacon on the snow-dusted path.

I paused; my heart was stilled by the silence and let the cold's sharp breath fill my lungs. In that moment, the frozen world felt suspended between what had been and what was yet to come—quiet, waiting, alive.

The chimney bellowed, sending fragrant tendrils of wood smoke spiraling into the sky. A rich, charred-wood aroma clung to the cabin's dark timbers, nestled among towering pines whose needles blanketed the frozen ground alongside brittle, fallen leaves. I stood merely from the low wooden fence, watching the smoke curl upward in lazy spirals against the deep-green backdrop of the forest.

I drew in a cold breath—sharp and stinging—then exhaled in a frosty plume, like a dragon's first gust of winter fire. With each step, the snow crackled beneath my boots, the only sound in the near silence.

Then—a woman's cry pierced the hush, frantic and raw. My heart leapt, and I halted, straining to catch the echo inside the cabin. Another scream followed, urgent and fearful.

I crept closer to the cabin wall, my pulse thudding in my ears. That's when I sensed them: two wisps of white smoke drifting into view behind me, hovering like ghosts summoned by the shout.

My breath caught, tension coiling in my chest, as I stared at the spectral forms before me—silent witnesses to the terror unfolding beyond the door.

I froze as two figures materialized inches behind me—Daniel and Elias.

Daniel's frame was rigid, the firelight glinting off his eyes. Behind him, Elias stood with his wild, unkempt hair plastered to his forehead by sweat. His white frock shirt hung open at the collar, revealing a smudge of chest hair and a smattering of dried blood. Mud caked the hems of his brown trousers, and snow crusted the tops of his boots.

My gaze drifted to his forearms: jagged streaks of crimson crusted along his sleeves and wrists. The hem of his shirt was flecked with bright red—proof of bloodshed. My heart pounded as I took an involuntary step towards the cabin door.

The remnant of the man I thought I knew and the monster he'd always been, curse or no curse. Elias's jaw tightened, his lips pulled back in a silent snarl of malice. His eyes, dark as storm clouds, fixed on the broken figures within the cabin.

I tore my gaze from Elias and glanced at Daniel. His dark hair was pulled back into a taut ponytail, revealing the high planes of his cheekbones. He wore a simple white linen shirt beneath a weathered brown leather coat that creaked softly as he shifted his weight. His trousers, too, were of supple leather, disappearing into scuffed boots that left dark prints in the snow.

With each frantic scream from inside the cabin, Daniel's brow furrowed more deeply. His storm-blue eyes, usually so controlled, flickered with helpless concern. A tremor ran through his jaw as the yells grew louder—rage, fear, pain: he didn't know which.

Suddenly, a heavy crash echoed behind us. Both brothers spun toward the door—Elias with predatory speed, Daniel just a heartbeat behind. Elias thundered inside, ripping the door from its frame, while Daniel vaulted over the threshold.

My heart tightened as a woman's panicked voice rang out, "Get out! Please—get out!"

I stood rooted in the snow, ears ringing, unable to tear my eyes from that shattered doorway. The world had narrowed to darkness beyond the threshold—and the horrors it hid.

Suddenly the air grew oppressive, each breath tasted cold and moisture. The snow—once drifting lazily—now blasted down in angry torrents, whipping across my face in stinging sheets. I tilted my head back, eyelashes gathering frosty clumps that blurred my vision. My hair, already dusted with the first flakes, soon became a frozen lattice, each strand heavy with snow's weight.

Beneath my boots, the powder's surface thickened rapidly, muffling the world in a vast, white silence. Tree branches bowed under the growing burden, their twigs snapping like brittle bones. The sudden storm swallowed the cabin and its horrors in a swirling veil of winter, leaving me alone on the threshold, heart hammering, torn between the safety of the storm's camouflage and the terror I'd just witnessed inside.

A bone-chilling wind whipped through the doorway as I stumbled inside, each breath freezing in my lungs. My teeth chattered uncontrollably; I could feel icicles forming on my eyelashes. Desperate for warmth, I pressed my palms to my mouth and exhaled, hoping the steam would thaw my stinging fingers.

Snow clung to my boots in heavy clumps, each step forward weighted by the drifts piling ever higher. At the cottage's threshold, I froze. Elias stood over her, blade poised at her throat, as pale as the moonlight through the window.

Panic eclipsed thought—I lunged. My shoulder slammed into his broad chest, sending me crashing through the gap between them. My form falling right through Elias like a phantom. The world spun as I hit the floor, a sharp crack exploding at my collarbone. Pain flared, white-hot, rushing up my arm to my neck. I screamed, the sound swallowed by the storm outside, knowing instantly that my collarbone had shattered under the impact.

Tears burned my cheeks as I watched Meridith pressed against the rough-hewn wall.

"Do it," a woman's voice hissed from the shadows.

Suddenly an unleashed tremor of power—a black wave of force— that slammed Meridith into the splintering wood. Her spine arched with each brutal impact. Splinters snapped free, raking her back. I flinched at the sickening thuds, unable to look away.

Blood blossomed at her nostrils, her eyes fluttered—and then stilled, emptying of life. Elias stood back, lips curved in triumph, his eyes glittering with perverse delight.

Across the room, Daniel's face was pale as ash. His jaw clenched; the flicker of guilt in his eyes was almost as sharp as the crack of Meridith's shattered ribs. Yet he said nothing, his hands hanging limply at his sides.

I pressed my hand to my chest, feeling the dull ache beneath my palm—her broken body had broken something in me. My own tears soaked through my shirt as I rose unsteadily to confront them both.

That's when I saw her—Rebecca, the witch from my dreams and that fateful council. She stood lit by a flickering torchlight, her platinum hair braided tight against her skull, ebony robes swirling around her like living shadow. In one graceful motion, she extended her hand over Meridith's chest. Dark tendrils of magic snaked from her fingertips, lancing through bone and sinew with a sound like tearing silk. Meridith's ribs cracked in a soft, grotesque chorus as her body convulsed against the rough-hewn timber. Blood fountained from the shattered cage of her sternum, soaking the floor in a dark, spreading stain.

"Elias—enough!" Daniel staggered forward, desperation cracking his voice.

But Rebecca only laughed, a low, cruel sound that echoed off the log walls. She snapped her wrist again, while a wave of onyx light hurled into Daniel's chest. He flew backward, crashing into the wall with thunderous impact, splinters flying as his form slumped to the ground, unmoving.

For a heartbeat, Elias stood transfixed. His eyes, once alight with violent hunger, filled with shock at his lover's brutality. Then Meridith, broken yet unbowed, lifted one trembling leg—her gown shredded, skin bruised purple—and kicked him squarely in his groin. The force drove the air from his lungs in a pained groan. He doubled over and dropped limp beside Daniel, both men felled by the witch they'd underestimated.

In the sudden, eerie silence, torches guttered, and sparks drifted upward, leaving Rebecca's silhouette carved in shadow against the wall—and Meridith, collapsed but victorious, clutching her blood-soaked gown, the last of the coven's strength burning bright in her eyes.

Meridith didn't relent—she slammed both palms onto the rough-hewn floorboards. At her touch, the earth itself trembled. Cracks spidered out beneath her fingers; the cabin shuddered as if about to uproot itself.

Rebecca lunged forward, black magic crackling at her fingertips, but her footing gave way on the heaving floor. Meridith's eyes—burning with equal parts rage and desperation—held Rebecca's as the tremors intensified.

Each thunderous shake rattled the walls; dust and splinters rained down in gritty showers. Bundles of straw and frayed twine dislodged from the roof, plummeting into the room. Outside, heavy snow began to cascade through shattered windows, blanketing the chaos in cold white silence.

In that moment, the witch's magic and the vampire's fury collided—and the old cabin groaned its final protest before collapsing inward, sealing both hunter and hunted in a maelstrom of destruction.

Rebecca's body lay half-buried beneath a tangle of broken beams, straw, and fresh snow. Each flake that drifted down muffled her gasps for breath as she fought to free herself from the wreckage.

Elias knelt a few feet away, windburned and reeling from Meridith's fierce kick, his hands curled tight over his head as snow pelted him. The great cabin around us was now a ruin of splintered wood and hanging rafters, its collapse echoed by the storm's howl.

I pressed my back into the safety of a fractured wall, watching Meridith channel every ounce of her magic. Her hair whipped around her face, alive with the electricity of her anger. With a commanding sweep of her arms, the snowfall intensified—ice crystals caught in her palms, swirling upward in a blizzard that bent saplings and sent a swirl of white into the night sky.

Snow drifted around us in living waves, the world reduced to frozen motion and roaring wind. Then, as suddenly as it began, the whirlwind stilled. Meridith's eyes, bright with grim determination, scanned the wreckage one last time before she pivoted on her heel and bolted through the gaping hole in the wall.

I sprung to my feet, heart hammering, and sprinted after her across the debris-strewn clearing. Her boots carried her over fallen beams and jagged stones with impossibly graceful speed. The forest swallowed us; its tall pines loomed like dark sentinels, their branches heavy with snow.

We raced past rotting stumps and moss-clad boulders, each step taking us farther from the broken cabin—and farther into the gathering shadows of the wood. At last, the trees parted to reveal a moonlit glade, the snow-blanketed ground shimmering like glass. Meridith paused at its center, chest heaving, eyes aflame with the raw.

The snow lay undisturbed around her—soft, cold, silent—until her ragged breathing broke the hush. I collapsed to one knee; each inhaled a white cloud of pain as my broken shoulder protested every breath.

Her sorrow turned raw, a sound that tore through the stillness: a keening wail that bounced off the pines. Hot tears-streaked Meridith's frozen cheeks, her slender shoulders trembling beneath her coat. She crouched low, pulling a small, curved knife from the top of her mud-caked boot. In one swift, trembling motion, she slashed the inside of her palm. Scarlet rivulets snaked down her wrist, pooling where snow met earth.

Her voice was a harsh whisper, choked by tears:

"A curse set takes blood and love, a curse broken takes heart and peace."

She closed her eyes as if to steady herself, pressing that heated, bleeding palm into the snow-dusted ground. Each syllable came slower, heavier, as though bleeding into the frozen earth itself. Tiny tendrils of steam curled up from the contact point, hissing against the knife's edge and sizzling into the cold night air.

Behind me, a crack of twig snapped like a gunshot, and Daniel stepped from the tree line—his broad shoulders tense, eyes wide with shock.

"Mer, what are you doing?" His voice reverberated through the woods, equal parts alarm, and urgency.

Meridith's head jerked up. The wound on her hand dripped fresh blood onto the snow, but her eyes blazed—not with panic, but with fierce rage. Snowflakes clung to her lashes as she stared down the path he'd appeared on, her pain warping into pure, unguarded fury.

For a heartbeat, the only sound was her ragged breathing—and the faint drip, drip of blood melting into the snow. Then she rose, blade still in hand, her posture rigid with resolve. The wind picked up, rattling the bare branches overhead as if nature itself braced for what would come next.

"You were just going to let them kill me, Daniel?" Meridith's voice cracked like a whip, each word driving a shard of ice through her heart.

Daniel's knees buckled. He stared at the snow-choked ground, tears freezing on his lashes. He couldn't meet her gaze—couldn't face the searing hurt he'd inflicted. His chest heaved as though each breath was laced with regret.

Meridith's sobs erupted then, raw, and ragged. They shook her to the core, wracking her body with pain so fierce she could feel her ribs splinter. She pressed one hand to her side, as if bracing against an invisible blow, while the other curled into a fist that dug into the bloodied snow.

"You—" she gasped between sobs, voice hoarse and broken, "—you'd watch me die for their hunger of power." Each word was a knife, carving grief into her bones. The wind whipped her hair across her face, mixing tears and frost until she could barely see.

Daniel trembled, his own agony thunderous in the silence that followed. He reached a handout, but froze halfway—too ashamed to touch her, too late to offer anything but sorrow.

Meridith's grief turned to fury. She inhaled deeply, steeling herself even as her knees trembled and the tears refused to stop.

"Since you crave power, then you shall have it," she murmured, her voice laced with both threat and promise.

"May you never rest. May peace always elude you. May love remain forever beyond your reach—and may your soul ache with unending hunger." Her curse crackled like lightning, and in its aftermath the world felt colder, hollower.

Her final scream was pure, unfiltered pain—an echo of a life betrayed—then drifted away on the wind, leaving Daniel and me standing amidst the swirling snow, haunted by the echo of her heartbreak.

He lifted his chin and watched her chant the riddle one last time: May you never rest. May peace always elude you. May love remain forever beyond your reach—and may your soul ache with unending hunger. A curse set takes blood and love, a curse broken takes heart and peace.

Her voice cracked on the final word, as if the very syllables tore through her chest. Crimson rivulets snaked down her palm, pooling in the snow and steaming in the cold air. She looked at Daniel then, her eyes raw glimmering with love, with hurt, with the memory of all she'd lost and all she'd hoped for.

A brittle smile flickered at the corners of her mouth, fragile as frost on glass. And in that instant—one heartbeat before the world shattered—she drove the blade into her heart.

The thunder broke in an earsplitting roar, lightning fracturing the sky in jagged white veins. I staggered back as the shockwave of sound rattled my bones. Daniel leapt forward, his grief-stricken cry swallowed by the storm, and caught her as she collapsed in his arms.

She went limp against him, each breath departing like a sigh of surrender. Daniel's sobs tore through the night, raw and unrestrained—his body convulsing with the weight of an impossible loss. He pressed her close, clutching what remained of her warmth, as if holding her together could defy death itself.

I sank to my knees in the driving rain. My own tears mingled with the downpour, burning hot on my cheeks. Every hope I'd ever carried—of freedom, of redemption, of love—crumbled into shards of ice in my chest.

The forest around us trembled in the tempest, and I felt my heart fractured a little more with every drop of rain that fell.

The world narrowed to the two of them and the ruined clearing beyond. Through the thinning veil of snowfall, Elias and Rebecca emerged at the tree line, silhouettes against the storm's fury. Elias's shoulders were taut as steel struts; his lips pinched into a hard line while Daniel knelt, trembling, cradling Meridith's broken body. The crimson stain on her lips glistened in the lamplight as her blood seeped onto Daniel's coat.

Elias's fury was a living thing, coiling in his glare, but it never touched Daniel. Rebecca, pale, and silent, gripped Elias's arm—her eyes distant—then led him wordlessly back into the swirling pines. Their departure only deepened the silence.

My heart twisted in my ribcage and tears sprung unbidden.

I shot to my feet—my chair skidding across the stone hearth—and the air crackled around me. Daniel's calm veneer shattered as he pressed flat against the wall, arms drawn tight, as if shielding himself from my wrath.

Magic thrummed under my skin—electric, molten. A low hum filled my ears, louder than the storm. I felt it surge up my arms, hot and insistent. My fists clenched the rough-hewn table so hard the wood splintered beneath my nails. I lifted my head, eyes blazing, and Daniel flinched, his wide, worried gaze locked on mine, desperate to know what had ignited this blaze within me.

"You're the reason for the curse," I choked out, my voice breaking under the weight of every life lost.

Daniel's pupils went from shock to sorrow in an instant. His jaw slackened, and the soft red glow returned to his eyes—anguish pooling in their depths. He swallowed hard, the rasp of his breath the only sound above the storm outside.

For a heartbeat, we simply stared at each other: me, trembling with accusation; him, fractured with guilt. Then he reached up and rubbed a hand over his face, as if trying to erase the truth he'd just heard. His shoulders slumped.

"I—" he began, voice raw.

But the words caught in his throat, unspeakable, unredeemable. In that silence I understood: the curse had not been born of magic alone, but of choices made, loves betrayed—and he, more than anyone, bore that burden.

Daniel's confession hung in the air like a dying ember. I could see the weight of his centuries laid bare in those weary eyes. He pressed his palms against the stone wall, as though bracing himself against its cold permanence.

"I've spilled more blood than I care to remember," he rasped. "Each century, each life—it was a sentence I chose, and one I've lived a thousand times over."

His voice cracked. "I… I don't want another sunrise, Maeva. Not like this."

My breath caught. The man who'd felt so invincible—who'd sought to harness my power—now trembled with mortal despair. The grimoire lay between us; its leather cover dull beneath the flickering torchlight.

In that moment, everything shifted: predator and prey, captor, and captive, bound together by the same longing for release. I glanced down at my blood-stained hand, then back to his face.

"Then we end it," I said, my voice steady despite the whirlwind within me. "No more bargains—just truth and the price it demands."

A fragile peace settled between us, fragile as the first light of dawn that neither of us would see. Sympathy flooded through me, coiling around my anger and melting it away. His confession—years of regret, centuries of regret—felt painfully true, yet a small voice inside whispered that words alone could be a trap. I closed my eyes, inhaled slowly, and let the riddle echo in my mind one more time:

"A curse set takes blood and love; a curse broken takes heart and peace."

Meridith's final act had been one of terrifying clarity—her blood mingled with the love she bore for him, and in that sacrificial moment, she wove the first strand of this terrible curse. My heart pounded as understanding bloomed.

I lifted my gaze to meet Daniel's. His eyes, rimmed with sorrow, searched mine for absolution—yet there was no judgment in their depths, only shared grief. But was that grief genuine, or just another mask? I let the pages of the grimoire drift close between us and found my voice, raw but uncertain:

"A curse set takes blood and love—it begins with her death, Meridith's own blood, poured out for the man she loved."

He froze, as if expecting relief to wash over me. Instead, doubt coiled cold in my chest. "You say you want an end to this curse," I continued, my tone harder now, "but words aren't enough. How do I know you won't use my blood—and my trust—against me, just as you all once did?"

Daniel's shoulders sagged, the flicker of emotion in his eyes genuine—or so I told myself. The chamber fell silent, the only sound the distant echo of my heartbeat drumming in my ears. We stood on the brink of something, perhaps salvation, perhaps betrayal. And I realized that, more than ever, I would need to guard my own heart.

Daniel's brow furrowed, the words hanging between us.

"But a curse broken takes heart and peace," he repeated, voice tight with uncertainty.

I leaned forward, tracing the grain of the leather cover where my finger had just drawn ink from my blood. The firelight trembled across his face as if afraid to settle.

"It means love will be your peace," I murmured, softer now, as if confessing a hope rather than a truth.

His deep blue eyes searched mine—were they eager or hesitant?

"Love will bring your peace."

I closed the grimoire with a deliberate thump and sank back into my chair. My vision swam; the room tilted. Every thought felt like it was dissolving into smoke. I shut my eyes, desperate for a moment's respite from the weight of ancient spells and fragile promises.

Daniel's voice rang out, sharp against the headache that was forming.

"But how do we break it?"

I barely managed a murmur before exhaustion claimed me. My lids fluttered like wounded birds, and the world went soft around the edges.

He swept to my side in an instant, the grimoire dropping from my fingers as he lifted me into his arms. His strength was gentleness incarnate—every step back to my cell measured, every breath a promise of safety. The familiar whisper of hickory smoke curled around us, warm and protective.

Nestling into him, I let the last of my defenses melt away, my cheek pressed to the steady thrum of his heart. His fingers tangled in my hair as he bent close, inhaling my scent like a benediction. My own heartbeat slowed, comforted by the nearness of him.

At the cell, he laid me on the thin blankets, tucking me in with solemn care. His large hand hesitated at the door's edge, then brushed my forehead in a soft benediction before it swung closed with a final, echoing click.

"Vampire," I murmured, my voice a fragile thread between us.

His breath barely a whisper: "Witch."

Chapter Twenty- One

Lori Whittens

Night's chill clung to the abandoned inn as the last of our Raven Coven drifted through its broken threshold. Moonlight slipped through gaping window frames, illuminating splintered beams and graffiti—crude warnings scrawled by frightened children. But we knew the truth: this crumbling stone house, once a proud welcoming inn, was now our sanctuary.

Outside, I'd traced protective sigils into the mossy mortar and buried blessed stones at the compass points—north, south, east, and west—ensuring only true Ravens could cross our thresholds. One by one, coven members stepped into the cavernous lower chamber. They formed a loose circle around the hearth I'd rekindled—a small bonfire of driftwood crackling defiantly against the dark.

Each witch advanced in turn, presenting the Raven mark on her finger to the warded walls, the blue-black sigil glowing faintly under the flickering torchlight. Some faces were seasoned and grave; others, barely more than girls, trembled with anticipation

The air tasted of ash and damp earth. A lone branch tapped against a broken pane, echoing like a summons.

I swallowed hard, my heart drumming in my ears as I faced the assembled sisters of the Raven Coven. Every breath felt borrowed, every second stretched thin by the weight of what I was about to say. I sucked in a trembling breath, my voice barely more than a rasp.

"Please," I choked out, stepping forward until the flickering firelight danced across my tear-streaked face. "They've found her—Maeva. They know she's Meridith's blood. If they break this curse with her magic… she'll die." When the final witch stepped into the circle, I drew in a steadying inhale.

"They've found her," I began, voice quivering with equal parts dread and determination. "The Knight family—they discovered Meridith's descendant. They plan to use her to break their curse… or worse."

"I haven't heard from her, but I think I know where she is" I said with anxiousness in my throat.

"There was a shadow" my voice quickly cut off from another.

"Why should we heed the ramblings of someone who can't even guard her own sister?"

The accusation slithered through my mind like a venomous snake. My hands curled into fists as heat scorched my cheeks. Every eye felt like a blade, slicing through my trembling resolve. I raised my chin, fighting back tears and rage both.

"You think I failed?" My voice cracked, louder than I intended.

A thunderous crack filled my skull, pain exploding behind my eyes. My fingers clawed into my temples as I sank to my knees, body trembling. Tears carved hot rivers down my cheeks—shame, fear, desperation all bleeding together. I forced my gaze upward, blurred torches casting long shadows over my sister's faces: some twisted in judgment, others frozen by fear.

Then she appeared. From the far corner of the ruined parlor, a silhouette in midnight black glided forward. Her coat was cut of the finest cloth—sleek and severe—with a dramatic flare at the waist. A broad-brimmed hat, crowned with a single raven feather, hid most of her face in shadow, yet I could catch the glint of her eyes beneath its brim. White fox fur draped around her shoulders, stark against the darkness of her ensemble, and her slender arms were encased in elbow-length satin gloves. Each step she took was measured, the soft swish of her skirt the only sound against the crackling hearth.

Every breath felt impossible as my sisters parted, creating a corridor of stunned silence. My pounding head stilled for a fraction of a second as her gaze swept the room—calm, unyielding, and somehow ancient.

Even in agony, I sensed the shift in the air: this woman wore authority as easily as her mourning-black finery, and in that moment, I knew she alone held the power to decide my fate.

I staggered as my vision blurred—an echo of that shadow at Maeva's door. A searing headache pounded behind my eyes, each pulse drowning out my thoughts.

Then I saw them: the cloaked woman in black and, beside her, that impossible man—Elias—slipping past my wards as though they were nothing. Fury and fear tangled in my chest, but the pain was too fierce to think.

Suddenly, my sisters in the coven closed in, their whispered incantations drifting on the stale air. They grasped each other's wrists, forming a ring around me—hands pressing into my shoulders, binding me in their silent ritual. Their eyes were cold with conviction. My heart thundered: they meant to destroy me here and now.

I slammed both hands together in a forceful clap. A blast of orange wildfire surged from my core, shattering their circle. My magic erupted, hurling them backward—women and man alike—to sprawl across the dust-choked room. Pain receded enough for adrenaline to take hold.

I scrambled up and bolted for the door, each step fueled by raw terror. Barely three yards from the threshold, a jagged force hurled me to the ground. Elias's hand closed around my throat, lifting me off my feet. His eyes were voids of darkness as his fingers tightened, stealing my breath.

Panic flared. My fingers clawed at his wrist. But his grip was iron, his intent clear: he would break me here, in front of the coven.

My lungs screamed for air as his grip tightened fingers like iron bands crushing my throat. My vision blurred at the edges, dark spots pulsing like warning lights. I thrashed, heels clawing at the empty air, but gravity pulled me down.

His jaw yawned wider—a hellish canyon lined with gleaming ivory spikes. Saliva dripped in slow-motion beads, each one a promise of pain. My heart thundered so loud I thought he'd hear it, each beat echoing against my ribs. My panting breaths rattled in my ears like a storm.

Fear exploded through my veins, a wildfire of terror scorching every nerve. Sweat stung my eyes as the shadow of his fangs loomed ever closer. My hands shook uncontrollably as I slammed my palms into his shoulders, bracing for impact, for any break in this nightmare. Every instinct screamed, "fight, run, anything but this.

His growl deepened, primal and hungry, as the world narrowed to the harsh rasp of his breath and the glitter of those impossible teeth. I was drowning, suffocating in panic, clinging to the flimsiest hope that somehow, some way, I could wrench free.

I squeezed my eyes shut and channeled every ounce of panic into my palms, pressing them harder against his scorching flesh. His ragged breath whipped across my neck, each exhale a hot, fetid gust that made me gasp. I thought I would black out as his fangs hovered millimeters from my throat, but then—he hesitated.

Opening my eyes, I saw confusion flash across his twisted features. Before he could recover, my hands surged with searing heat. Red-hot flames roared beneath my skin, burning through his cursed hide in blistering handprints. He howled—a sound so raw it rattled my bones— and flung me aside like a ragdoll.

I hit the ground hard, pain blossoming in my tailbone, but I barely registered it. Above me, his monstrous cry ripped through the night, an inhuman bell toll that scattered ravens from the treetops. He clawed at his arms, blackened skin peeling away in charred ribbons. The stench of burning flesh choked the air as he staggered back toward the wrecked cottage, smoke trailing from his shoulders in ragged plumes.

My chest heaved, lungs burning as I struggled upright. The forest fell silent around me, broken only by the echo of his agony. My heart pounded like a war drum—fear and exhilaration coursing through my veins: I had survived.

"Rebecca!" the monster yelled out in agony.

My heart pounded as I made it to the safety of my car, I wrenched the wheel left, tires gouging deep ruts into the gravel. The roar of the engine was a lifeline, drowning out the ragged breaths I'd barely managed when he had me in his claws.

I needed to get to Maeva.

My legs trembled as I lifted my foot from the brake and slammed it down again—iron fused against iron as the gates buckled beneath my car's momentum. Sparks spat out in angry showers, showering the courtyard in molten diamonds.

I yanked the wheel around and skidded over the scattering stones, kicking up a roiling cloud of dust and gravel that stung my cheeks. The manor's massive doors loomed before me like a promise of sanctuary. Two silhouettes carved from nightmares waited for me as I arrived.

The first was Mistress Abigail, small but impossibly fierce, her beautiful hair swept into an austere bun beneath a cage of black iron filigree. Her slate green eyes blazed with predator's focus; long, lacquered nails curled into talons, ready to riddle my body with pain.

Beside her stood Daniel, his frame now monstrous fangs bared into a razor grin, his eyes molten onyx. The air around him crackled with dark magic, tendrils of shadow flicking at the edges of his jaw.

My breath came ragged as I ground the car to a halt, door flying open. Every instinct begged me to bolt—but my legs refused. I was pinned between the shattered gates and two of the deadliest monsters I'd ever faced. The gravel at my feet rattled with the echoes of those who'd hunted me here before, and I realized: there would be no easy escape this time. The roar of my engine faded, leaving only the pulse of my own fear—and the promise of their inevitable strike.

I eased out of the driver's seat, one foot finding purchase on the gravel. My chest tightened as I straightened, eyes locked on the two figures flanking the shattered gates. Every instinct screamed to run, but I planted my feet and squared my shoulders. If they wanted a fight, they'd find me ready.

"I'm looking for Maeva Sinclair," I said, voice steady despite the tremor in my limbs. "I know she's here. I won't hurt anyone—unless I have to."

My palms flickered with orange firelight, sparks dancing along my fingertips. The Raven sigil on my ring finger burned into life, a promise, and a warning in one.

Mistress Abigail's lips curved in a slow, cold smile. "She's in no danger."

Anger flared through me, heat spiking in my veins. "Funny," I spat, "one of you tried to rip my throat out—some "Rebecca" and her pet vampire." My laugh was brittle.

At my words, the man—Daniel—stilled. His eyes widened, disbelief flashing in their depths. He glanced over at Abigail, but her face gave no emotion; confusion etched into his chiseled features.

"She's been dead for centuries" he said slowly.

"Then she's haunted me real good," I shot back, stepping forward, the gravel crunching beneath my boots. "And your…whatever he was— he left his mark." I lifted my arms to show my neck. "Now give me my friend, or I'll level this entire place."

The air between us crackled as my hands pulsed with raw power. Tiny embers leapt from my fingertips, gathering into a fierce glow. My heart hammered against my ribs, each beat fueling the fire in my veins.

They stood frozen, Abigail's fur-trimmed coat rustling in the night breeze, Daniel's jaws clenched beneath that lordly mask. The night stood silent, heavy with anticipation.

Their eyes locked onto my glowing brand—mine isn't inscribed like hers, but it's unmistakably Raven.

Silence stretched between us until Abigail finally spoke "I'll fetch her," she said, voice soft but unyielding.

I nodded once and dropped my hands to my hips, waiting. Daniel watched her leave, his brow furrowed as if a question burned his lips. My patience snapped.

"Say it," I demanded.

He exhaled, searching for my face. "If Rebecca truly walks, I've never sensed her. She's… elusive."

I rolled my eyes. "You want to drink my blood?" I snapped, tone sharp. "Like the other?"

Daniel shook his head. "Just a small cut. I need to see if you're telling the truth."

I laughed—harsh, bitter. "You really are cursed, aren't you? Meridith poisoned your line good."

His expression flickered with annoyance, proof enough I'd spoken the truth. I didn't soften, though. This wasn't the time for mercy.

Moments later, the heavy iron door groaned open, and Abigail reappeared, guiding Maeva through the gloom. Relief flooded me—at least she wasn't gone for good. But as Maeva stepped into the torchlight, trembling and wide-eyed, the weight of everything to come settled on my shoulders.

My arms trembled as I held her, the gravel crunching beneath us a distant echo compared to the pounding of my heart. When her sobs finally slowed, I felt the last of my tension melt away in a rush of relief so deep it felt like my bones were sighing.

I leaned back just enough to look into her eyes—still red-rimmed but softer now—and let out a shaky laugh, half sob, half exhale.

"You're okay," I murmured, my voice cracking.

The weight of days spent worrying, the nightmares of what might've happened, all drained out of me in that single moment.

Her arms tightened around me again, and I let myself relax completely for the first time in what felt like forever. The knot in my chest unraveled, leaving me achingly grateful, overwhelmed by the simple, astonishing fact that she was here, alive, and safe.

"Are you okay?" I whispered, pulling her tighter as relief buzzed through me.

"I'm better now," she replied into my neck, her voice trembling like a fragile leaf in a storm. "What are you doing here?"

I straightened and searched her eyes. "Bitch, you have no idea what kind of mess you're in," I said, voice low but urgent, gripping her shoulders.

Before she could answer, a brutal shove knocked me backward. The ground rushed up to meet us both, and we landed hard—faces smashing into gravel, shards biting into our skin. The wind was knocked clean out of my lungs; my ribs thundered with impact. Maeva's gasp was muffled by the crunch of stones beneath her cheek.

For a split second, everything went white: the roar of blood in my ears, the sting of pain radiating from my side, and the cold shock of earth against my face.

Then I felt Maeva's hand clutch my arm, grounding me. Her heartbeat fluttered against my palm—still alive, still fighting.

I rolled onto my back, coughing as I fought to catch my breath after the blast. Maeva lay beside me, her body trembling from the impact, but she forced herself up onto her hands. Before we could steady ourselves, another strike slammed into my face and drove Maeva into the manor's cold stone wall, sending us both sprawling across the hard floor.

I hit the stone with a sickening thud—my skull planting a bloody kiss on the rock. Warm blood trickled into my hairline and streamed down my cheeks. Maeva lay motionless in the gravel, her chest rising and falling so faintly I could barely tell she was alive. Fear and relief warred in my chest: relief that she wasn't gone, terror that she might be. I scrambled to her side, heart hammering as I pressed my hand to her neck, searching for a pulse.

"Maeva!" I whispered, the panic strangling my voice.

I dropped to one knee beside her, gripping Maeva's wrist for a pulse. When she didn't stir, panic ignited in my chest.

"Maeva!" I screamed.

No answer.

I forced myself upright—and froze. Emerging from the tree line, illuminated by torchlight, were my sisters—each bearing the Raven brand—and behind them, Elias, and his monstrous lieutenant. Gravel crunched under their deliberate approach.

I squared my shoulders and raised my hands, palms glowing with orange magic. The air crackled as power gathered at my fingertips.

They fanned out around us, glowing hands at the ready, betrayal burning behind their eyes.

I took a full breath. "You won't touch her," I warned, voice trembling with both fear and fury. "I promised to protect her—and I will."

The woman in black stepped forward, magic flickering like flames in her palms. My coven—my sisters—stood poised to strike. But as their wards glowed, I realized: I was the only Raven that stood against them.

Warm blood still trailed down my temple, each throb of pain a reminder of how close I'd been to losing her. I swallowed back a sob—I wasn't the strongest witch, but I was Maeva's only hope.

"You're nothing to me—or this coven!" Rebecca's voice sliced through the tension. Her palms flared crimson, glittering sparks dancing between her fingers.

I stood my ground, chest heaving.

"Does our sisterhood mean nothing?" I screamed, thrusting my hand forward to flash the Raven brand on my finger—our shared blood oath. Across the circle, my sisters' faces remained stone-cold, their hands mirroring Rebecca's readiness to strike.

"It means you belong to me," Rebecca hissed. Her fist clenched, and I felt my magic drain away—the world went black around the edges, the ground rushing up to meet me.

"Maeva!" I gasped as I crumpled.

Her eyes snapped open, panic and something fiercer igniting in their depths. She lunged forward, wrapping me in a desperate embrace.

I clutched at her chains, summoning the last of my strength. I forced my hand against the cool iron cuffs.

Heat blazed from my palms, red-hot magic eating through the sigils. The iron glowed and warped, melting into a molten pool at our feet. A hiss of steam rose, and for the first time, I felt the full force of Maeva's power surging beside my own.

She was free.

The instant the last cuff melted away in a hiss of steam, Maeva inhaled sharply—her lungs flooding with a freedom they'd never known. I knelt beside her, heart pounding, as she flexed her newly liberated wrists and rose to stand at my side.

Moonlight caught the Raven sigil on her finger, igniting it in brilliant blue. Tiny arcs of electricity danced along her skin, crackling like distant thunder. Her eyes blazed electric, pupils alight with power and purpose. Relief washed over her features—softened relief that hardened in determination the moment she met the coven's stunned gazes.

One by one, the women recoiled mouths agape, eyes wide with disbelief. Rebecca, ever the picture of twisted elegance, let her fur-trimmed cloak slide from her shoulders and tossed her ornate hat to the floor. Hat and fur pooled at her feet, a silent concession to the raw force Maeva now embodied.

Maeva stepped forward, the ground beneath her seeming to tremble in anticipation. Her shoulders squared, her stance unshakable, she held the coven's attention—and mine—with the promise that nothing, no ancient curse nor iron shackles, would ever bind her again.

Chapter Twenty-Two

Maeva Sinclair

I hovered over Lori's crumpled form, her once-radiant skin paling to lifeless gray. My heart twisted in agony—every ragged breath she drew felt like a wound to my soul.

Around us, the courtyard's cold torchlight flickered against the gaping faces of Elias, Rebecca, and the others—but all I saw was the friend I'd failed, slipping away under my watch.

The weight of helplessness pressed down on me, each second stretching into unbearable sorrow. Rage began to creep up my spine, fists clenching the gravel underfoot as waves of grief crashed through me. Every instinct screamed to lash out at the monsters who'd stolen her life.

Elias and Rebecca stood opposite me in the courtyard, flanked by a ring of other witch-women. Sparks flickered between my trembling fingers, each one a flash of righteous fury—until I saw Rebecca's cruel laughter at Lori's fallen form and something hollowed out inside me.

I staggered forward, the urge to destroy them burning like acid in my veins, but Daniel's broad hand closed over my abdomen, another on the small of my back, gently but firmly anchoring me in place. His touch was a lifeline, a reminder that even as my power roared beneath my skin, I was not beyond compassion—or beyond grief for what I'd almost forgotten, my own humanity.

Daniel's breath ghosted against my ear. "Don't."

His single-word plea cut through my storm of rage like a life vest. I tore my gaze from Elias—who stood across the courtyard sneering, his crooked fangs bared in savage delight—and looked back at Daniel. Blue sparks still crackled along my fingertips, thunder rolling in my chest, but his steady, worried eyes held me. Carefully, he lowered his hands from my sides and retreated a step, as if trusting me to choose my own fight.

I felt the full weight of my power—and the promise of what I could become if I unleashed it. Yet, looking at Daniel's quiet faith, I realized that even monsters deserve mercy. I stilled the lightning in my veins, letting the electricity fade into the night air.

Elias's cruel laughter echoed in my ears, but I stayed rooted beside my friend knowing that compassion, not wrath, would be the true measure of my magic tonight.

My magic flowed freely within my veins like a river of electricity. Her gentle hands caressed my skin, reminding me that she was with me.

Rebecca stepped forward, her fingers aflame with crimson light, the Raven sigil on her ringed hand pulsing in time with the thunder overhead. Above us, storm clouds churned over the manor, a conspiracy of midnight blue pierced by the moon's pale glare.

A shiver raced up my arms, as if my very veins were drenched in ice and fire at once. Magic roared beneath my skin—hot, restless, begging to break free. I stood my ground in the center of the gravel courtyard, heart hammering, breath caught in my throat.

She closed the distance with a mocking smile, red sparks dancing around her palms like hungry embers. Hatred flared inside me, bright as the moonlit sky, threatening to spill over. Yet I held myself taut, a wire strung too tight, refusing to feed her a show of fury. Let her revel in her cruel triumph—whatever happened next, would be on my terms.

I tightened my stance as Rebecca swept into view, hands on her hips, a cruel smirk playing on her lips.

"So, this is the great Meridith's descendant," she mocked, leaning in so close I felt her warmth. "The little witch who holds the last key to the lock."

She spun theatrically to face the assembled coven, arms raised in triumph, hurling barbs like firebrands. Insults danced from her tongue, but I didn't give her the satisfaction of a flinch. My gaze stayed fixed on hers—calm, unblinking, predatory.

When her performance finally stalled, she pivoted back to me, amusement draining from her face. She was only a few inches taller, yet her vaunted confidence wavered under my stare.

From behind her, Elias stepped forward, sliding his arm around Rebecca's shoulders as if she were a trophy. His grin was sharp, all fang and triumph, as though capturing me were the crowning achievement of his immortal life.

His scent—once intoxicating—now reeked of rot and decay. Elias's hand slithered possessively around Rebecca's waist, staking his claim while I watched, stomach knotting.

They stood like royalty: the perfect Queen and King, basking in the adoration of their court. Fury ignited in me, fierce and white-hot. Elias's eyes flicked toward me, a challenge, but I held him with my own unyielding gaze. He tensed, lips curling in annoyance clearly unused to being ignored—and for the first time, I felt free of his manipulations.

All my attention centered on Rebecca. Sparks danced across my palms, lighting my skin with electric promise. In that moment, she wasn't just Meridith's betrayer or a pawn of this cursed lineage—she was my target, the one I needed to stop. And nothing, not even the King at her side, would deter me.

I stiffened as Rebecca's breath ghosted across my ear.

"You think you're the only one who can unravel a mystery, baby witch?" Her lips curved into a knowing smirk. "From one old witch to a new one, when you claim a coven, you inherit its magic."

She pivoted, sweeping her arm toward the circle of women. Their faces were pale, hollow—far fewer than any coven of legend should number. Each held up a hand, the Raven mark blazing on their fingers, magic crackling at their fingertips like coiled lightning.

Each one bared the mark of Raven Coven on their finger matching Rebecca's. All their hands brightly lit with magic, waiting for an order. I tilted my neck to Rebecca in confusion. My mind dissected her words.

A chill rippled through me as Rebecca's words sank in:

"Magic equals life, and I have lived a very long time."

Her voice curled around my thoughts like a serpent, and suddenly everything clicked. The odd uniformity of her coven's mark—so unlike my own—wasn't a fluke. It was her design.

She'd murdered the other Raven women one by one, draining their magic to bind herself and Elias to life beyond mortal years. In the aftermath of Meridith's death, Rebecca had seized the mantle of elder, her bloodstained path clearing the way to unimaginable power—and near immortality.

I staggered back, the moonlight catching the cold gleam in her eyes. She had not only usurped Meridith's place but had twisted our very sisterhood into her personal fountain of youth. And now, every endangered heartbeat in this courtyard beat at the mercy of her own cursed ambition.

The realization settled over me like a frost: to save myself—and to save what was left of the true Raven line—I would have to confront Rebecca's centuries-old treachery head-on.

The truth ignited something fierce in my chest, the righteous fury of a thousand betrayed sisters. I barely registered the tears burning at my eyelids as I thrust both palms forward.

A surge of cobalt magic—Meridith's bloodline roaring through me—erupted in twin waves. Elias and Rebecca were torn from their feet, hurling skyward like rag dolls caught in a storm. Their bodies slammed into the gravel below with bone-crushing force, sending plumes of dirt and broken rock swirling into a choking barrier around them.

Elias staggered up first, as unshakable as the curse that bound him, muscles coiled to strike. Rebecca scrambled upright next, the moonlight revealing dirt-cake silk and tangled hair. Her eyes blazed with fury—and fear.

Beyond them, the false Ravens closed ranks, hands ignited in angry ruby light, palms aimed squarely at me. Their magic trembled in the night air, electric and menacing.

But I would not yield. I stood shoulder-to-shoulder with Rebecca—my heart no longer hollow but burning with the legacy of every sister lost to Rebecca's lust for power.

The gathered witches' palms shimmered with pinpricks of light—emerald sparks dancing atop a torrent of barely contained magic. It piled behind them like water against a dam, every heartbeat swelling the pressure.

My glare swept the circle of faces: blank, unreadable masks. Not one showed the flicker of doubt or compassion I'd hoped for. They were empty vessels brimming with power—and poised to unleash it.

Then a crushing pulse of energy rocked me like a tempest, slamming into my chest with the force of a landslide. Air whooshed from my lungs in a ragged gasp as I was flung backward into Daniel's arms. His broad shoulders caught me, the rough weave of his coat biting into my ribs, but his strength saved me from the hard ground. I hit the packed gravel with a jarring thud, stones skittering beneath me, and pain exploded along my side in searing bursts.

Daniel's eyes—wide and frantic—hovered over me, his breath misting in the cold night air. For a fleeting second, I saw his fear, before I wrenched free of his support. Each movement felt like dragging splinters through my bones, but adrenaline roared in my veins, sharpening every sense: the metallic tang of blood in my mouth, the hiss of magic crackling around us, the distant whisper of wind through skeletal trees.

I forced myself to my feet, legs trembling like saplings in a storm. My chest heaved, sweat chilling on my skin even as my heart thundered. Then—a gentle warmth, like a soft hand pressed to my shoulder. My eyes fluttered closed against the pain, and in that stillness, a delicate reassurance bloomed in my chest. It steadied me, reminded me I was not alone in this fight.

When I reopened my eyes, Rebecca was already there, arms raised. She conjured a sphere of raw power: a bleeding-red orb veined with silver sparks, hovering before her like a heart about to burst. The heat of it rippled through the air, distorting the torchlight around us. My hands instinctively ignited, bright blue flares dancing across my skin as I squared off—ready to meet her fury head-on.

I dropped to one knee and drove my fist into the gravelly earth. My knuckles split on the jagged stones with a crack, and in an instant the ground buckled under my command. A surging wall of dirt, pebbles, and fractured rock burst outward like a miniature landslide, obliterating Rebecca's crimson orb before it could form.

Around me, the remaining coven raised their hands in unison— palms up, fingers trembling with magic. Their wards flared to life, bristling like invisible shields, halting the earthen deluge inches from their faces. Gravel spat upward in a frozen arc, then settled in the deep cracks I'd carved into the courtyard—a spiderweb of fractures leading straight to them.

Rebecca's lips curled into a slow, triumphant smile. She crouched low, fingertips skimming the gravel as though coaxing music from stone.

"Not bad for a new witch," she purred, her voice velvet dark.

A tremor ran through the pebbles at her touch. I swore the ground breathed beneath us. Then, before I could blink, darkness pooled around her feet—an oily black mist that oozed outward like ink dropped in water. It thickened into a shapeless shadow, rippling and pulsing until it slithered free of the earth.

A surge of dread knotted in my chest. My heart pounded so violently I thought my ribs would fracture. The shadow—no more than living night—flowed toward me in slow, deliberate waves. I raised my fists, sparks of magic crackling along my knuckles, but doubt clawed at my mind. What if I'm not strong enough?

The creature halted mere inches away, coiling upward like a serpent poised to strike. Its formless head loomed before me, eyes—if they could be called that—voids of absolute black. A scream clawed up my throat, but I swallowed it. Panic burned at my temples, sweat slicked my skin, and the world narrowed to that dancing shadow and my own ragged breath.

I felt every failure; every moment I'd doubted my magic rush in— was this the end? Yet even as terror threatened to swallow me, a spark of defiance flared. Claws of fear still raked at my spirit, but I would not let them win. I squared my shoulders, every nerve blazing with raw, desperate resolve, and braced to fight a darkness that seemed more ancient than time itself.

I staggered backward as the world wavered through the formless vortex of shadow. It reared up, its inky tendrils rippling like dark water— yet through its body I could still make out the manor's stone and the courtyard trees, warped by its presence.

Fear locked my legs in place, and when it struck my chest, I flew backward, slamming against the cold wall.

My knees buckled under their weight; air evacuated my lungs in a brutal whoosh. I tasted copper on my tongue as stars danced at the edges of my vision. My back ached, bruised and raw from the impact. A crushing heaviness threatened to drag me under—every muscle trembling, every breath felt borrowed. The cruel gravity of defeat weighed on me: I wasn't ready, my power was still raw, unshaped, and I wondered if I'd ever stand again.

Tears pricked my eyes as hopelessness pooled in my chest. But then—a finger, delicate yet insistent—pressed into my arm.

Lori's voice was a ragged whisper: "Light."

Summoning all I had left, I planted my hands into the gravel, shards biting into my palms. Through the haze of pain, I forced myself upright, willing my spine to straighten. My palms rose, shaking but determined, toward the dark sky. The shadow quivered and advanced once more, close I could feel its chill—but this time I met it head-on, heart hammering, ready to ignite the darkness with my own.

I traced slow circles in the air, summoning every ounce of will I had. The courtyard answered: wind shrieked to life, whipping leaves and kicked-up gravel into a dizzying vortex. The ancient oaks groaned as their roots strained against the gale. Above us, ink-black clouds boiled in like a tide, thunder drumming a furious cadence across the sky.

My palms crackled with raw electricity, tiny arcs dancing along my fingertips. Lightning split the heavens—a searing white slash that gilded the manor's stones for a heartbeat before vanishing, plunging us back into shadow. The next flash revealed only one thing: the shadow-creature recoiled, its form flickering like a dying flame.

Then it lunged. But before it could reach me, the sky answered my command: another bolt—brighter, closer—struck the inky mass. With a sound like shattering glass it dissolved into mist, sinking into the earth from which it had come.

I lowered my arms and let the dying crackle in my veins fade. Standing tall, I met Rebecca's furious glare with bright blue eyes charged by the storm. Her lips twisted in rage—her own darkness had just been drowned by my lightning.

"Anything else before I end this?" I bellowed, chest heaving with defiance.

Rebecca's eyes blazed with fury. She balled her fists at her sides—and then, one by one, the coven collapsed.

First their knees buckled with hollow thuds, then their spines straightened, heads thrown back, and they crumpled onto the cold earth like discarded dolls. Their glowing palms dimmed as she siphoned their magic away.

I took a reflexive step forward, horror rooting me in place. Each fallen witch lay motionless, drained of every spark of power. At Rebecca's side, Elias laughed—a low, predatory chuckle. He moved in a blur, snatching a body from the ground. His jaw unhinged grotesquely, ivory fangs sinking into her neck. Blood sprayed as he drank, ruby rivulets tracing his lips.

Beside him Abigail didn't hesitate. She seized another victim, ripping her throat with a savage rip. Warm liquid gurgled down her chin. The scent of iron and fear filled the air.

I glanced at Daniel. He stood rigid, eyes flicking between us and that horrific feast. I saw the battle raging behind his gaze—hunger clawing at his restraint. His jaw worked; a single tremor of desire ran through him, but he fought it back, every muscle clenched against the pull of his dark family's violence.

In that moment, the full horror of the curse revealed itself: a hunger so primal it eclipsed even the thirst for blood and power.

My gaze found Daniel's. He gave me a barely perceptible nod—his only way of reassuring me that he would not give in to the madness around us. In that small gesture, warmth kindled in my chest: a fragile ember of hope that he truly meant it.

I tore my eyes away from him and watched as the courtyard became a slaughterhouse. Each ravenous mouth sloshed through the mud—once rich earth, now stained a rotting crimson—like starved beasts tearing at carrion.

Rebecca stood apart, her lips curving into a smile of triumph. She didn't even glance at the carnage; she was too proud of the monsters, of her accomplices. Her eyes locked on mine, cold and self-satisfied, as though this tableau of violence were the proof of her genius.

My mind raced, flipping through the fragments of Meridith's grimoire I had memorized—any incantation, any clue that might end this atrocity. But the pages blurred in my thoughts, offering only empty riddles.

A sickening crack cut through my panic. I spun toward Daniel and saw it before I could process anything else: a great, gnarled root—dark as fresh blood—had burst from his chest and pinned him against the earth like some twisted totem. Mud and blood dripped from its tip. His eyes, wide with betrayal and agony, locked onto mine as he sagged to the ground, the life draining from him in ragged gasps.

My mouth fell open in horror. A scream caught in my throat and died there as I stumbled backward, eyes locked on the root impaling Daniel.

From behind him, Elias emerged—his hands caked in dark mud and sticky crimson. He stepped over his brother's lifeless body with the slow, deliberate grace of a predator. With each footfall, my heart pounded against my ribs like a trapped bird. I lurched back into Lori's trembling form; she clung to me, her own strength all but spent.

Abigail flanked Elias on his other side, her small frame lit eerily by the torches' flicker. Both she and Elias wore expressions of perverse triumph, their white teeth bared in wicked smiles. Dried blood crusted at their lips; flecks of flesh caught between their teeth—trophies of the innocent women they had devoured.

Beside Abigail lay a pair of iron cuffs etched with warding sigils— ready to bind me, to strip away every ounce of power I still possessed. I realized, with a pit of dread in my stomach, that I stood utterly alone and outmatched. Three monsters advanced, and I had nowhere left to run.

"I don't know how to break the curse," I croaked, voice hollow against the carnage around us. Every ounce of strength had drained from me—my limbs trembled, my heart pounded in my ears, and Daniel's lifeless form lay just feet away, a brutal reminder of my failure.

A sudden rustle split the night. Rebecca stepped forward, gliding between Elias and Abigail as though parting a curtain. Her lips curled into a victorious smile.

"I don't want to break it," she purred, eyes glinting with cruel satisfaction.

"I can't lift the curse outright—but I can adjust it to suit my needs."

I pressed my shaking hands to the gravel, fingertips digging into cold stones. The world felt impossibly heavy, my chest tight with grief for Daniel. Warm tears stung my eyes as I fought to control my voice.

"Adjust it?" I managed to make each syllable rasping like broken glass.

"Yes," Rebecca said, stepping closer—her presence a shadow that seemed to swallow the moonlight. "All I ask is for you to swear fealty to me as your true leader and grant me Meridith's power. I need only the immortality the curse grants."

A fresh wave of despair crashed over me. My shoulders slumped— how could I bargain with this witch, when her demand meant betraying everything I believed? And yet, here I was nakedly vulnerable, cursed by blood and bound to a fate I didn't understand.

I closed my eyes against the horror in Daniel's still face, a single thought twisting in my chest: perhaps I too had been a pawn in someone else's game, just like Meridith. And now, faced with impossible choices, I lay broken at Rebecca's feet—ready to swear allegiance, or watch the last hope I had bleed away.

"Meridith was a scorned woman—hurt, betrayed," Rebecca breathed, amusement slipping into her voice. "But in the end, I won. Not her."

"You killed your own family" I whispered, barely able to meet their eyes.

She laughed—a cold, mirthless sound. "aw, how cute" she sneered, nodding at Elias and Abigail, whose stony expressions gave no hint of remorse.

My world tilted and I felt the earth yawning beneath me, ready to swallow me whole. Anguish tore at my chest—for the fallen women, for Daniel. I wanted nothing more than to curl into a fetal ball and disappear forever. How could I, with all this power coursing through my veins, feel so utterly defeated? I'd let my guard down, trusted Elias, and now I was trapped in the wake of his corrupt ambition.

Even as shame and grief threatened to crush me, I felt ancestral fire ignite in my blood. I reminded myself: I am a Raven witch. Meridith's legacy runs in my veins. I would not die here, curled on cold gravel, while these living corpses claimed eternity with their brutality.

I forced my feet under me and rose, shaking off despair like a cloak. My limbs trembled, but my gaze locked on the cursed trio before me— Rebecca's cruel smile, Elias's predatory leer, Abigail's silent complicity. A spark of defiance flared in my heart.

For fuck's sake, I thought, if I can curse others, then I can damn well fight back. I may be bruised, bloodied, and terrified—but I am not broken. Raven witch or not, I refuse to lie here and let them win. I'd spent my whole life shackled by fear—every waking moment a tightrope walk over the abyss of my own anxiety.

But now, as I rose to face them, I felt a strange calm settle in my bones. I straightened my spine, lifted my chin, and let the thunder outside answer the furious storm roiling inside me. My fingers tingled, then flared cobalt blue, the electric warmth snaking up my arms like a molten river breaking through its banks.

Around us, the sky shuddered in sympathy: low clouds boiled across the moon, and distant thunder boomed like a war drum. Rebecca's cruel smile faltered as her crimson glow dimmed against the growing pulse of my power. Elias and Abigail staggered back, claws and fangs bared, their eyes black as empty wells—yet even they sensed the shift.

With a swift twist of my wrists, I shattered the night's silence. The ground trembled as long, gnarled roots—rich brown, studded with clinging earth—shot from the soil, wrapping themselves around their ankles like living chains. Elias gnashed his teeth in fury; Abigail's claws scraped uselessly against damp clay. But the roots only tightened, feeding on the raw magic thrumming beneath my skin.

In that moment, I was not the frightened girl I'd always been—I was the heir of the Raven Coven, and the storm I'd summoned would not be denied.

Roots writhed up their limbs like living serpents, coiling tightly around legs first, then clutching wrists and forearms. Elias and Abigail thrashed wildly—claws scraping despairing arcs through the air—but each frantic movement only made the bindings squeeze harder.

From a cracked fissure in the courtyard, a thick root shot out, wrapping around Rebecca's ankles. With a deafening thud, her slender form tumbled across gravel, sending pebbles and dusty leaves swirling skyward. She screamed, black-gloved hands flaying at the undergrowth as more roots slithered from the earth, dragging her blood-streaked figure deeper into the forest's shadows.

Abigail's guttural roar echoed as colossal tendrils hoisted her off the ground, hoarding her struggling weight like a trophy before spiriting her behind the trees. The underbrush swallowed her growls, leaving only faint rustles as the roots pinioned her fast.

Only Elias remained. I beckoned the roots back with a slow, deliberate flick of my wrists. They surged forward, coalesced around him in a living cage. Inches from his snarling face, I let a smirk curve my lips. In my eyes, bolts of electric blue lightning danced and fractured—each flash mirrored in his dark pupils like a warning.

Then, with a single, powerful motion, I flung the root-bound curse into the forest's edge. He landed among the gnarled roots and moss, limbs splayed and bound, his rage as hopeless as the wind's whisper in the trees.

I sprinted to Daniel's side, my heart hammering in my ears. Kneeling, I thrust both palms into the soft earth and willed the roots to obey—felt them loosen and slither free from the remnant still buried in his chest. In one swift, sickening pull, the root slid out, leaving behind a ragged tunnel of torn flesh.

Blood gushed from the wound in a furious spray, hot and metallic, drenching my hands within seconds. I clamped my small palms over the gash, pressing with everything I had to staunch the torrent. His ribs creaked beneath my grip as crimson welled between my fingers, pooling onto cracked stone and muddied gravel. Daniel lay limp, eyes half-lidded, breathing ragged whispers. My own pulse thundered as panic clawed its way up my throat—if I didn't act, he would bleed out here in the cold moonlight.

"Shit Daniel" I said frantically.

I cradled his head in my lap. Gently, I tapped his temple—once, twice—calling his name into the night's hush. He lay impossibly still, pale as marble despite the life I knew roiled within him. Immortality or no, I couldn't shake the terror that this wound might finally beat him.

Tears blurred my vision as hot sorrow pooled in my chest. I brushed a trembling hand through his hair, the softness of each strand a cruel reminder of all I stood to lose.

"Daniel, please," I whispered, my voice ragged with fear and regret. The words felt hollow against the pounding of my heart—each beat crying out his name.

Hope felt fragile, slipping like sand through my grasp, but I refused to let it go. Even as the weight of despair threatened to crush me, I held tight to that single, desperate promise: I would not let him slip away. Not tonight. Not ever.

Lori's voice trembled as she knelt by our side. "He needs your magic," she croaked, each word a ragged whisper against the night's stillness.

My shoulders shook with fresh sobs. "I don't know how—"

Her cold fingers reached for mine, curling around my wrist with surprising strength. With gentle urgency, she lifted my hand and pressed it to Daniel's blood-slick lips. "Your magic," she rasped, "give him yours."

I froze, tears trailing down my cheeks as I looked from Lori's haunted eyes to Daniel's still face. The weight of the moment crushed me—my best friend, this cursed man, lying broken. My chest tightened with grief and guilt. Could I drain myself to save him? Was I willing to pay that price?

Lori's grip tightened, beckoning me forward. The ragged rise and fall of her breathing stuttered with effort, as if each heartbeat were a battle.

"Now," she urged.

Shaking, bright sparks flickered at my fingertips, tiny embers of life desperate to pour into him. Lori's eyes closed in concentration, her hand steadying mine. In that fractured moment, under the torchlight's flicker and the chill of the night, all I knew was that I would give everything I had to bring him back.

And so, trembling, I willed my magic—heart and hope—to flow from me into him, praying it would be enough.

I knelt beside him, heart hammering as I took in the sight of his pale, blood-speckled face—every detail seared into my memory. A fierce warmth bloomed in my chest, a wild hope I didn't know still lived in me. He was as broken as I was, and I needed him alive as badly as he needed my magic

Trembling, I eased his jaw open, my breath catching at the glint of those marble-white canines. They looked more like weapons than teeth—long, razor-sharp fangs that sent a fresh tide of fear tumbling through me. My gut screamed at me to pull back, but my heart pounded louder, demanding I try.

I pressed a fingertip against one fang, coaxing it forward, until its tip hovered just above my wrist. The torchlight danced across its surface like a mirror, and tiny beads of liquid gathered instantly—his venomous saliva, or perhaps my own blood already pooling. I knew it wouldn't be enough.

Steeling myself, I let go of his tooth and positioned his fang on my skin. A furious rush of pain flared as I forced that needle-tip into my wrist. For a frantic moment, I thought I'd torn apart my own veins. Then, warm blood welled up and dripped straight into his open mouth, a crimson tide washing over his fangs. It poured down his throat in steady leaks, and I held my breath, willing him to live.

Silence stretched—until, finally, his chest rose. I pressed my hand to his side, feeling life return in ragged breaths. Relief crashed through me, sharp as the wound on my arm, but sweeter than any victory. Despite every warning in my bones, I had saved him.

He hesitated for a heartbeat—those deep blue eyes heavy with regret—then closed the distance at last. His fingers brushed my knuckles, cool against the fever of my skin, and I let out a soft, unguarded breath. The brush of his touch sent warmth flooding back into my chest, knitting the ache into something fierce and tender all at once.

"Maeva," he rasped, voice thick with something I couldn't name—relief, guilt, hope—and in that moment he wasn't monster, nor captor, but the man whose life I had just saved. I saw him there, trembling over me like a guardian, and every doubt I'd ever held dissolved in the courtyard.

Lori melted away into the shadows, giving us space. Daniel guided my wounded arm gently to his shoulder, leaning close enough that I could feel his steady heartbeat beneath my palm. The pulse was slow, even— so achingly human.

"It's… it's okay," he whispered, as if afraid I might vanish.

I swallowed past the stick of blood in my throat, mustering a shaky smile. The rough fabric binding my wrist cut into me, but it felt sacred now—a symbol of the life that still ran through my veins.

"You're alive," I breathed, surprised at how soft my own voice sounded. "Because of you."

He pressed his forehead to mine then, that familiar warmth rising from his skin. In the hush between thunder and crackling flame, I let my eyes close, soaking in the safety of this single touch.

All around us, the wilderness waited, but here—beneath the ruined arch of the manor's torches—I felt something else blooming in the darkness: a fragile, terrifying, hopeful first step toward peace.

Lori's cough ripped through the stillness, her face flushing a fierce red as every ragged breath rattled her small frame. Fear knotted in my chest the moment she bent over me, her head cradled against my shoulder, as if seeking the last comfort only a friend could offer. I gathered her closer into my lap, rocking her gently, heart breaking at how frail she'd become.

Tears blurred my vision, hot with anger and sorrow. I threaded my fingers through her tangled hair and brushed it behind her ear, each stroke an aching plea for her not to slip away. Her eyes, once bright and full of mischief, now hovered between life and shadow. She turned her gaze to Daniel, and in that lingering look passed something profound—an unspoken promise I could not yet understand.

"Lori, please—no," I gasped, reaching for her trembling hand.

She pressed a cold palm against mine and managed to make a watery smile. "This is for you, Maeva," she whispered, voice ragged but unwavering.

My world spun. My best friend, my protector, is now offering herself to save me. Panic surged as I fought the truth I saw etched into her hollowed cheeks and the gray depths of her eyes—Rebecca's curse had already stolen so much from her.

"Why?" I cried, tears flooding down my face and soaking into her gown.

"To help you, fight" she breathed, voice nearly gone.

Above us, thunder rumbled like a tormenting drum. I surrendered to her choice, knowing arguing would only deepen the wound. Lori lifted her frail arm toward Daniel, whose face twisted with agonized hesitation. She nodded, fragile as a sparrow against the storm, and closed her eyes in trust.

He leaned down, his great hand cradling her wrist. Two ivory fangs slid from his lips—gentle, precise—and pierced her skin. Trembling, as her life's warmth welled and spilled into his mouth. Each crimson drop on his tongue was a betrayal of everything I loved and feared.

Lori met my gaze one last time—her lips curved in a sad, satisfied smile—before her body went limp. Daniel's head dipped, sorrow and guilt flooding his dark eyes as he drew into the life she so bravely gave. I wrapped my arms around her still form, shaking with grief and fury, the distant thunder echoing the storm in my soul.

Like a cork blasted from a bottle, a tidal wave of magic erupted from me, tearing into the night. Pain convulsed through my limbs, and I wept uncontrollably—sobbing into the dirt, my tears carving rivers of grief across my sodden shirt. Daniel's hand closed tightly around my arm, but I was beyond comfort; the world had shattered.

Another pulse of raw power hurled itself outward, slamming into his chest with the force of a freight train. He soared backward into the tree line, carried on my anguish-fueled blast. Behind me, the ancient stones of the manor groaned under the assault: hairline cracks spiderwebbed across its weathered walls, widening into gaping fissures.

As my grief poured out, each surge of magic fractured the fortress anew. Roof beams splintered and fell, walls buckled and collapsed, and the very earth trembled beneath my fury. Dust and rubble erupted skyward, blotting out the stars, as torches crashed to the ground in showers of sparks.

But amid the ruin, I felt the emptiness most keenly where Lori's gentle warmth had been. I closed my eyes on her sacrifice—her last, whispered blessing still echoing in my ear—and my chest ached with the hollow left behind. Every shattered stone, every shattered dream, bore her memory: the way she had offered her own life to save me, how her final breath had been for my future.

Only the moon remained unwavering, its pale light filtering through the ruins. The glow highlighted the crumbled stones that lay in heaps—a testament to broken curses and broken hearts.

Beyond the wreckage, the lake lay untouched, its silken surface reflecting that same silver moon, as if she alone bore witness to a friendship that death itself could not truly erase.

Chapter Twenty-Three

Maeva Sinclair

Daniel and I lowered Lori's makeshift cross of broken sticks into the damp earth by the moonlit lake. The stones covering her shallow grave were slick with dew and flecked in emerald moss—soothing to some, but to me they felt like a tomb of my own failures. I pressed my fingertips into the cold rock as every pulse of my blood burned with fury rather than peace.

Beside me, Daniel's shoulder brushed my arm. A flicker of warmth—a shared grief, perhaps—flared in my chest, only to be snuffed out by the bitter ache of betrayal. I straightened, glaring down at the fresh mound.

"What did you see?" I asked, my voice sharp as broken glass. I wouldn't look away from Lori's makeshift cross, tacked together with damp sticks and mossy stones.

Daniel's shoulders slumped. "She was part of the Raven coven since birth," he said quietly. "Assigned to keep an eye on you."

"You mean from you," I spat, turning my cheek so he couldn't read my expression. His gaze lingered there, heavy with something I couldn't name.

He swallowed and looked back at the grave. "She didn't know much—only what the elders told her. They asked about you every time, and always said you were in no danger."

I forced myself to study Lori's resting place again. The wind stirred the water behind us, sending ripples that distorted the moonlight. A hollow ache bloomed in my gut.

Those "reports" had come from the same coven that had fed Lori into that machine of blood and betrayal. My throat tightened.

Doubt coiled in the pit of my stomach, biting at me. I was part of something far larger than I'd ever imagined—and suddenly, I realized how little I actually knew.

My mind tried to piece together the puzzles of her curse and somehow all I could think of is that she wanted them to be imprisoned for eternity for a reason. Anger seeped up again; this time I couldn't catch it.

"You know, Rebecca said she was going to adjust the curse to her liking" my voice laced with suspicion.

I folded my arms, heart hammering. Daniel's shoulders sagged against the moonlit night.

"I never trusted Elias or Abigail to have my back," he confessed, his voice thick with regret. "Unfortunately, we're the only ones who live long enough to have to stay together."

My breath hitched. The truth in his tone cracked something open inside me—and yet only fueled my suspicion further.

"Loyalty to family…" I echoed, stepping closer. "Or loyalty to the curse?"

His expression froze; the wind hushed in response, and a nearby torch guttered as if recoiling. Magic thrummed through my veins—a low, insistent drumbeat warning me to question every syllable he spoke. I caught the ghost of a smirk at the corner of his mouth, a flicker that vanished too quickly to be innocent.

My skin prickled at the faint chill in his gaze, as though he were sizing me up rather than speaking from concern. Every nerve quivered with suspicion, each heartbeat echoing the doubt I tried to suppress. Though part of me still yearned to lean on him, I clenched my jaw and crossed my arms tightly over my chest, pressing my palms against my ribs to steady the tremor of uncertainty. My heart was guarded now, even if he secretly meant more to me than I dared admit.

We picked our way through the wreckage of the old fortress, stones and splintered beams jutting out at all angles. Daniel worked in grim silence, hoisting massive timbers as easily as if they were driftwood. I watched him move through the ruins—each muscle in his arms flexing under his coat, each breath controlled and purposeful—as he cleared a path deeper into the heart of the collapse.

I paused beside a partially intact wall, its jagged stones still clutching at one another despite everything that had fallen away around them. My legs trembled from the climb, and when I tried to haul myself up to sit on that rough seat, my arms shook too violently to support my weight. I bent my knees for a running start, lifted off with a hopeful thump—then felt strong hands wrap around my waist.

Warmth and steady strength carried me effortlessly onto the wall's narrow shelf. Heart pounding, I turned to meet his eyes—grateful, breathless, and a little afraid of how easily he could lift me into place.

Daniel stood so close I could feel the heat radiating off his body—and smell the faint tang of sweat clinging to his shirt. His dark hair, damp at the temples, fell forward across his forehead as he shifted, muscles barely flexing under the weight of my unconscious form. With a careful motion, he lowered me to the narrow ledge, then stepped back into the ruins.

I swallowed against the sudden rush of warmth in my cheeks—my pulse still thrumming from being carried—and forced myself to watch as he hunched over the rubble. For a long, tense moment, he seemed frozen in concentration, jaw clenched, fingers brushing through the dirt. Then, finally, his hand closed around something half-buried: a small wooden box glinting in the dappled moonlight. He lifted it into view, eyes dark with both relief and determination.

"What is it?" I spoke.

"Elias's box of secrets" his replied with a sound of relief.

I jumped down from the rubble and moved to stand beside him. He held a small wooden chest, its surface unmarred by the surrounding destruction—no chips or gouges from the falling stone. Intricate sigils were carved into the lid, their lines still crisp and glowing faintly in the moonlight. The chest looked almost untouched, a perfectly preserved secret amid the ruin.

"What's inside?" I said with curiosity.

"Meridith's grimoire and the cursed blade."

My eyes shot up to his at his words. I looked back down to the chest he was holding in his hands. My mind raced at the thought of the cursed blade.

"What do you mean, the cursed blade?" I said with tension in my voice.

"It is the blade that Meridith used to kill herself with. It was used to murder Elias's father and seems to be only thing that can kill us." He says coldly.

I thought you and your family were immortal—untouchable. Nothing about this adds up. The questions swirl in my mind.

"Why not use the blade on yourself, if you want to end the curse?" my curiosity peaked in my voice.

His face changed to a stern scowl and the softness that was resting on his eyes began to change.

"Only Elias can open this box." Daniel's voice cold.

I turned away from him trying to gather my thoughts. Finding where all the pieces have been laid and where the missing ones are. I began to talk to myself openly as I tried to find a sense of direction. Tension rose in my voice as I tried to put everything together.

"You needed me for Meridith's memories, That's one key. You needed me to read the grimoire to find the clues to the curse. That's another key. What are we missing?"

I began to pace back and forth hoping a missed clue would pop into my mind.

A sudden female voice pierced the haze, sharp as a knife: "You need to be at the exact location of her death in order for me to twist it."

I snapped my head up. Barely ten feet away, Rebecca, Elias, and Abigail materialized out of the gloom—each one caked in mud and streaked with old and fresh blood. Their limbs bore jagged slashes where my roots had lashed them, muscles taut over open wounds. Dried rivulets clung to their skin; fresh droplets still wove slow rivers down arms and thighs. They stood perfectly still, glaring at me through the swirling dust, every inch of their battered forms radiating defiance.

Blue-white sparks of magic crackled around my fingertips, each spark an echo of my fury. I drew in a ragged breath and advanced—every step fueled by rage; every sinew coiled for the strike. This time I wouldn't hold back: I'd unleash everything I had on them.

A sudden crack like a falling branch echoed at the back of my skull. Pain exploded across my scalp as I collapsed to my knees, hands flying up to cradle the wound. Warm blood seeped through my fingers, slick and coppery, matting my hair and dripping onto the stones. My vision swam; each heartbeat thundered in my ears as the world tilted. Darkness pooled at the edges of my sight, dragging me under.

I tried to fight it—tore ragged breaths into the night air, but my limbs slackened, and my knees gave way. The last thing I registered before the blackness took me was the cold certainty that only one of them could have struck me from behind.

Daniel.

Chapter Twenty-Four

Maeva Sinclair

Soft voices drifted through the haze, distant and urgent—whispers carried on the night wind. My eyelids fluttered open, each blink heavy as though weighed with lead. Pain throbbed at the base of my skull, the world tilting around me in a blur of broken stone and moonlight. I forced my head to lift, every movement sending fresh jolts of agony across my forehead, as if a slab of granite pressed down upon me.

I realized I was seated on the cold earth, the ruined walls of the fortress looming in fractured silhouettes around me. My scalp stung where warmth pooled beneath my fingers; blood, thick and metallic, coated my hair. The whispers grew louder—a frantic chorus echoing off crumbling stones. Though my vision swam, I made out ragged shapes moving just beyond my focus: shadows draped in tattered robes, circling like vultures.

A pounding behind my eyes threatened to consume me, but amid the pain a spark of awareness ignited. I was alive—though battered—and still here, at the heart of their desecrated stronghold. My pulse steadied as I forced myself upright, every breath a razor-sharp reminder that I had been struck down… and whatever came next, I would no longer be caught unawares

My fingers curled into fists, summoning every ounce of will as I directed my magic toward the dancing torch flames. I willed the air to chill, the embers to die—but before I could cast even a whisper of power, a cold clink sounded at my ankles. My blood froze in my veins. I dropped my gaze and there they were again: the iron cuffs, wicked sigils burning faintly into the metal, pinning my wrists and ankles in unbreakable embrace.

A lump rose in my throat as a wave of shame and despair crashed over me. My chest tightened, each breath coming in shallow, ragged gasps. Tears welled in the corners of my eyes, smudging the grime of battle into blurry streaks down my cheeks. Defeat settled like a lead weight in my belly—I, a Raven witch, chained in my own ruined stronghold, powerless to even comfort my own scorched skin. The world tilted, the heat of the dying embers mocking me, and all I could feel was the scorching ache of captivity.

The three monstrous silhouettes closed in around the dying fire—Rebecca's sinuous frame, Elias's towering bulk, and Abigail's lithe form. Tears blurred my vision, but I recognized them by their outlines alone. With each measured step, the stench of decay and dark magic crawled up my throat, forcing a gasp from my chest.

They kneeled before me, faces inches from my own. I spat out a shaky breath, matching their leer with my own defiance, though my heart thundered with betrayal—Daniel's absence was a knife twisting in my ribs. Lantern-fire danced in Elias and Abigail's eyes, turning their gazes into empty wells of hunger. Shadows flickered across their cursed features, and for a moment I saw them not as people, but as predators savoring my downfall.

I swallowed hard, the bitter taste of tears and hurt on my tongue and met their hollow stares. My magic lay chained at my wrists and ankles—useless. And yet, I refused to look at them.

"He's still around," Elias murmured, his lips curling into that familiar, predatory smile. "Don't worry—your boyfriend isn't going anywhere."

A hot surge of anger rolled beneath my ribs, but I forced my jaw shut. He was baiting me, daring me to break. I wouldn't give him that satisfaction.

"He's not going to miss this," Elias added with an amused chuckle, the sound echoing off the shattered stones.

That of a hand barb—so casual, so cruel—landed like a blade at my heart. For a heartbeat, I felt the sharp sting of betrayal. I'd convinced myself Daniel was different, that somewhere beneath the centuries of curse and cruelty there was something true between us.

But now doubt clawed at my mind: had I really seen warmth in his eyes, or simply projected hope onto a monster? I shoved the question down, burying the ache, and forced myself back to the present—surrounded by predators, magic shackled, and danger breathing down my neck.

The three of them rose as one, their silhouettes towering against the fractured glow of the moonlit courtyard. I pressed my back against the crumbled stone, hands still chained, heart pounding like a drum in my chest.

Rebecca's smile stretched too wide—hungry, triumphant. "Here's how it goes," she purred, voice smooth as poison. "You will swear your fealty to me—your Coven Leader—then I'll siphon your magic, forge a new curse in my image, and, finally, I will kill you. And because I'm generous, Elias will do it swiftly. "

The cold night air burned in my lungs. My jaw worked, searching for words, but all I could taste was betrayal and defeat.

My chest tightened as a cold tide of panic rolled over me. Sweat beaded along my hairline and my pulse thundered in my ears. I needed a way out—now. My fingers rattled against the iron cuffs, probing each link, searching for a weakness. But these chains were brutal—thicker, colder, their sigils glowing with forbidding strength. I closed my eyes, pressing my palms into my temples, willing my magic to spark beneath my skin. Nothing. A raw, desperate fear shivered up my spine. If I couldn't call on my power.

A sudden crack—twigs snapping—shatters the night's stillness. Every head whip toward the dark tree line. Then, like a wraith drawn by moonlight, Daniel steps into the flickering glow of the fire. He crosses Lori's fresh grave without a second glance, the bright light of the moon catching in his eyes and making them burn with an otherworldly intensity.

Daniel's approach was silent but impossible to ignore—each step a hammer blow to my racing heart. Anger flared alongside betrayal as he skirted past Rebecca, Elias, and Abigail, closing the distance between us. He crouched down beside me, the rough gravel under his knees reminding me of every wound I carried.

His familiar scent of sweet hickory washed over me, stirring something raw in my chest. He leaned closely, and his warm breath brushed my ear, soft and dangerously intimate. My jaw tightened; I couldn't bring myself to meet his gaze, even as his presence pressed against the cold weight of those cursed cuffs.

"I'm sorry, you wouldn't understand" he whispered into my ear.

Hot tears welled and carved salty rivers down my cheeks. Each drop stung as it fell, a slick reminder of how utterly shattered I'd been made. The air tasted of iron and lies—his whispered words ricocheting inside my skull until all I could hear was the thunder of my own heart, every beat hammering me with one undeniable truth: I'd been played, just like Meridith.

My legs buckled, and the world tilted as the weight of his betrayal crushed me from the inside out. I wanted to scream, to lash out, to crumble into nothing—but my body went numb, paralyzed by devastation. How could I have been so stupid?

"Shall we get this over with?" Rebecca said with a sigh.

Elias clutched the rune-carved box to his chest like a priceless relic. Abigail stalked at his side, claws extended, every sinew coiled for violence. Daniel—grim and silent—hoisted me to my feet, then slung me over his broad shoulder like a lifeless sack. I thrashed against his grip, the shackles at my wrists rattling uselessly.

He marched us into the forest's throat, where the firelight shrank behind us and night closed in. Branches whipped at my face; the cold press of Daniel's shoulder blades dug into my ribs, stealing each breath. I tried to wriggle free, angling for even an inch of comfort—only to be slammed harder against him and snapped back into silence.

"We're almost there," Daniel murmured, each word unnervingly calm against the pounding of my heart.

Closer now, the moonlight carved silver paths through the trees— and with each step, the forest grew eerily familiar. My breath caught in my throat. This was it: the very clearing from my nightmares, the place I'd raced through in my dreams, desperate to catch Meridith before the curse snapped shut.

I craned my neck, pressing my back against Daniel's broad shoulder to peer around him. My pulse thundered in my ears, the world narrowing to moonlit trunks and the distant rustle of undergrowth.

My voice trembled as the truth settled over me like a shroud.

"It was here," I whispered, pressing my palm against the rough bark of the oldest oak. "This whole time… I was this close."

Daniel's breath was soft in the night air. "You were drawn here because your ancestor needed you," he said, voice low but certain. "Meridith led you back to the very place her life—and her curse—began."

The forest seemed to lean in around us, the moonlight flickering through leaves as if to confirm his words. A heavy wind stirred the branches overhead, carrying with it the echo of a long-ago heartbeat— my own, entwined with hers.

At last, we stepped into the moonlit clearing where Meridith's life— and her curse—had ended. Daniel lowered me gently to the ground, and

I pressed myself against the rough bark of a great oak, my knuckles whitening as I gripped it for balance.

Before us lay the still, glassy expanse of the lake, its surface reflecting the silver light in fractured diamonds. Velvet-green lily pads floated along the shoreline, each punctuated by a single bloom: delicate petals of alabaster and blush unfurling toward the sky. Tiny insects danced in jittery arcs above the water, while distant frogs answered each other in mournful chorus.

Towering pines formed a silent amphitheater around the water, their ancient branches drooping as though weighed by centuries of secrets. Here, on this same spot, I could almost see Meridith kneeling in her final agony—her lips moving in a dark litany of blood and betrayal. The very air quivered with the echo of her despair.

A tremor ran through me—cold, thrilling, almost like Meridith's own power stirring beneath my skin. I closed my eyes and let that echo wash through my veins. This was the place where past and present met, where my ancestor had woven her pain into the land itself—and where I would at last confront the curse she left behind.

This was it, the finally resting place of the one who started this entire curse. My heart began to ache for the torture that Meridith had to endure for love. My eyes glossed over to the thought of her heartache and pain she thought was real but wasn't. That seemed to be the common point of view for any woman that chose to get close to those men.

I pressed my palm to the cool earth, as though touching Meridith's own final breath. My chest tightened with grief and awe—here I stood, the last tether to her life and power, at the very spot she chose to end it all.

The moonlight painted the ripples of the lake in silver, and I felt her sorrow echo in every quiver of the water. It was almost… beautiful, in its tragedy—that the line of our lives, separated by centuries, should meet again at this moment of sacrifice. The universe had woven this cruel symmetry: Meridith, betrayed and broken, her death a promise that one day I would rise to carry her burden. Now, I carried not only her magic and memories but the weight of her final choice, and as I inhaled the frosty night air, I understood at last that fate had chosen me to finish what she began.

"Now what?" Abigail's voice sounded off like an impatient child.

"Bring her over here, we need her to be near the site of Meridith's death. Her residual magic still lingers. I can feel it." Rebecca said, pointing to the far side of the lake—exactly where I'd seen Meridith kneel.

The three of them advanced, their predatory silhouettes cutting through the moonlit mist. Panic knotted my stomach, and my heart pounded so hard I feared they'd hear it. I tried to scramble backward, only to discover my feet shackled together—there was nowhere to go.

With a thud, I collapsed into the mud at the water's edge, cold, grimy slush splattering my face. The fetid scent of stagnant water stung my nostrils as I tried to pull myself up—only to sink deeper under my own weight.

Daniel's hands fell away, and I let the mud drip from my hair without a second thought. I shrugged out of the clearing sludge on my own terms, flicking grit from my palms. His smile remained hopeful, but I simply met it with a cold, steady gaze. When he reached out—tucking a strand of dirt-smeared hair behind my ear—I didn't flinch. His touch hovered against my cheek, but I kept my expression blank, as if he were nothing more than a bothersome insect. Better to let myself break my own heart, than to have someone else do it for me.

"Let's get this over with" I snapped while looking directly into Rebecca's gaze.

Rebecca's grin stretched across her face—sharp and gleeful. Daniel exhaled, lowering me into his arms once more, then shouldered me toward her. His boots sank into the muddy shore as he carried me forward; each step shook loose droplets of cold water from my clothes.

Beyond us, the lake's rippling surface pulsed with Meridith's ancient power, just out of reach—but unmistakable. Centuries of magic had seeped into these still waters, and I could feel it thrumming beneath the moonlight. No matter how hard I pushed against my chains, I knew that without her blood—without my own mark to call it forth—the magic would remain tantalizingly beyond my grasp.

Daniel hefted a slick, moss-covered boulder onto the lake's embankment and gently set me atop it. The stone was cold and uneven; I had to wedge my boots into its natural grooves just to stay upright. My arms wrapped around my knees, my chained wrists — raw and bruised — bore the full weight of my posture, gnawing at my resolve with every shift.

In the gathering gloom, Rebecca stood directly before me, Abigail to her left with claws half-bared, and Elias to her right, cradling the ornate wooden box. Daniel lingered just behind his brother's shoulder, his expression unreadable in the wavering torchlight. Their eyes—all four pairs—fixed on me like hungry stars in a midnight sky.

Beneath our feet, the lake's surface shimmered with Meridith's long-dormant magic, just beyond the reach of my blood-heavy chains. I realized how utterly alone I was—surrounded, bound, and at the mercy of their waiting power.

Chapter Twenty-Five

Maeva Sinclare

Elias lifted the box reverently before us. Slowly, he brought one pale finger to his fanged mouth and bit down—just enough for a bead of crimson to form. With deliberate care, he smeared that drop of blood across the carved wooden sigils, tracing their ancient lines in a scarlet offering. The box trembled in his palm, then—almost imperceptibly—a soft, amber glow began to pulse beneath its lid, like embers stirring to flame.

Our collective breath caught as the glow grew brighter, illuminating every rune until the lock clicked open. Elias tilted the box forward. There—nestled in folds of velvet—lay Meridith's own grimoire, its leather cover still unmarked by time, and beside it the slender, curved blade that had ended her life.

My heart twisted tight in my chest. I stared at the knife, white and terrible, and felt a fresh pang of grief for Meridith—her death, my betrayal, the countless innocents whose blood had been spilled to claim these artifacts. Each helpless victim had been a step on Elias's path to power; each life taken to feed his unquenchable hunger. The soft glow of that box, once so wondrous, now felt like a beacon of all the darkness it had demanded.

My eyes flew wide at the sight of Meridith's grimoire—its familiar leather binding almost mocking me now that it rested in their hands. A cold fury twisted in my chest as I shifted on the mossy rock, the iron cuffs cutting cruel crescents into my wrists. Rebecca's fingers, streaked with mud and dry blood, closed around the hilt of the knife.

The blade gleamed; its six-inch steel edge jutted from a bone-white raven's head, the carved beak cradling the metal as if born for violence. Rebecca drew it from the box with deliberate slowness, then leveled the tip at me. My breath stalled in my throat.

Sweat beaded at my temples, and my pulse thundered in my ears. I pressed back against the damp stone, clutching at the rock's rough texture for purchase. Below me, the water's surface lay still and silent—a mirror to this nightmare.

Rebecca's boots sank into the mud with each deliberate step toward me. A wet squelch rose around her ankles as she closed the distance. My eyes locked onto the raven-headed blade, its steel point aimed unerringly at my throat. Moonlight danced off the metal edge, flickering like a heartbeat in the darkness.

A freeze settled over me—my limbs heavy, my throat tight with unshed tears. Panic coiled around my ribs, but I forced it back, swallowing the tremor in my voice. My lashes fluttered as shame and fear blurred my vision.

"You will proclaim me your leader of the Raven Coven," Rebecca said, lips curved in triumph, her eyes alight with cruel satisfaction.

I glanced at the others standing sentinel behind her: Elias's cold glare, Abigail's sharp smile. Their faces were masks of hollow devotion, all traces of humanity drained by centuries of the curse.

In their distorted reflections, I saw the monsters Meridith had fought so hard to contain. I inhaled, hands clenched at my sides, and braced myself for the choice I could not avoid.

Abigail's claw hovered mere inches from my heart, the wicked curve of it glinting in the moonlight. My breath caught in my throat. I dared not flinch.

"What happens if I don't?" My voice quavered, the single question tumbling out like a plea.

They each leaned in—their shadows closing around me like a noose. Elias's grin split his face, fangs bared. Rebecca's eyes burned with hungry triumph. Abigail's nail grazed my chest, sharp enough to carve my skin. I tasted copper on my tongue and my pulse thundered in my ears.

Abigail's voice was ice. "I can force you to do it." She snapped her claws, and I felt the air slice where they would strike. My spine prickled; every nerve screamed to run, but the iron cuffs held me fast.

Rebecca stepped forward, the raven-headed knife still glinting in her hand. "It begins with shared blood," she intoned. "Then you must utter the words—swear your allegiance. Believe that I am your true leader. Only then will the curse bend to my will."

A cold wave washed through me. Shared blood. A vow. My own magic betrayed me—my wrists stung where the chains bit in, and I could almost taste the rusted iron on my skin. Outside, the lake whispered its sorrow, and the trees shivered in the wind.

I closed my eyes for a heartbeat, gripping the edge of the moss-slick rock. My mind raced for any escape—any spark of power I could claim.

My gaze dropped to the mud, the ink-like ripples in the shallow water mocking my defeat. Shared blood—what monstrous demand was this? A cold panic seized my chest; every heartbeat pounded like an execution drum. I was drowning, suffocating beneath the weight of inevitability.

I curled into myself, knees to my chest, arms locked tight as if I could squeeze out the terror. My tears pooled in my lap, warm and bitter, each drip a testament to my helplessness. This was the pit Meridith had fallen into centuries ago—trapped, betrayed, and forced to yield.

"I… I'll do it," I whispered, voice cracking against my thighs.

The words tasted like vinegar on my tongue. Silence stretched—a suffocating pause in the night's breath. Daniel's eyes burned into me, flickering with desperate hope and unspeakable sorrow. I sensed his surprise mirrored my own. I should have fought, should have clawed at those cuffs until my nails bled, but the knife's cold promise at my throat stripped me bare. There was no defiance left—only the final, bitter surrender of my free will.

I closed my eyes and let the night sky cradle me. My breath slowed until it matched the gentle pulse of the earth beneath me. Anxiety drained away, leaving only the soft chorus of crickets and the distant shimmer of the lake. I raised my face to the stars—the same stars that had watched over my ancestor in her final hour—and found a strange kinship in their cold light.

"Rebecca you are the Raven Coven leader" I said to the moon as if it needed convincing.

The words tasted like iron on my tongue, but as they left my lips, I felt a curious weight lift from my chest.

In that moment of submission, the moon slipped behind a cloud, and for a heartbeat the world held its breath—then exhaled. The clouds parted to reveal her pale glow once more, and I knew that whatever came next, I had met my fate with clear eyes and a steady heart.

I felt the salt of that tear warm my cheek as it pooled at my ear— then, astonishingly, nothing. No searing pain, no flash of magic, only the cool night air brushing my skin. I dared to open my eyes. Rebecca's narrowed gaze met mine, confusion rippling through her perfectly poised mask. Around us, Elias and Abigail exchanged uneasy glances, the hush of the forest pressing in like a silent jury.

At last Elias cleared his throat, his deep voice cutting through the stillness.

"Perhaps it's these cuffs," he ventured, stepping forward.

Relief and suspicion warred in my chest as I stared at the cold iron on my wrists and ankles. Rebecca's lips twitched into a reluctant nod.

Abigail—her jacket sleeves slipping back to reveal ordinary, human nails—fished a small, tarnished key from her pocket. For a moment, her hand hovered over the lock, the key's metal glinting in the moonlight, and I realized that this very prison might be the shield that spared me.

Rebecca's hands, ice-cold and merciless, snatched the iron links from around my ankles first, tugging them with a cruel impatience. Agony shot through my wrists as she wrenched the chains free, the metal bit into raw flesh.

My world lurched, I was yanked from the mossy rock and hauled closer to their bodies, the rock's edge scraping my calves. She loomed over me, her eyes narrow slits of pure, predatory intent, daring me to struggle.

With a disdainful flick, she sent both sets of cuffs clattering into the lake behind us. In that instant, the restraints disappeared—but so did the barrier holding my magic in check. It surged through me like a storm: electricity crackled beneath my skin, igniting every nerve ending with icy fire. The hair on my arms stood on end as a wave of raw power washed over me.

I lifted my head, breathless, and met the fierce, expectant stares of Rebecca, Elias, and Abigail—nails lengthened to lethal points, fangs glinting with saliva. At the center of their circle, Rebecca's blade hovered at my throat, the moonlight dancing on its edge.

"Say it" she said with impatience.

My breath caught as I met her gaze—equal parts steel and fire. I knew that uttering those words would bind me to her forever, that saying them might very well seal my fate. And yet, refusal meant certain death beneath those claws. Panic pressed against my ribs; every plan I'd held dissolved in the weight of her stare.

"If I do this, will you promise to let me live?" I said with a gentle plea.

Her face softened but a touch and for a fleeting moment I thought I saw pity in her eyes. A moment passed and her eyes still gazed into mine, I could see thoughts roam behind her eyes like she was contemplating on something. Her cursed still ready for their order of command.

"Yes, if you do this. I will let you live" she said with a gentle smile.

Her hand lowered with the knife at my throat and down to her side. My heart almost leapt out of my chest at her promise to me. The light was near at the end of the tunnel of my demise, and it was my only chance out.

Hope began to sprout within my stomach, and it was slowly growing into my chest. My heart raced at the thought of freedom, and I was ready to embrace it.

"I just need to confess it, right?" I said eagerly.

I barely had time to register my own heartbeat before Rebecca's knife flashed out—cold steel across my palm. The blade bit in, slicing layer by layer through flesh. I jerked back, but her grip held fast, the pain a white-hot lance shooting up my arm.

Behind her, Elias and Abigail's low growls rolled like distant thunder, their razor teeth glinting at the scent of fresh blood. Rebecca pressed the tip of the blade deeper, then withdrew it swiftly, letting my palm gape open. I cradled the wound to my chest, watching crimson pool into the mud. The monsters growled low and deep behind her. Their beasts raged within them with only a weak lock that kept them at bay. I watched their eyes flare at the sight of the blood trail down my arm and into my clothes.

Without hesitation, she flipped the knife and drew it across her own palm—smooth as butter, her skin parting in a clean line. Not a wince crossed her face as her blood blossomed onto the earth beside mine, a silent pact forged in pain. She instantly grabbed onto my hand with a firm grip.

"*Say it*" she said with a deep voice that was no longer hers.

It was a darkness I'd never known in any fairy tale or myth—a living, breathing evil. Rebecca wasn't merely a witch; she was something far sinister. My gaze locked on hers, and time seemed to shatter around me. Each raindrop, cold as crystal, hammered the surface of the lake, ricocheting off my scalp like a thousand tiny darts.

Perched on that slick stone, I watched her and her cursed brood: faces twisted by centuries of bloodlust, eyes gleaming with predatory triumph. In them, I saw only Meridith's stolen future—her power appetite satisfied by slaughter. A comet of fury ignited in my gut, Rebecca might have thought she'd claimed victory over my ancestor, but she had no inkling who I was, or the magic that pulsed beneath my skin.

The air crackled around me—earth, water, and blood uniting in a silent oath. I wouldn't let this monster roam free, gutting covens to feed her twisted hunger. With every fiber of my being, I vowed to move my own pieces on this board, to unmake her reign of terror.

"Rebecca if you are the true Raven Coven leader take my power" I professed out loud for the world to her.

Rain exploded around us in sheets, blurring the world into frantic streaks of silver. Yet through the deluge I watched her—Rebecca's smile, all predatory confidence, wound itself into something far darker. Her head tossed back, and a low, triumphant chuckle rolled from her throat like thunder. In the flash of lightning her eyes flickered—first that cruel, fetid brown, then into obsidian voids identical to those of her savage brood.

The stench of decay curled through the storm's roar—an acrid miasma of rotted flesh and bitter bile that turned my guts to ice. Every breath felt like inhaling ash. A jagged bolt cleaved the sky, illuminating the rising waters at my back; the lake's edge lapped hungrily at the bank, its surface torn into whitecaps by the driving rain.

She leaned closer—too close—her victory radiating off her like a living thing. I braced my feet on the slick rock, until the weight of her triumph bent her in two. Even bent low, even under the storm's fury, her joy was unmistakable: she had won.

I clamped down on her wrist, staring into eyes darker than the midnight storm. Lightning flared, and I caught my reflection in their depths—alongside six other pairs of glowing, predatory eyes looming behind her.

I noticed the knife still clutched in her other hand, its blade sliding free from her hip—steel gleaming in every flash of lightning. Rain beads clung to its edge like frozen tears. I had only an instant. Dropping to my knees, I yanked her close, pressing my mouth to her ear in one swift, burning motion. Her eyes snapped wide in shock, rain-slick hair plastered to her forehead, as my heartbeat thundered louder than the storm around us.

"But if you're not, then I'm your leader" I whispered in her ear.

I leaned back just enough to see the knife's hilt buried at my ribs—its white bone gleaming stark against the spreading red. The Raven's beak jutted from my side, slick with my blood as it pooled between us.

My vision blurred instantly; a cold shock knifed through my veins, rooting me to the spot. Rebecca's triumphant smile flickered in and out of focus as Elias and Abigail caught her under each arm, their faces painted with victory.

Around us, the storm seemed to pause, waiting for my next breath. I tried to draw air in, but my lungs refused. The world tilted, and all I could feel was the knife's weight and the bitter betrayal of her promise.

Rain sluiced off the eaves in silver sheets, drumming on our shoulders like a relentless heartbeat. My tears mixed with the downpour as Daniel emerged through the mist. His claws receded; in their place were the hands I had once could call home—warm, steady, impossibly gentle.

He stepped forward, eyes soft with sorrow, and cradled my face against the chill. The lightning-bright rivulets racing down his cheeks only made him more achingly familiar. Then his lips met mine, tender and fierce all at once—a promise of refuge in a storm of betrayal.

I clutched his wrists. Each drop of rain that slipped between us felt like a benediction, washing away a fraction of my pain. My heart surged with hope: maybe this was the moment he'd tear away the blade lodged in my side, dismantle the lies, free me from this curse. I leaned in, seeking the warmth of his arms, ready to believe in salvation.

—and then I felt the razor's edge twist once more.

Every breath I drew burned like acid, my wound aching as if it had been torn open all over again. My heart fractured in pain, each shard twisting with the memory of his soft touch turning into violence. The rain pounded my face, indistinguishable from my tears, and every drop felt like a reminder that the one I could've loved could hurt me worse than any blade.

For a heartbeat, his soft smile hovered over me—an echo of the man I thought I knew. Then, without warning, he shoved me backward into the frigid water.

Chapter Twenty-Six

Maeva Sinclair

I hit the surface like a stone, the cold water roaring around me as I sank. I tumbled beneath the waves, the blade's razor edge still buried in my side, each breath now a gasp of pain. My limbs felt leaden, the frigid water seeping into my bones, dragging me toward the lake's muddy bottom.

Blood trailed from my wound, swirling into the dark water like ink. I clawed at the surface once—twice—but the world spun, my strength bleeding away. My fingers fumbled, powerless against the weight of the water and my own injury.

I opened my mouth for air—water flooded in instead. My vision swam, red halos drifting around the distant shapes. The last thing I saw was Daniel's hand brushing the surface, not reaching for me, but turning away. Then darkness closed in, and I drifted into cold oblivion.

The world above fractured with each jagged bolt of lightning. In those silver flashes, I saw them all—Rebecca's cruel watching tilt, Elias's predatory stillness, Abigail's silent leer—and Daniel, squatting on the rain slick rock, hand trailing just beneath the surface.

Below, the water closed over me like a tomb. My own silhouette flickered against the roiling waves, fingers grasping at shadows. Up there, Daniel's hand broke the surface—just enough to feel the lake's icy grip—before he pulled it back, wiping the dripping chill from his pants as if it could scrub away my very existence.

My own hand rose instinctively, fingertips brushing against phantom skin, drawn by a thread of desperate hope. Shame and grief coiled around my heart; I, too, had been fooled by a monster's promise. I wanted to drag him under, to make him share this dark abyss with me. But as his shape receded—looming for a moment in the cracked light, then vanishing—I sank deeper, humiliation and heartbreak tethering me ever down.

I tasted defeat—death hovered in every heartbeat. I let go of pain and sank into acceptance. My heart shattered; my mind blinked out like a dying star.

Then, instinct drove me: I yanked the knife free from my side. A white-hot shock climbed my spine, and the blade slipped from my limp fingers. It drifted beside me into the depths.

With my eyes closed, the roar in my skull faded. I floated weightlessly, untouched by sound. A quiet calm settled over me—too deep, I knew, to escape.

But then the current stilled. I hovered, motionless, as if caught in a hidden snare. Electricity split the sky above—flash after flash—each blast of lightning illuminating lily pads and ghostly roots.

Murky green water swirled around me, algae drifting past my vision. Tiny fish flickered in and out of the light. I was trapped beneath the surface, powerless and utterly alone.

Panic seized me. I thrashed my arms and kicked wildly, desperate to break free of whatever invisible iron held me down—but my limbs felt like lead. My chest burned for air as I fought the suffocating silence of the deep.

Then—an electric jolt coursed through me, as if the lake itself had reached in to seize my soul. A surge of icy water slammed into my ribs and dragged me feet-first into the abyss. I gurgled, clawing for purchase in the void, lungs screaming for oxygen.

Another powerful swell rose beneath me, lifting and flipping my body in a churning whirlpool. Vines of water coiled around my torso, squeezing with unrelenting force. All at once I understood: the lake wasn't just water—it was alive, and it intended to keep me forever.

My last gasp bubbled tortured bubbles through the muddy water—then I let go. My arms and legs floated uselessly as currents toyed with me, hair whipping across my face until I could scarcely breathe. Then came the searing jolts—dozens of them—each like a live wire coiling beneath my skin. The cold lake turned to ice against the heat of those shocks, my heart pounding a desperate drum as my lungs screamed for air.

Abruptly, a firm grasp seized my wrists and ankles—something alive in the depths. I felt a pulse of cerulean energy snake through my veins, and my eyes flew open at the sight of electric-blue filaments branching beneath my skin. A crackling sizzle raced along the length of my side where the blade had struck—hot as molten steel—sealing the wound in blinding white arcs of light. Tiny bubbles carried my muffled screams upward in frantic spirals.

Then, as if propelling me with inhuman strength, a surge of buoyancy rocketed me toward the surface. I slammed through the water with a rush of mud and reeds, lungs flooding with the sweetest, sharpest gasp of oxygen. My soaked clothes clung like a second skin, dripping cold relief down my spine. All around me, the lake rippled in the thunderstorm's glow. This had to be part of the spell where my magic is given to Rebecca.

Blinding jags of lightning struck me in rapid succession—each bolt a lance of pure white fire that stabbed through my bones. I couldn't sob or scream; my throat constricted as every nerve ending ignited.

The storm around me roared in triumph: thunderclaps rolled like cannon fire, rain pounded my skin so fiercely I felt each drop as a hundred pinpricks, and the ancient oaks groaned, their trunks bending under the onslaught as if they might splinter in half.

Yet beneath the violent storm I felt a deeper blaze: the Raven mark on my finger flared red-hot, an ember of wrath that twisted and churned beneath my skin. My fingertips snapped and sputtered with tiny electric darts, as though my blood itself had become a crackling grid of power. Cold rain sluiced off me even as adrenaline flooded my veins—my lungs greedily gulped the charged night air I'd been denied—and a feral strength coursed up my spine, loosening every fear, every shackle of doubt.

In that crucible of storm and pain I was reborn. Where once I had felt fragile and broken, now I brimmed with relentless vigor. My heart, once splintered by betrayal and loss, beat steady and unafraid. The lake's surface churned below me, reflecting the furious sky, and I rose on trembling legs transformed—new, unbound, and burning with the promise of vengeance.

I whipped my gaze back up to those four beings that tried to kill me. My eyes flared electric-blue, veins of raw lightning dancing across my skin in intricate, spider-web patterns. The last thunderclap still rumbled behind me, but the lake—once a roiling, boiling cauldron—recoiled at my power. I felt the water release its grip, dumping me from its embrace with a thunderous crash. A towering wave rose where I fell, then collapsed in on itself, its edges hissing as they met the shore—only to settle again into a trembling, rain-kissed hush.

As the storm's fury waned, my magic reached up through my ankles and calves, lifting me effortlessly. I hovered an instant above the glassy surface, suspended between sky and water, before drifting down like a weightless feather. When my boots touched, the lake's face froze solid in an instant: a matte sheet of frost cracked outward from my soles, spreading in jagged spokes until the entire expanse gleamed like a winter dawn.

Now I stood, statuesque on the ice, lightning still flickering beneath my skin, every breath of mine a plume of steam. Four pairs of watching eyes blinked back at me—Elias, Abigail, Daniel, Rebecca—each stunned by the raw, untamed power I'd wrested back from them. And for the first time, I felt in total command.

My arms hung at my sides, palms out—an unspoken challenge. I could feel every heartbeat hammering in my wrists, every nerve ending alive with electric fire. Around me, Elias, Abigail, and Daniel stared in stunned silence, their predatory masks slipping for just a moment as they realized I was no longer the frightened girl they'd caged.

I took the first step toward them, ice cracking softly beneath my feet. The sky answered with a salvo of thunder, bright knives of lightning carving the clouds overhead. Each flash revealed their razor teeth and velvet-black eyes—creatures of hunger set loose at last. But I felt nothing but ice-cold resolve.

My gaze locked on Rebecca. Her signature confidence had bled away, replaced by wide-eyed horror. I felt Meridith's ancient magic surge inside me—a tidal wave of ancestral power mingled with my own—and I knew this strength was ours alone. My fingertips sparked; tiny arcs of blue lightning danced up my sleeves. My Raven Coven mark glowed like a beacon, and every step I took toward her resonated with raw, crackling energy.

Rebecca sank to her knees on the frost-hardened lake, mud-spattered boots slipping in the puddles at her feet. She lifted her face— lips trembling, tears glistening like fractured stars—finally meeting my gaze in quiet surrender. In that moment, the storm held its breath alongside her, and I realized: this time, I held the power.

"I thought we had a deal?" I drawled, my voice dripping with mock sweetness.

Rebecca's lip quivered; filthy tears carved shiny rivulets through the grime on her cheeks. For an instant, my chest softened at the sight—but it snapped shut the moment I stepped closer. A chill slithered up my spine, frost biting through my blood.

She looked up at me like a beaten dog: no more haughty magic in her eyes, no more rancid stench of decay, no trace of that terrible pride she wore like a crown. Just a trembling woman in mud-soaked clothes.

A harsh, mirthless laugh tore free from my throat—so raw it felt like splitting my ribs. My sides shook with it, breath catching between ragged gasps, until I was forced to clutch my stomach just to keep standing.

Rebecca's face twisted in furious confusion, the last embers of her victory snuffed out. The ageless predator who'd claimed centuries of lives was now a shattered thing, bowed and broken before me.

I stepped forward onto solid ground, rain sluicing down my face, lightning crackling in my veins.

"Was this your great 'adjustment'?" I asked, voice low, mocking. A half-smile tugged at my lips. My eyes, electric blue, danced with stolen power.

Rebecca knelt, sodden and spent. Hateless defeat lined her features—once-proud, ageless hunter now a crumbling thing. She looked up at me, raw malice flickering in her tear-choked gaze.

"Unlike you, Rebecca," I said, voice calm, terrible in its restraint, "I'll let you live. But should our paths ever cross again…" I let the threat hang.

She rose unsteadily. Mud caked her skirt, her jacket twisted; she smoothed ragged lapels, as if recapturing dignity. I watched every muscle coiled for a final strike. But she did nothing.

"Why not kill me now?" she hissed, voice brittle with disbelief.

I paused, raindrops stinging my cheeks like ice. Her question—her arrogance—pierced me, however briefly. She'd slaughtered coven sisters, betrayed me, murdered countless for power. Yet as I looked into those desperate eyes, I recognized the truth: she was broken, stripped of the dark gifts that had made her monster.

"You already are dead," I said softly. "You've lost everything that mattered."

Her breath caught. Thunder rolled overhead, and for a single heartbeat, the ancient curse that bound us all seemed to shudder—and break—beneath the storm's roar.

I let the thunder answer her question. My gaze never wavered from Rebecca's pale face as rain streamed down her cheeks—washing away the last vestiges of her defiance.

She was the architect of horrors: Lori's death, Meridith's suicide, my family's slaughter. Every one of her victims cried out for justice, and for an instant, my spirit leapt to deliver it. But another voice—soft, insistent—gave me pause.

A trembling warmth brushed my shoulder, as though Lori herself reached through the veil to steady me. I closed my eyes and felt her presence: fierce, unyielding. What would she have done?

I opened my eyes and looked down at the broken witch. Rain pooled in Rebecca's hair; her lips quivered. Yet the storm's wild energy surged inside me, and with it came clarity.

"I'm no murderer," I said, my voice rising to cut through the wind. "You're mortal now—just a broken woman at the mercy of forces far bigger than any magic."

Rebecca's eyes widened. She dared not speak.

I raised a trembling hand and let the electricity crackle free, dancing along my fingertips like living light. A final bolt of lightning flared overhead, illuminating the lake's slick surface.

"Let the universe be your judge," I whispered.

Her features stiffened into an unbreakable mask of rage. Rain glistened on her muddied jacket as she straightened it with deliberate slowness, smoothing her skirt with trembling fingers.

For a heartbeat she remained rooted, embodying every ounce of indignity she still possessed. Then, without a word, she pivoted away from me, shoulders squared.

Elias's gaze met hers as if she wanted him to follow her. His feet planted firmly into the ground—not out of loyalty to her, but because his heart was torn. I watched the betrayal writhe across Rebecca's shoulders: her posture slumped, the elegant tilt of her chin falling away, replaced by raw, open grief.

Ellipses of rain ran down her cheeks as she swallowed back a sob. In that brief, wrenching moment, I knew her alone heartbreak: centuries of ruthless ambition undone by one truth, one word unspoken. Her face crumpled in grief when he refused to follow her—allowing her to walk away as though she had never been the one who placed the crown upon his head.

Her defeated frame dissolved into the black woods, the weight of her sorrow pressed into my chest, a lament I could never forget.

Chapter Twenty- Seven

Maeva Sinclair

My gaze followed her as she melted into the forest's inky embrace—her silhouette swallowed by gnarled branches and the snap of dry leaves underfoot. Relief and doubt warred in my chest: I'd spared her life, yet a nagging seed of unease rooted itself deeper with every passing heartbeat.

A sudden whisper of wind drifted across the clearing, cool and gentle—a momentary lull that left me unprepared for what came next. In an instant, Abigail was upon me. Her slight frame blurred into view, her obsidian eyes widening to reveal nothing but inky voids. Ivory fangs slid into place behind her curled lips, and claws—long, gleaming, and cruel—tore through the air toward my throat.

Panic exploded in my veins. My heart thundered as adrenaline jerked me upright. Instinct took over: I flexed my fingers, bracing for the slash, and then—without conscious thought—my magic burst free. A jagged bolt of electric blue lanced from my palm, striking Abigail's outstretched arm. She howled, the force of that sudden current hurling her backward into the underbrush.

I stood, trembling, as the crackle of fading sparks echoed around me. My lungs burned with the cool night air; my mind struggled to catch up with what my body had done. Her tiny frame caught a volt of electricity and sent her flying backwards into the lake. Her body skidded across the water like a flat rock, her arms and legs flailing around her as she couldn't brace herself. The ice splintering and breaking under her weight. Her body smoldering with smoke from the electricity. Her clothes frayed and her skin burned from the shock before finally sinking into the lake.

Daniel and Elias stood at the water's edge, their mother's scream still echoing in the trees. In the next moment, their attention snapped to me—those inky eyes narrowing to pin me in place.

I took a hesitant step back, heart hammering as they closed the circle. Elias prowled one way, Daniel the other, each mirroring the other's ruthless grace. Their claws hovered at their sides; their fangs gleamed like steel in the moonlight. My own hands flared bright blue at my hips, weaving sparks that crackled in the humid night air, and I felt the old familiar panic rise—only to be steadied by a gentle pulse of power under my skin, like a friend's reassuring touch.

They tested me, Elias shuffling his feet in a feint while Daniel lunged and then recoiled, each manacing bounce of their shoulders sending ripples of cold dread through my veins. A cruel chuckle drifted from their lips: a hunter's laughter. They were playing with me, savoring my fear. But this time, I wouldn't be bait.

Like lightning uncoiling, they sprang in perfect tandem—claws snarling toward my throat. I didn't hesitate. My fingers snapped together, and an electric wave of pure Raven magic burst from my palms. It slammed into them with the force of a tidal surge. Elias and Daniel were thrown backward into the slick mud, bodies hitting with bone-jarring thuds at the water's edge.

Only Elias recovered fast enough to stagger to his feet and race me again, every savage instinct bared. I planted my feet in the soft mud and steadied myself. He danced in and out, slashing in arcs meant to intimidate.

Thunder split the sky, and for the first time, I met their fury on equal footing. The storm obeyed my will; magic thrummed in my bones.

I planted my feet. Pulling my hands to my sides, I willed the electricity to obey. Tiny sparks ignited at my fingertips, coalescing into sinuous blue veins that snaked across the earth. Each filament struck the ground like a living wire, probing outward in search of prey.

My eyes, now the color of storm-lit cobalt, locked onto Elias. He stood beyond the arc of my electric field, his black irises reflecting each flicker of lightning overhead. Rage rolled through me, cold and sharp, a blade at my spine—every betrayal, every shattered promise, coalescing into a single, unyielding purpose.

He charged without warning, limbs coiling like a panther's, fangs bared in a vicious snarl. In that moment he ceased to be human—only predator, honed by centuries of dark magic into a beast craving blood. The ancient curse had warped him, knitting his soul to a hunger that knew no end.

But I did not flinch. My barrier shimmered into being—a crackling wall of electric blue that crackled and pulsed between us. Each surge was a promise. Elias skidded to a halt at its edge. Sprinkles of rain hissed as it struck the barrier, steam rising in ghostly plumes.

He circled, claws clicking like ivory knives, eyes calculating every flicker of my field. He knew he could not breach it without suffering for it. A cruel smile curved his lips—a challenge, a promise of violence. I met his glare, chin high, unafraid.

I edged along the muddy bank, my crackling halo of power flexing with every step. The water's surface shimmered under the lightning—just shallow enough to supercharge my storm if I could lure him in. Elias mirrored me, trapped at the very lip of the lake, annoyance flickering in his coal-black eyes.

A grin split my face—until I caught movement out of the corner of my eye. A hot breath at my neck, and Daniel's iron grip snapped around my jaw and chest, pinning my arms. Instantly my world went crimson as his fanged mouth claimed my blood. I couldn't move—could only feel the cold slick escape through my skin.

Then, reflex took over. I stomped my heel so hard the bank trembled. A surge of electrical force slammed into Elias like a battering ram, launching him backward into the lake with a thunderous splash. Daniel's hold loosened; needles of pain shot through me as he fell away. I twisted free, elbowed him in the ribs, and scrambled to my feet as his ragged gasp echoed in the night.

Blood dripped from my throat, each heartbeat hammering ice through my veins. Fear clutched me—but I couldn't stay. I tore into the woods, branches tearing at my clothes, roots snagging my heels. The moonlight was a blur; every breath burned in my lungs. Behind me, the silent night swallowed my pounding footsteps.

When my legs finally gave out, I collapsed beneath a gnarled root arch. Mud oozed beneath me, cold seeping into every bone. Pressed into that tiny hollow, I clutched my bloody side and forced ragged breaths— knowing that this fragile pocket of shadow was the only thing standing between me and their jaws.

Surrounded by mud and fallen branches, I huddled against the gnarled root, every shred of cover barely concealing me. The copper tang of my own blood still clung to the air—and to my fingers pressed against the ragged wound in my side. I wasn't safe here, but I couldn't move yet.

My heart pounded so violently I thought it might burst free of my ribs. Each breath came in ragged gasps; every footstep I imagined sent fresh panic crawling up my spine. I pressed myself flatter into the dirt, knees drawn tight to my chest, willing the shadows to swallow me whole.

Tears blurred my vision, hot and sharp on my cheeks. But I forced myself to still my shaking hands and slow my ragged breathing. In… and out… In… and out. I felt my pulse steadying, the pounding in my ears easing away. Beneath the thrum of fear, I sensed it—my magic, quiet and patient, nudging me back to myself.

Eyes closed, I centered my mind on that steady presence. My breath came easier now; my heart, though still racing, had found its rhythm again. There, in the muddy hollow, I began to piece together my next move.

The knot in my chest—tight as a noose—finally unraveled, slipping away like tide-washed sand. Relief blossomed in its place, warm and enveloping, as my magic thrummed beneath my skin, a silent promise that I wasn't alone. No longer the frightened girl trapped in that cell, I was Maeva Sinclair—the witch whose power pulsed through every vein.

I pressed my back into the rough bark, eyes closed, savoring the steady beat of my heart. When I opened them, the world looked sharper, brighter under the moon's argent glow. Crimson slicked my fingers; I tore a jagged strip from my sleeve and bound my side to staunch the flow. I couldn't stay hidden forever.

Behind me, laughter curled through the trees—low, predatory. Abigail's mocking voice drifted through the underbrush, and I knew they were close. Every footfall I'd taken was tracked; I would never outrun them. Instead, I darted into the night, weaving between gnarled roots and slick stones, my breath ragged but determined.

When I could no longer run without falling, I spun around a broad oak and leaned against its trunk, gasping in the icy air. My lungs burned, but my spirit soared: I'd stolen my freedom, if only for a moment. Ahead lay darkness—and on the wind, the soft, sinister whisper of the hunt. But I would not be their prey. Not tonight

Chapter Twenty-Eight

Maeva Sinclair

I again pressed my palms to the gnarled bark and exhaled, feeling the pulse of my own magic echo through my bones. Beneath my touch, the wood vibrated—like a heartbeat synchronizing with mine. White-blue motes of arcane light flickered between my fingertips, drifting down into the roots at my feet.

First, a single tendril shuddered, then dozens. The roots coiled tighter, thickening as if plumping themselves for war. They glowed briefly—veins of luminescent cerulean—pulsing in time with my breath. Each pulse sent ripples of energy through the living wall, making the barrier itself hum in low, resonant tones, as though the forest were awakening to my command.

Along the trunks, bioluminescent fungus bloomed, trailing delicate lacework of glowing tendrils that wound around the ridges in intricate runes. Every leaf above shivered, and droplets of rain caught in the canopy refracted the moonlight into dancing prisms that scattered across the mossy floor.

When I finally stepped back, the barrier was complete: a living palisade of twisting wood and glowing roots, its surface rippling with faint currents of magic like waves on a phosphorescent sea. The very air inside that circle crackled—charged with energy—drawing even the smallest mote of dust into gentle spirals. Here, I was sovereign: the raw power of the earth itself bound to my will, shielding me from those dark shapes just beyond its edge.

I stumbled back another half-step, and there they stood—three silhouettes carved in the silver moonlight, their forms rigid beyond the living trees. Their eyes glowed an eerie emerald, not merely reflecting my barrier but seeming to draw power from its very magic. Each blink sent twin flares of luminescence, like watchfires kindled in the gloom.

Rain-slicked branches overhead swayed as if sighing with approval, each leaf's edge tracing arcs of light before settling quietly once more. Beneath their watchful stare, I felt the barrier's heartbeat throb in harmony with mine—speaking in a language of root and sap that pledged its fierce protection so long as I willed it so.

As their serrated claws raked across the living wall, the roots shuddered beneath each slash, splintering into glistening shards of wood and clay. With every desperate wrench, the barrier's pulse faltered—its pale-blue glow dimming in ragged eddies where bloodied talons bit deep. Thudding crackles echoed like breaking bones, and tiny motes of light winked out, one by one, as if the roots themselves were dying.

Heart pounding like a war drum, I wrenched free of the final intact fern-root, vaulting past the split in the fence just as it gave way entirely. A tangle of broken roots snapped shut behind me, sealing the splintered gap with a final, muted groan of surrender. For a heartbeat I faltered—mud slick underfoot—then the glint of moonlight on water lured me forward again.

The forest dissolved into a wide, shadowed clearing. The lake lay before me, its surface black glass shot through with silver—each ripple etched by raindrops that still fell in steady sheets. My lungs burned for air, every ragged breath a reminder of how close they were behind me. I could almost hear their ragged panting, smell the acrid tang of their bloodlust on the wind.

Relief flooded me as I burst free from the tangled trees, the moon's silver spill illuminating the path ahead. My lungs heaved, heart hammering in my chest like a frantic drum, but I forced my legs onward, each stride carrying me closer to open air. Roots and brambles clawed at my clothes, but I broke through the final curtain of foliage and found myself on the rocky shore.

The water lay before me, black as obsidian, its surface shattered by a thousand raindrops into dancing diamonds. I stumbled over slick stones, scraping my palms raw against their jagged edges, and fell to my knees at the water's brink. Behind me, the forest yawned—a dark maw I'd escaped. Ahead, that serene lake, whispering promises of sanctuary.

My breath came in ragged gasps as I pressed trembling fingers into the glacial water. The cold bit at my skin, but beneath that sting there was a pulse—a living heartbeat echoing my own. Summoning every last ounce of strength, I wove my magic through my veins, a soft hum that merged with the lake's ancient power. Where my fingertips lingered, ripples glowed faintly, fracturing the moonlight into a thousand dancing shards.

Behind me, the forest lay silent and long behind; ahead, the ruined manor loomed. But for a moment my gaze fell instead upon Lori's grave, across the water—a simple cross of weathered sticks bound with twine. My heart clenched so violently I thought I might double over, tears pricking at my lids. I didn't have time to mourn again. Survival waited on the far shore.

I ran the length of the shoreline, sand sucking at my feet, water lapping at my ankles like a promise of sanctuary. Each surge of magic at my call sent the lake's chill up through me, turning the surface beneath my steps to frosted glass. My Raven mark blazed bright blue on skin and waves alike, guiding me like a torch.

The fortress came into view: jagged stone walls half-buried in brambles, torn tapestries fluttering from collapsed doorways. I could almost feel the echo of every betrayal, every stolen life, seared into those broken halls. And yet—here I was, heart pounding but unbroken, magic humming through me like a battle cry. One more sprint, one more desperate push, and I would leave this nightmare behind forever.

My triumph was blistering in my veins—Lori's car, parked where she'd left it, gleaming under the moonlight just beyond the blade of grass. I was three strides from freedom when a crushing blow slammed into my ribs. Pain exploded through my side as I tumbled off the shoreline and skidded across the wet grass, blades slicing into my palms. I choked back a cry as a hulking shape loomed over me—Daniel, his eyes black as a starless sky, his jaw locked in cruel determination. The ground beneath me trembled with the weight of his approach.

My head slammed into the ground, stars exploding behind my eyelids as I lay tangled, hands trapped beneath my body. Hair plastered across my face and neck like a cruel scarf, I lay limp, lungs heaving shallow, every inch of me screaming with pain.

A low groan escaped my throat as the impact throbbed through my bones. I tried to roll free, to slide my arms out from under me, but the ache in my ribs stole what little strength I had left. Darkness swam in my vision; my head pounded so fiercely I couldn't find purchase to push myself up.

Then a cold grip closed around my throat like an iron clasp. I was yanked upright, limbs dangling, chest stretched tight beneath the weight of an unseen force. A heavy palm smothered my eyes; fingers tangled in my sweat-slick hair. Panic slammed into me—another hit would surely kill me.

I kicked and thrashed, claws scrabbling at the hand choking me, but my attacker's grip only tightened. Warm breath ghosted along my neck, the faint rasp of teeth brushing my skin. Recognition flared: Daniel's scent. His betrayal from the forest returned in an instant, fueling my terror. He drew me closer—his arm a steel bar across my windpipe—and I convulsed against him, but his hold was absolute.

With a low whisper in my ear, it felt like a trickle of ice drip down my spine.

"I wish I met you in a different life," he murmured, his voice a tremulous whisper against the shell of my ear—soft as a lover's confession. His breath feathered over my skin, warm and hesitant, while the tip of his nose brushed the delicate curve behind my lobe. I felt his pulse in the gentle press of his forehead against my hair, as he inhaled deeply one last time, chest tightening with the ache of it.

When I dared to meet his eyes, I saw raw pleading flicker there—lakes of sorrow rimmed with salt. His lashes glistened with unshed tears, and the taut line of his jaw betrayed the storm of regret roiling beneath. For a suspended heartbeat, the cruelty of this world fell away, leaving only the quiet agony between us.

I stilled in his hold, the fight draining from me like color from a fading sunset. Vulnerable and trembling, I let my limbs go slack—no longer struggling.

"What?" I spoke with confusion.

I was expecting another game of him toying with me; to make me bring my walls down once more so he could crumble my fortress, but he didn't say another word. He looked at my wound on my neck and back into my eyes. Regret washed over his face.

He drew back just enough that I could see the conflict in his eyes—an anger tempered by something deeper, something he wasn't letting me in on.

"She sent you," he said, voice low and heavy with disappointment.

My heart skipped. Meridith's magic had revealed something when he bit my neck… something more than just blood and power. I studied his face, searching for the shadowed hollows beneath his eyes for a crack in his sincerity. His jaw clenched; for a heartbeat, he looked away, as if afraid I'd read the truth in his expression.

I forced my voice steady. "I don't understand?"

He swallowed, his Adam's apple bobbing. The moonlight caught in his eyes—bright, searching—before he finally met my gaze again.

"Unleash all you got Raven." He stood there, every muscle taut with regret and unvoiced longing—as though he feared if he spoke more, he might betray what he'd tried so hard to hide. And I realized then that the same magic binding us had woven a web of secrets far deeper than either of us dared admit.

I never saw Abigail move—one moment I was collapsing against the rough bark, the next I was sprawled on the cold ground, every breath a jagged gasp as my spine trembled with the impact. My back sang with fire, ribs protesting under the sudden weight. I clawed at the earth, coughing up shards of pain, hands scraping tiny stones as I struggled upright.

Before I could brace myself, a razor-sharp scrape ripped across my shoulder blades. Abigail's claws, long and wicked as bayonets, carved through fabric and flesh in a single, brutal arc—four crimson gashes searing into my skin. I tasted iron on my tongue as blood pooled between my shoulder blades, hot and sticky against the chill night air.

The sting was overwhelming, lancing down into my core, and I doubled over in agony, my stomach twisting with bile and shock. Gritting my teeth, I forced my vision upward: there they stood, the three once-human horrors formed by betrayal and carved by the deepest blackest magic.

Twilight flickered across their twisted shapes, revealing claws dripping, eyes hollow with centuries of ravenous hunger. Rebecca's promise echoed in my mind—there was no breaking their curse, only matching cruelty with cruelty. A fierce calm settled over me: if pain was the spell they thrived on, then pain would be my answer.

Their footsteps were silent, stalking closer like wolves circling a lone fawn under the moon's cruel glow. Every shallow breath I drew burned in my lungs; every heartbeat thudded in my ears, echoing the promise of this final stand.

Meridith's vengeance thrummed through me—years of betrayal, stolen lives, shattered covens, all fueling a fire I thought had long since burned out. These monsters had tasted love and spat it back in blood, craved power without price, and left innocents broken in their wake. They believed themselves invincible; they'd never faced my fury.

I willed the last vestiges of my strength to rise, my coven's ancient magic humming beneath my scars. My hands, still trembling where Abigail's claws had scored me, cracked open with electric sparks that danced along the wet earth. The Raven mark on my finger burned brilliant blue, each pulse a promise: here I stood, alone, but unstoppable.

The three of them closed in, silhouettes etched against the dancing firelight. Their ragged breaths and low snarls cut through the hush of the woods, but I felt nothing of their menace now—only the steady drum of my own heartbeat, the fierce pulse of power coursing through every vein.

I inhaled again, slower this time, feeling that same sorrow and rage coalesce into purpose. I raised my arms—flames licked at my fingertips, crackling like captive thunder—and let the fire spiral outward in a living arc. It swept between us, carving a circle of light so bright the trees themselves seemed to recoil, leaves hissing in heat.

Elias and Abigail froze, claws half-drawn, as the blaze wrapped around their ankles, licking upward like a hungry serpent. But there was no panic in me—only clarity. This was what Meridith's power had meant for me: not just to avenge, but to protect. I stepped towards the beasts. Herding them into their prized lake.

Flames roared to life, leaping from my fingertips in roaring tongues of sapphire and gold. The underbrush crackled as each ember touched dry grass and fallen leaves, igniting them in a hissing wave that raced toward the trunks of the surrounding trees. Smoke curled upward in thick black ribbons, blurring the moonlit canopy overhead.

I thrust my arms skyward, and the blaze answered—bursts of heat pulsed outward like a beating heart. Sparks scattered into the night, falling like fiery rain onto the roots that writhed beneath the soil, turning earth to molten glass in my wake. The acrid scent of burning wood filled my nostrils, but beneath it all I could hear the steady hum of my own power, a living force that surged through every cell.

The inferno rippled outward, a living thing hungry for fuel. One by one, tree after tree erupted in roaring flame—leaf canopies collapsing, trunks glowing ember-red before snapping and crashing earthward with bone-shaking thuds. Sparks raced ahead of the firestorm like angry fireflies, igniting new patches of tinder under the breath of the gale that howled through the burning pines.

A black column of smoke towered overhead, blotting out the moon, turning night to crimson haze. The acrid heat pressed in on me even through the ash-choked air, but I stood firm—my magic the spark that had set the whole forest ablaze.

Elias swept his arms wide; his grin split with amusement.

"You really think burning down the forest is going to stop us?" His voice slithered through the crackling flames, mocking.

I raised a single hand, the firestorm pausing—an obedient beast obeying its mistress. Around us, the blaze dimmed to smoldering glows, the wind's fury quelled at my command. The contrast between his sneer and my sudden silence was stark: three monsters poised to strike, and I alone who could hold this conflagration in my palm.

Behind me, the forest burned in my name—each tree's collapse exhaling a plume of smoke into the night sky—a reckoning no curse could contain.

Boiling steam hissed around them as the lake transformed into a white-hot cauldron. Each monstrous form writhed in agony, their claws clawing at blistering water and seared wood alike. Elias's howl – part man, part beast – shattered the night, echoing against the burning shore. Abigail's scream cracked like a dying match as her blackened skin bubbled beneath the flame's wrath. Even Daniel, caught between mercy and duty, recoiled as the heat coursed over him, tears carving clean lines through the grime on his cheeks.

I stood at the water's edge, chest heaving with raw power. My arms glowed cobalt, veins of lightning snaking up my shoulders. Every ember in the forest bent toward me, drawn by my will; the fire was both my shield and my sword. And in its roar, I heard my ancestors' voices – Meridith's calm strength, Lori's gentle laughter – guiding my hand.

Steam curled around my ankles in soft eddies as I waded deeper into the lake's wreckage. Every footfall — once mossy stones, now slick bone, and ash — sent shivers of heat up my spine. I hovered my palms over a fractured skull: it glowed blue for an instant, then crumbled to dust beneath my fingertips. Each vaporizing touch sent out a hiss like ghosts exhaling their last breath.

Above me, the moon slipped behind a drifting cloud, flicking the scene into sudden shadow. In that half-light, the steam became living ribbons, weaving between the jagged silhouettes of shattered limbs and charred vertebrae. It was as if the water itself mourned, rising in ghostly wisps before bowing back to the flames.

My heart thundered in my chest at the sheer weight of what I'd uncovered. These remains weren't just bones — they were the stories of every victim who had trusted their lies. Now their stories were mine to carry, etched into the bones beneath my feet.

Elias lunged toward the rippling water, desperation twisting his features—yet not a single droplet would answer his plea. I willed the lake itself to rise up in defiance: the surface trembled, then held firm like a living shield. Every time his fingertips brushed that cold dark mirror, it recoiled, springing back to glassy stillness under my control. His dark eyes flashed with furious betrayal—how dare the water he once commanded refuse him now? Behind me, Abigail and Daniel pressed closer to the edge, their claws scraping at the lake's mirror-smooth face, carving silver arcs that vanished the instant they formed.

All around us, the air crackled with the grief of buried secrets—centuries of sisterhood betrayed, hidden beneath these depths. But tonight, the veil had been torn, and I alone would choose what lay buried. As they thrashed, I let my magic seep into the shore: the sand grew slick and mud rose like a living tide, swallowing their protests inch by inch. Not one drop of that once-sacred water would grant them solace—only my will held sway here, and I was its mistress.

My pulse thundered in my ears as the lake's haunted groans mingled with their ragged breaths. Killing them felt impossible—but I could still end their reign of terror.

My gaze flicked to Lori's makeshift gravestone, its humble cross half-buried in soft mud, and a fierce resolve flared in my chest. If I couldn't destroy their immortal flesh, I would entomb it forever—far from any innocent life.

Beneath the water's surface, their wails had dimmed to ragged moans; above, the lake's edge rippled as if recoiling from their very presence. They lay slack on the rocky bottom, framed by rotting roots and skeletal remains, eyes wide with helpless dread. I turned fully, drawing in a lungful of the damp night air, and summoned the last of my strength.

Whispering an old coven chant—words that flickered on my tongue like embers—I pressed my palms to the wet earth. The ground shuddered, thick mud roiled and then surged toward the shoreline in a living tide. Vines and roots erupted, entwining their limbs and dragging them slowly into the soil. With each stifled scream, the earth swallowed them deeper, until nothing remained but a trembling expanse of mud: a burial chamber of my own making, sealing away their darkness for eternity—and ensuring no more would ever suffer by their cursed hands.

"I can't kill you," I bellowed, voice cracking over the roar of the wind and the crackling shoreline, "but I can hide you."

At the edge of the water, their gaunt faces drained of malice—only raw terror remained. I unclenched my fists, letting the last of my blue-white fire flicker out, and felt the tremor in the earth as something ancient answered my call. The mud beneath their bodies pulsed and split, and thick, sinuous roots erupted from the lakebed, writhing like living chains.

First, they snaked around Elias's ankles and wrists, lifting him helplessly into the air; then Abigail and Daniel were bound in the same arboreal snare. The roots slick with brackish water and flecked with algae, held them mid-air, limbs splayed, their claws clicking in desperate agitation.

I planted my boots firmly in the wet earth, raising one hand to beckon the power beneath my feet. A massive, spear-like root, gnarled and sharpened to a cruel point, shot upward with terrifying speed. Their eyes widened in silent dread as it hovered at shoulder-height, dripping lake water and ancient silt.

"You've stolen so much blood," I whispered, voice low but unyielding, "now it's your turn to bleed."

With an almost casual motion, I drove the root forward. It pierced Elias's shoulder with a sickening slide of wood through flesh; crimson welled and spilled across the polished grain. His scream echoed across the water, a raw, shuddering note of agony. One by one, the root's dark siblings struck—a chorus of splintering timber and anguished cries. Warm rivulets of their blood snaked down to mingle with the lake's silt, turning the shallows a deep, mournful red.

Their eyes met mine one last time—Elias's blazing with silent fury, Abigail's wide with helpless dread—before I spoke the words that would seal their fate forever:

"You will never see the light of day again. For as long as I live, my purpose—and the purpose of every Raven descendant after me—will be to keep you buried and hidden. The kingdom you craved is mine now."

At my command, the earth convulsed. Thick, mud-dark roots writhed upward, weaving themselves over their bound limbs. Abigail's struggles slowed as the roots cocooned her entirely—first her arms, then her legs, until only her neck remained free. In a final, merciless twist, a root sharpened like a stake pierced her heart; her muffled gasp echoed through the night as her body stilled. The roots continued their sacred work, rising to enfold her head, silencing her forever beneath the earth's unyielding grip.

Elias, too, was caught in the same living web. His feet and hands, once so poised for domination, were bound fast by sinewy tendrils. He glared at me, a storm of betrayal and rage in his unseeing black eyes, as the roots climbed higher—across his chest, over his shoulders, until a final spear of earthen timber thrust through his heart. His body fell limply into the muddy cradle, his head soon swallowed by the living tomb.

I brought Daniel closer to me, wrestling his bound form until I could bring my face close to him. His ocean-blue eyes—once so alive—now reflected only sorrow and resignation as the living roots crept inexorably higher.

My chest tightened with conflicting emotions: relief that the others could harm no more, grief for the man I once thought I knew, and a dull, bitter ache at the realization that some darkness cannot be redeemed.

"In a different life," I whispered, voice quivering with unshed tears. His lashes fluttered, as if he fought to believe me, to grasp at the sliver of hope in my words. But the roots were relentless.

Slowly, almost mournfully, they wound around his thighs—thick coils of clay and earth—then snaked up to bind his waist and ribs, pinning his arms tightly to his sides. Each tendril felt like a verdict, a sentence delivered not by me, but by the very earth he once prostituted for power. He gasped, not for breath but for forgiveness he would never earn.

"I saw it, in her memories," he whispered, voice cracking like thin ice.

Confusion clouded my face.

"Meridith sent you, Maeva," he pressed on, each word rasping out of him. "She sent you—to me."

My pulse thundered in my ears.

"But why, if you were cursed?" I demanded, searching his expression for any glimmer of truth.

He offered me a small, sorrowful smile—far too practiced, far too secretive—and his eyes darted away, guarding whatever truth lay behind those dark pupils. In that moment, a cold suspicion coiled in my chest.

I watched the last coils of root slip beneath the water's mirrored surface, sealing them in their silent tomb. My breath caught in my throat, lungs tightening as grief—so sharp and unbidden—clawed its way up from my chest.

Daniel's yearning gaze haunted me: the man I'd once reached for, betrayed me over again, yet remained the only soul I'd ever longed to save. Now, beneath that dark glass, he lay forever still. My own magic—my gift—had bound him, too.

A tremor ran through me, and the world shifted. The lake stilled, the wind died, and in that fragile silence I felt the weight of what I'd done. I had saved the innocent, but at the cost of what little remained of my heart. Tears slipped free as I sank to my knees on the muddy shore, the fabric of my soaked sleeves pressed against my cheek.

I lifted my hands over the lake's surface, the air humming with lingering magic. With a breath, I willed the water to reclaim its purity.

Slowly, the ripples drew back the crimson stain—each wave erasing the final traces of their blood. Bits of ash and debris drifted away, carried out into the moonlit expanse, until the lake lay smooth as mercury once more, reflecting the cratered moon without blemish.

Behind me, the forest still smoldered—charcoal pillars where proud pines once stood, their skeletons bowed and blackened. Ash danced in the breeze like lost spirits, settling in delicate swirls across the scarred earth. I could almost hear the hush of mourning, the trees themselves grieving what had been lost.

A single crack of falling timber broke the silence, and I started—realizing how alone I truly was. The weight of my victory settled cold in my chest. I had undone their reign of terror, but at a terrible cost, and the forest's ruin around me mirrored the hollow ache within.

Kneeling at the water's edge, I pressed my fingertips to its glassy surface one final time. Its cool touch washed away the last tremors of rage, leaving only clarity—and an unyielding resolve to guard this place, and all its hidden depths, against any who would unleash such darkness again.

I sank onto the stones by Lori's grave, the weight of my body matching the crushing ache in my chest. The moment my knees hit the cold rocks, the dam broke—I couldn't hold back the torrent of tears. They fell in hot, stinging rivulets, soaking into the earth, as raw grief and a strange relief wrenched through me in equal measure.

Clutching my chest, I collapsed onto my side, letting the forest floor cradle me. I felt every shard of my broken heart pressing sharp against my ribs, my breaths shallow and ragged. In a guttural cry, I hurled my pain at the sky, the echo tumbling through the silent pines.

Far above, the first pale blush of dawn crept over the horizon. Night's navy depths gave way to swaths of rose and amber, chasing away the last stars until only the promise of morning remained. My tears slowed as I lifted my head, watching the sun's fingertips gild the treetops.

I pushed myself up onto trembling knees. Overhead, a flight of birds traced perfect Vs across the brightening sky, their calls weaving through the light. A single warmth—a tender touch like a mother's hand—settled on mine. My magic, my constant companion, whispered its presence through that gentle pulse against my skin.

I was the only one now—last of the Raven, guardian of a terrible secret. But the dawn was new, and so was I. My purpose stood clear in the soft glow of morning: to keep these monsters buried, to shield the innocent from their hunger, and to honor the memory of those I've lost.

This is my vow, and this is what I intend to do.

Acknowledgements

First and foremost, thank you. Thank you for taking the time out of your busy life to read my story. Your love and support in diving into these magical pages with me means more than words can express.

To my wonderful family—including the "wolf pack"—your unwavering encouragement and boundless faith in me have carried me through every twist and turn of this journey. I couldn't have asked for a more incredible support system.

And to my hardest-working, most dedicated husband: your sacrifices made these pages possible. Thank you for believing in me (and for tolerating all the "vampire sex" research). I love you more than I can say, and I'm endlessly grateful for you.

About the Author

Jana Cser lives in Alabama with her family and two mischievous pups Margeaux and Nova. When she's not lost in a dark romance or weaving new worlds of fantasy, you'll find her curled up with a good book and steaming cup of tea. She believes that every day should be Halloween and fall year-round. Also, you can find her on her motorcycle dancing like no one is watching and singing like she's on stage.

Ticktock: Jana.C.Cser
Instagram: @Jana_Conerly